This book is a work of fiction. The names, characters, places, and incidents are products of the writer's imagination or have been used fictitiously and are not to be construed as real. Any resemblance to persons, living or dead, actual events, locale or organizations is entirely coincidental.

Editor, Cindy DeJager, Words Are My Business

for my husband

Thursday

Chapter 1

Detective Louis Baker slams the door to the car. She sheds her blazer, "I'm not ready for the heat this summer." She gazes at the large, run-down Victorian house.

The otherwise plain large pink house has fancy, but broken, scrollwork and delicate spindles. The front door's four doorbells indicate that this Victorian house has been converted into apartments. Above the door a wrought iron sign reads "Smokey Point" with a no smoking sign tacked on haphazardly. She smiles at the irony.

Her partner, Detective Robert Hicks III, a mighty presence at six and a half feet tall, slightly overweight, holds the door open for her. "Are you kidding? It's not even technically summer yet."

"The heat is pushing the nineties and the humidity makes it feel like we are walking inside of a sauna. More like we are the main dish at a clam bake."

"Don't start talking about clams. It's hard as hell to find good clam dishes here in Rochester, they are always overcooked."

She looks down the brown walled and wood floor hallway, completely void of any personal touches one normally sees in old Victorian houses. On either side of the hall are two plain doors both with tarnished brass numbers. "Alec said apartment four; it must be upstairs."

The detectives walk up the flight of stairs to the apartment, each stair giving away its age with a loud creak. The landlord probably thought of himself as quite the accomplished carpenter, as each stair is beautified with a tiny, off kilter, wooden molding, not matching the color of any other of the dozen or so differently shaded brown moldings that can be seen in the foyer.

Hicks opens the door to the apartment and feels a rush of icy cold air. "Wow did someone leave the freezer door open?"

"Actually Detective, a freezer cannot cool a room since it produces as much heat, if not more, than it does to cool the inside of the freezer." Says a skinny, redheaded, freckled-face uniform police officer standing next to the closet.

"And you are?" Hicks frowns.

The young officer fumbles with his pen, dropping it. He looks down, but doesn't pick it up. His cheeks redden. "Quinn, Patrick Quinn." He reaches his right out to shake the detective's hand.

"Pleased to meet you. Detective Robert Hicks, and this is Detective Louis Baker."

"Oh, Detective Baker. We've met." He grins. His bright red cheeks match his red hair.

"We have?" Louis looks at him curiously. Surely, she thinks, she would have remembered this geeky guy.

"Yes, I reported that dead guy in his beat-up pickup last summer? Well, I thought he was dead."

"Oh yeah, old Pete." Louis smiles. "Old Pete has been reported dead a few times, but always seems to snap out of it."

"He's like a cat with nine lives." Hicks elbows Quinn.

"What are you doing at my crime scene Quinn?" Louis asks.

"I, well, I transferred to robbery homicide on Wednesday."

"Well, thanks for the physics lesson, Quinn. But why in the hell is it so damn cold in here?" Hicks looks around the room.

One of the crime scene technicians in the kitchen addresses the question. "The victims turned the A/C on full blast. We didn't want to disturb anything until you got here, detective." His lanky tall frame is awkwardly compact while taking pictures over something on the kitchen floor.

Hicks shakes his head, "Thanks Mike. I think we can turn it down now."

Louis shivers a little. She puts her blazer back on, wincing as her right arm goes into the sleeve. She takes a moment to stare at Quinn who is fiddling with his pen and staring off into the kitchen. She clears her throat to get his attention, "What do we know so far?"

He bites his lower lip, "Two victims." He looks up at the ceiling, taps his forehead with his pen, and then looks at the notebook, "Victoria Wallace, age thirty-two. Tim Sherman, age thirty-eight. Both of them, I mean the victims, are in the bathroom."

A voice echoes from the next room, "Detectives?"

Louis makes her way past the Quinn toward the sound of the voice, "Yes?"

The tiny bathroom is crowded, with both victims in the tub. Steve, the coroner's assistant is crouching by the toilet. Tim is fully dressed, in shorts and a tank top, in an overflowing tub of water. The water has a red tinge to it, like someone dropped in a few drops of red food coloring. His body lies with his head barely fitting between the back wall and the faucet. His long hairy legs dangle over the side. His cheeks are red, as if he had been running around outside just a moment ago.

Victoria's face rests on her arm near Tim's knees along the edge of the tub. Her white shirt is so wet the Louis can see right through to her lacy white bra. Her gray eyes are fixed and staring at the doorway, right at Louis.

She's struck by how rosy red Victoria's cheeks are, by how alive both victims look.

She looks at the coroner's assistant fiddling with some of his tools when she asks, "How long ago did they die, Steve?"

"That's why I called you in here, Baker. Her liver temp is a hundred and eight." Steve says shaking his head and grimacing.

"A hundred and eight? How is that possible? How can a dead body register a fever?" Louis turns to wave her partner into the bathroom's doorway.

"I don't know, never seen one this hot." Steve says, shaking his head. He writes a few notes into his tablet. "Wait, I've never seen one this hot."

Louis recognizes the panic on his face.

"Everyone stop what they are doing right now! I'm shutting this down! Get everyone out of here!"

CHAPTER 2

The sound of Kristine's knitting needles click and slide outside the coroner's office door. She checks her watch. She starts counting the minutes she's now been waiting for the coroner to meet her for their scheduled appointment.

She goes back to concentrating on her knitting, a less frustrating subject. She started knitting when she was five, just over thirty-four years ago, but quit when she was in law school. A few years ago she picked it back up to clear her mind, like when she is working on a trial and inevitably has to wait.

She's working on a pair of socks for her nephew, Bryan, and she remembers him as the cuddly baby he was ten years ago. The socks are for the awkward ten-year-old she visited at Christmas. A simple repeating pattern, twin rib, that she can keep in her head and knit, even when she is distracted. The project is small enough to fit in her briefcase to be pulled out whenever she has to wait. He always seems to treasure the little tokens of her affection, no matter what form they come in. She wonders when that will subside.

She looks at the clock. She's been waiting now for nearly half an hour. Whatever he is going to tell her, at this late stage of the trial, is going to ruin her case, or at least her weekend.

"You could come back later." The receptionist says. She has been glaring over her partitioned wall for nearly a half hour.

"How much longer will he be?" Kristine asks.

"I don't know." She shrugs.

"Then I'll wait."

Why the constant rounds of budget cuts did not cut someone who hasn't answered a phone in almost an hour is beyond her comprehension. Her own paralegal was let go because of budget cuts six months ago. Her new paralegal, hired in a fit of budgetary spending spree has been nothing but a pain.

A short, squat, balding, and deeply wrinkled man pokes his head out from his office door. "Oh Miss Rocha, I'm sorry to keep you waiting." His voice is far from convincing.

Kristine packs up her knitting, straightens up her blouse and pencil-line skirt. She strides into the office. Her heels make an echoing sound in the bleak hallway. She turns to see the receptionist staring at her. As she passes the office threshold she's straight to the point, "Your email indicated that you are planning to change your testimony on the Mercedes Hewitt case."

"Yes, I believe that the DNA on the case has been, well-"

Kristine cuts him off, "Well what Dr. Vaughan?"

"Miss Rocha. Please, have a seat." Dr. Richard Vaughan points toward the brown leather Chesterfield Queen Anne chair dotted with brass tacks. Kristine expects the chair to swallow her small frame. Vaughan takes his seat and she reluctantly takes hers.

"Well then, there was a problem last fall when we tested the sample, it is possible that it may have been," Vaughan lets the air out of his lungs like a punctured tire, "contaminated."

"How was it contaminated? Who tested the sample? Why on earth is this just coming out now?" Kristine's questions come out in machine gun rapid fire.

Vaughan pauses, absently nodding at her questions. "Well, the trial is set to begin in a few weeks. I had my assistant pull it up. I noticed that Dr. Young took the samples."

"Yes, Dr. Young, I remember that from my notes as well."

"Well, Dr. Young is no longer with us. I asked him to resign a few months ago. There were some problems with his work; I found it to be perfunctory. He was having issues around that time."

Kristine's eyes nearly bulge out of her head, "You asked him to resign because he did sloppy work?"

"Yes."

She is awash with questions, but her brain cannot seem to focus on just one of them. Kristine is stunned into silence. Dr. Vaughan looks down and shuffles a few papers at his desk. The seconds click off on the foot tall wooden clock that sits on the bookshelf.

Kristine straightens the creases in her skirt. She looks up directly at Dr. Vaughan. She speaks clearly. "What evidence do you have that the samples were contaminated? Can we test the samples again?"

"Yes, we can ..." His voice trails off, but she hears the last bit anyway, "And I have." He shifts his eyes back to the papers on his desk and frowns.

From his expression she knows she doesn't want to hear the answer to the next question, "What were the results, Doctor?" she asks.

"Negative. I tested them myself, three separate times. There is no evidence of Mr. Baxter's DNA in the sample taken from Miss Hewitt's vaginal swab."

"Dr. Vaughan, if you haven't already, please go through all of the forensic evidence in the case with a fine tooth comb. Please write up a thorough report on this incident. I have an appointment to talk to Mr. Baxter's lawyers next Friday. I want to make sure that there are no more surprises." Kristine's shaking voice gives away her frustration, even if her words do not.

"Yes, Miss Rocha, this is now my top priority. I will make sure that the remaining evidence holds up to the utmost scrutiny."

Kristine gets up from the enveloping chair with some effort. "Thank you Doctor. Please call me if anything at all comes up in this case."

He walks around his large oak desk. He walks her to the door, "I will Miss Rocha. Your number is in my speed dial."

CHAPTER 3

"Well this is fun." Hicks' muffled voice comes through the duckbill protective mask. "I feel like Donald Duck."

"Somehow I don't feel all that comforted by the mask and these super strong gloves." Louis says.

"Yeah, especially when the HAZMAT team over there is wearing full gear." Hicks points to the crowded bathroom.

Hicks walks over to the crime scene technician in the kitchen holding up a small baggie. "Jake?"

"Hey Hicks." Jake's extremely low baritone echoes off the walls.

"Who's having that baby; you or your wife?" Hicks asks, pointing to the black man's bulging midsection.

Louis estimates he's at least twenty or thirty pounds heavier than the last time they saw him, which couldn't have been that long ago.

"I know. It's the late night refrigerator raids. She doesn't want to eat alone." He pats his midsection, making a crinkling noise with the sterile white coveralls.

"So when are you expecting?" Hicks laughs.

"Next week, June twentieth." Jake says. His full belly jiggles as he laughs "Then I start on the diet."

"Congrats man. Good luck." Hicks looks down at the baggie that Jake set on the countertop, "What have you got there?"

"Looks like purple pills." Jake replies.

"Pills? Any label?" Hicks leans over to see if he can find any distinguishing marks.

"No label, but the letters 'L' and 'T' are etched into them." Jake hands Hicks a small magnifying glass from his kit.

"Interesting, have you seen these before?"

"Nope, never." Jake shakes his head, "We also found blood here, and here." He points to the oven door and the floor. "Drops of blood lead from that spot on the floor all the way to the bathroom."

Louis, listening from the living room, follows the faint bloody trail from the kitchen to the bathroom, "Yeah, and it looks like the carpet has two streaks in it. Like, someone was dragged." She thinks out loud, "So, Tim has a head wound, maybe he fell in the kitchen, hit his head?"

"But then why does she drag him to the bathroom? There's not enough blood here to indicate the wound as fatal."

"No, maybe he passed out? And what's up with those fevers?" Louis asks.

"Jake here found some pills."

"Did you see ones like that back when you were in the drug squad?" Louis asks Hicks.

"Nah, but it's been two years, there are new players in the drug market just about every month. Once you bring a drug dealer down, two more take his place."

"Hmm, drugs. Yeah, that might explain the fevers. Maybe they overdosed?"

"People who overdose generally look like they are into drugs pretty heavily." Hicks points out.

"I didn't see any distinguishing marks on Victoria. She's well kept. And I didn't see any marks on Tim either." Louis thinks for a moment and looks around the room. "Drug dealers need to be contacted." She picks up the first phone she sees. It's pink and shaped like a classic phone of her great-grandmother's era, outfitted with a fake rotary dial. She works through the phones little digital directory while it emanates trilling electronic sounds, unlike her

11

great-grandmother's phone. She makes notes of recently called numbers and all of the speed dial entries.

While Louis is fussing with the phone, Hicks wanders into the bedroom looking for an address book. He opens the nightstand drawer and pulls out a tiny pink vibrator. He smirks, thinking about couples and their commonalities. He digs further through the nightstand and finds heated massage lotion and Penthouse magazines. He takes a moment to flip through one of the magazines. The word 'police' grabs his attention and he skims through the lusty article concerning an officer and a woman trying to get out of her speeding ticket. She's over her limit and afraid her license will get taken away. He snorts a laugh, nothing so interesting happened in his speed trap days.

He walks back into the living room. He finds Quinn, who is staring at Louis, "Quinn, we need to find out where they worked. Talk to their coworkers, maybe some friends. See if this couple had a history of drug use."

"Where … they … worked …" Quinn says, sounding out each syllable in each word scrawled.

Louis is finished fiddling with the phone, "I've got a few numbers here. We can start calling them when we get back to the station. Wait, look at that." Across the room she spots a flat pink object hidden under a newspaper. It catches her eyes.

"What is it?" Hicks asks.

"I'm pretty sure it's a laptop." Louis lifts up the newspaper and pulls out the pearlescent pink laptop, covered in white swirls.

Hicks walks toward her, "Nice find."

"Thanks." She looks at Quinn, "Make sure this gets to Aria in the squad's computer lab as soon as possible."

"Right." Quinn walks over to Louis, grabbing a large plastic evidence bag from the pile on the kitchen counter next to Jake.

"Quinn, who called this in?" Hicks asks.

"... woman downstairs. Her name is ... ..." he fiddles with his notebook, flipping pages until he gets to the first page. He makes a pained face and flips back a few pages, "her name is Barbara Wellington. She lives in ..." he flips a few more pages, " ... apartment 1," he states excitedly.

"Have you spoken to her yet?" Louis asks.

" No. I haven't." His eyebrows knit together, "Was I supposed to?"

"No, Quinn, we like to do that." She points to the door, "The techs will find anything else we need in here, let's go talk to Ms. Wellington." She stops halfway through the door and whips around, " - and Quinn, don't forget to bring the computer to Aria."

"Right." He scribbles into his notebook.

Louis rips off her duck mask. She looks over to see a ring around Hicks' mouth from the mask. "What's got you smirking?"

"Just thinking. Maybe I should do some undercover work in highway patrol, or I could volunteer to do speed patrol school zones."

"What?"

"Oh nothing." He whistles.

Louis finds the door with the rusty brass number '1'. She takes her turn knocking on the door. "Ms. Wellington?"

There is a long pause until the door opens with a crack and a thud. A short, older woman with a peach turban peeks out from underneath the taught chain. "Who's askin'?" Her penciled-in orange eyebrows curl together.

"Ma'am, I'm Detective Baker and this is my partner Detective Hicks." She holds up her badge through the crack in the door for the woman to look at.

"Yeah? So?"

"Ma'am we need to talk to you about your upstairs neighbor."

"Didn't see nothin'."

"Yes, well, do you know them well?"

"Nope." The woman slams the door shut.

Louis isn't one to give up easily and knocks on the door again. "Ms. Wellington, we need to ask a few more questions."

There is a much louder crack and thud. The woman pokes her head out from between the door. "I said I don't know 'em. What else is there?"

Louis, who is just a few inches taller than the woman, can see over her head and into an absolute sea of newspapers. Tiny spaces between the stacks mark out her routes through the apartment. "Ma'am, we won't keep you long, but we'd like to know what made you call the police."

"There was a lot of yelling."

"Anything else?"

"Stomping around the house, but not stomping 'clicky-clack'. I don't know what the hell they had going on up there."

"But that's not why you called the police?"

"No, I heard a scream. But, right before that it sounded like someone dropped a bag of cement."

Hicks is intrigued, "Cement?"

"Yeah, my husband, God rest his soul, he used to work in cement. It sounded just like when he was throwin' those big heavy bags from the truck. Only, it was right over my head. In fact, some of that damn plaster came down. They're going to have to pay for the repairs. I'm going to send them a bill."

"Ma'am, they aren't going to be able to pay you for repairs, they're dead."

"I see, I'll send the bill to the landlord then."

"Yes ma'am, do you know if they were into drugs?"

"Aren't all them hippies into drugs?"

"Hippies?"

"Yeah. He had long hair."

"But you aren't sure?"

"I said I don't know them. And hell, I don't want to know them."

"What about some of your other neighbors?"

"The Chinks across the hall, they make foul smelling food. At least I think it's food."

"Yes ma'am, what about apartment 3?"

"Nobody lives there, not since the kitchen fire. Landlord still hasn't cleaned that up."

"Well, I think that just about does it. Ma'am, if you think of anything else please give us a call?" Louis fishes into her breast pocket for her card and gasps as she brushes against her chest. She hands the woman her card; tears running down her face. "Are you all right?" The woman snatches the card.

"Yes, I'm fine. Thank you for your -" The door slams shut. "- time." Louis exhales deeply.

"What's wrong Baker? Did you get a glimpse of your future?"

"Hicks, if I start penciling in my eyebrows and collecting an ocean worth of newspapers, will you promise to kill me swiftly and without warning?"

He bows, "It would be my honor."

The rush of hot air when they walk outside is enough to take some of Louis' breath away. The seatbelt scrapes against her left shoulder. She sucks in air between her teeth and her stomach sinks.

"What is up with you?" Hicks asks.

"Nothing. Where to?" She looks over at her partner.

"Maybe I should drive?"

"When you beat me at the advanced driving course, I'll be happy to relinquish the wheel."

"We should go talk to my buddy in drug enforcement. Perhaps he'll have an idea about these designer drugs." He says.

"What makes you think they are designer drugs?"

"Because they have designs on them." Hicks reaches over to fiddle with the radio.

CHAPTER 4

Kristine walks into her office and places her briefcase on the desk. She flips through the pink 'While You Were Out' messages.

She turns around to find Marcie Hoyle, her new paralegal, making a call. Her feet are propped up on the desk and she has new strappy silver shoes and freshly painted bright orange toenails. "No, I need to deal with some stuff here… yeah… Tschüs."

"I keep hearing you say that. What does Tschüs mean?" Kristine asks.

"It is an informal 'good bye' in German."

"Where were you this morning?" Kristine asks. She spots a glowing orange 'sale' sticker on the bottom of Marcie's shoes. $599 isn't much of a sale for shoes. *And I thought that only Cece would pay so much for shoes.*

"Out." Marcie says. "I had some things to do." She puts her feet back on the floor. She shuffles through a short stack of papers.

"I need you to pull the evidence on the Hewitt trial from storage. Use the van. I need every box."

"Why?"

"Because we have to go through all of the evidence again."

"Why?" Marcie asks again.

"Because the DNA evidence is no longer solid."

"So what are you going to do?"

What am I going to do? Kristine huffs, "Well, as soon as *you* pull all the evidence from storage *you and I* are going to go through the boxes and look for any leads that were not followed up on."

"I've got that deposition on the -"

Kristine cuts her off, "None of that matters now. We have to get this case back on track or both our jobs are on the line." Kristine's phone rings. "Can you get that? Take a message."

"I guess." Marcie picks up the phone, "ADA Rocha's office... Mr. Pucket?... Yes, sir, she's right here."

Kristine glares at Marcie, "Sir? ... Yes sir, I'll be at your office in five minutes." She slams the phone on the receiver. "What part of 'take a message' is confusing?"

"I'm going to have a cigarette." Marcie walks off, slamming the door behind her.

***

Kristine slips into her plain purple speed suit. Her weekly routine has been interrupted more times than she can count. Today she decided she was going to enjoy a nice lap swim at the new outdoor pool. It's her favorite pool in the summer, as long as she gets there on time for the afternoon lap swim. She steps into the cleansing shower, ready to wash away the day.

Her discussions with the district attorney went about as well as she thought they might. She's sure the other attorney's could clearly hear the shouting from their desks. Apparently the botched forensic evidence is as much her fault as it is anyone else's. She should have seen the inconsistencies. She suddenly realized that because of her incompetence, the man who raped his step-daughter is apt to get away with it. In an election year, someone is going to have to take the fall for such a high profile case.

Kristine steps out from the shower room. The only noise is from two swimmers in the pool and the flapping of her flip-flops on the concrete pool deck. She looks up to see the young svelte lifeguard, lit from behind by the late afternoon sun, at his high perch. His muscular thighs bulge out of his tight red shorts. His skin is tanned and his hair looks already bleached by the sun. He nods his head at Kristine.

She looks over to see the other two people in the pool. Kristine chooses the lane furthest away from the other swimmers, removes her flip-flops and glides into the pool. She's happy that there is a free lane. She breaks the quiet with an "Oh" from the sudden cold feeling. It's the first time she's had a chill in days. She places her goggles on, and adjusts them a little. She thinks she hears a ringing sound just before ducking her head under water and pushing away from the wall.

After a few laps she gets into the rhythm of breathing. All of the crazy thoughts of the day become paper-mache walls that she punches through one at a time. It's not her fault the ME's office put an incompetent fool in charge of processing Emily Hewitt's DNA. It's not her fault that the incompetent fool wasn't properly supervised. It certainly isn't her fault that the ME just got around to telling her the sample was compromised. If the district attorney is unable or unwilling to see these facts as they are, it's not her problem. Her case is not shot. There is plenty of other evidence to back her up. Marcie can go work for someone else. Kristine would prefer to do the work herself and not have to deal with that tongue wagging, chimney smelling, walking, attitude problem.

Her mind settles and she starts dreaming about that lifeguard. His little shorts and tank top sit next to her bed on the hardwood floor. His kisses touch every part of her body. His lips are supple from constant application of lip balm

She pops her head up out of the water and looks at her watch. A half hour has past. She hears a faint ringing sound and looks around the pool. The two other swimmers have left and the svelte lifeguard waves at her from his perch.

"I think that's your phone, it's been ringing every couple minutes or so." His voice, a higher pitch than she is expecting, refuses to match his beautifully toned body.

"You're the only one left. Process of elimination." Her fantasy of an evening with a hot lifeguard is instantly quelled by his logic. A lawyer just can't over look these things.

"Thank you," she jumps out of the pool and slips into her flip-flops. The phone rings again. She makes it to the changing room and hears a combination of her nephew laughing as a toddler and the sound of an older style phone, a ring tone composed by her brother-in-law, a theatrical sound engineer. It's a ring tone she only uses for her mother. Just as the lock opens the phone stops ringing. She digs around in her purse and finds the phone. The screen says she has fifteen missed calls from her mother and ten voice mails. This can't be good.

The phone starts ringing again. "Mom?"

"Kristine! Thank God I got you!" Hearing the stress in mother's voice is strange and unnerving.

"What's going on?" she asks.

"Your sister …" Her mother sobs uncontrollably.

Kristine waits. A small pool of water is forming from rivers of water running down her body to her feet. Her mind fills with the possibilities of her sister's situation. What did she do to make her mother so upset? What was it the last time her mother called? Something about their disagreement over discipline for Bryan, her sister's son. He ran off to the park without telling his grandmother.

Her thoughts are interrupted by her mother's sobbing words, " …she's … she's been in an accident." The word 'accident' comes out in her mother's voice as if it were extruded from her stomach.

"What? Is she okay? What about Bryan... and Ethan?"

"Kelly is in surgery now. Ethan …" Her mother hesitates. Kristine can hear the sounds of a hospital intercom in the background. "Ethan passed away."

19

"What about Bryan?" Kristine feels a rush of panic. She plops down on the bench, not ready to hear the news about her nephew. Her body quivers.

"Bryan is with me. Kelly and Ethan were out on a date." Her mother begins to sob.

"Where are you?" Kristine asks.

"Fairfax Hospital," Her sobbing continues and Kristine hears Bryan's sweet, tiny voice consoling his grandmother.

Kristine's teeth start to chatter, "Mom, I'll be on the first plane down to D.C. Call me when Kelly comes out of surgery."

Her mother is barely able to choke out "Okay" before sobbing more.

"Give Bryan a big hug and tell him that Aunt Kris is going to be there soon." Her mother sniffles an incoherent response. "I love you, Mom. It'll be okay."

Kristine stares at her phone incomprehensively. *An accident*, she thinks, *of all the things, an accident. Maybe she wasn't driving, maybe it was Ethan. Maybe it's not her fault.*

Her mind pulls back from the hard memories. She dresses swiftly, making a checklist in her mind. She has everything in her purse and gym bag she needs. She could always pick up clothes in Alexandria. She makes a quick call to her go-to airline, Trans-American, and gets a pretty good deal, just a five hundred dollar hit to her "dream vacation fund."

Her next call is not as easy however, "Mr. Pucket?"

"Ms. Rocha. I'm glad you called." Hearing the district attorney's voice reminds her of the argument in his office earlier in the day. The walls she knocked down in her swim are building back up again.

"Sir, my sister -"

"I don't know who leaked our discussion today, but I have a Motion to Suppress sitting here on my desk." Mr. Pucket interrupts.

"Wait, a 'Motion to Suppress' what?" Kristine's mind is reeling and her voice is strained.

"The DNA evidence in the Hewitt case."

"What?" She swallows hard.

"It seems someone in our ranks has been discussing the case with the defense attorney." Mr. Pucket puts an emphasis on the words 'our ranks,' a clear indictment pointed at Kristine.

"Sir, I -"

"I'm sure it isn't you, but you need to find out who's been leaking information to Mr. Baxter's attorney."

"Sir, my sister has been in an accident, she's in the hospital. I'm afraid I'm going to be out of town for a while."

The District Attorney clears his throat, a habit she knows he picked up whenever he got into a conversation that he didn't expect, which was rare. He clears his throat again.

She leaves a long pause, "Yes, well, I have my laptop and cell. I'll do what I can from here and direct Marcie to find anything else I need." *Not that she's been any help at all.*

This is just the answer that Mr. Pucket is expecting, "Very well, but get to the bottom of this … this mess."

Kristine's phone beeps indicating she's been disconnected. "Asshole," she whispers under her breath.

CHAPTER 5

Louis has met Hicks' old drug enforcement partner, Peski, a number of times. However, Peski never seems to remember her.

"Hey Hicks." Peski shouts from across the room. He strides up to them. His breath is labored, as though he scaled an eight-foot wall to get there. The buttons on his shirt strain to stay together. Louis wonders how he is able to complete the mile and a half run for his yearly physical exam.

"Hey Peski, got a little problem." Hicks holds up a plastic evidence bag with two tiny pills inside.

"Whoa, what have you got there?" Peski asks.

"We think it's some sort of designer drug." Louis says.

"Do you now?" Peski looks at her, "Detective..."

"Baker." She says.

"Right, Louise Baker."

"It's *Louis*." She corrects.

"Oh yeah, you have a guy's name. I never remember."

Hicks smiles. "They've got a little 'L' and 'T' etched in them. Have you seen anything like that?"

"Yup. Sure have." Peski holds up the bag to the light, "Looks a little different though. Not the right color, or something."

"What is it?" Louis asks.

"It looks like 'Lilac Trance'. Coupla kids sell the stuff at dance clubs."

"Anyone I know?" Hicks asks.

"No. Probably not. They started dealing about nine months ago out of Polyester." Peski continues to stare at the bag, "They call themselves the 'Chemistry Brothers'.

They're both Asian, and have degrees in chemical engineering. The drugs they are producing are just on this side of legal. I've brought them in twice, but the drugs check out every time. Maybe they changed their formula."

"What do you mean by 'just this side of legal'?" Louis asks.

"Their blends don't contain any illegal drugs, but they make you high anyway." Peski says.

"Can you have these tested?" Louis asks.

"Yeah. Don't worry." Peski says, "Our team will check them out."

"Where did you say these guys hung out?" Louis asks.

"Why, Detective Baker, you haven't heard of the new dance club called Polyester?" Hicks' single life is full of random adventures he rarely tells Louis.

"No, Detective Hicks, I have not heard of any club called Polyester." Louis plays along.

"It's a sorta retro-seventies place, off of West Pine, almost to Greece."

"So you've been there before?" Louis raises an eyebrow.

"Yes, yes I have." Hicks grins.

Louis checks her watch. Just after eight, so a dance club would just be getting started. "I'll drive." She kicks out her father's favorite tag line, "Let's went."

***

Louis and Hicks walk up to the brightly lit nightclub. The marquee spells out bands she's never heard of. "The Yourself Simulators" are supposed to be playing tonight and "The Vernacular Fasteners" are warming up for "Cocky Magpie" tomorrow night. They pass a few scantily clad young women, all congregating behind an area roped off with red leather. A tall man with a tattoo that looks like a vampire bit him stands at the front door. He seems overly skinny for a bouncer, but becomes a formidable force as Louis turns to walk into the club.

"Hey," his voice isn't deep, but commanding. "You need to get in line."

Louis rolls her eyes slightly. "I'm Detective Baker and" she points to her partner, "this is Detective Hicks. We need to speak to the Chemistry Brothers."

The skinny faux vampire victim purses his lips to the left toward the bite tattoo. Louis can see he is thinking hard about the consequences of both letting the police officers in, and not letting them in. It could be his job, a somewhat easy, likely moderate paying job. If he lets them in his boss could be pissed because the clientele would be skittish, maybe leave. If he doesn't let them in, his boss could be pissed for causing trouble. She watches the wheels turn.

Hicks asks, "Why don't you use that little radio?" He points down at the vampire victim's hip.

"Ah," The bouncer exchanges glances with both detectives, looking at him expectantly. He pulls his radio from his studded leather belt. "Team Edward to Back Room," he shouts into the radio.

"Go ahead Team Edward," the crackling sound of the reply comes through.

"Got some cops here, says they want to talk to Chemistry Bros." The skinny man talks into the radio, keeping eye contact with the detectives.

"Well, let them in, we don't want trouble with the cops. Chemistry Bros have their own get-out-of-jail-free card anyhow." The voice on the other end of the radio seems annoyed that 'Team Edward' had even bothered to ask such a stupid question.

"Go, right on through. The Brothers are usually hanging out in the Velvet Lounge, it's kinda in the back." The vampire victim points toward the inside of the club.

Louis hears a girl, from the gaggle of girls behind the red leather rope, let out a frustrated scream and whine,

"Now why the hell you let those two assholes in and not us?"

The bouncer sneers, "They had reservations."

***

The flashing lights and pulsing music drill through Louis' head in an instant. A flailing dancer bumps into her arm and she nearly jumps out of her skin with pain. She can't imagine what would cause so much pain. She's sure her little scream can be heard over the music and looks over for Hicks' reaction.

"Louis, what's going on?" She strains to hear Hicks over the loud music.

"Would you get a tattoo like that?"

He looks puzzled, but then has a sudden realization, "Oh! You got a tattoo?"

"No!" She says loudly in a break in the music. A few of the bell-bottomed, glowing makeup covered young women turn to stare at her. "Would you get a tattoo like the one the bouncer had?" She points to her neck with two fingers to indicate the vampire bite and rubs her neck with one finger to imitate the fake blood running down the bouncer's neck.

Hicks laughs, indicating he finally understands what she's saying, "Honey, this body is perfect," he mimes his hands up and down his tall, slightly overweight frame to show it off, "I don't need a tattoo."

Louis has considered getting a tattoo on a few occasions. She even made an appointment with one of Rochester's finest tattoo artists, but found she was unable to commit to one image being drawn on her body forever. Handcuffs? "26.2" for the miles covered in a marathon? Stars? Some fancy saying? Maybe a saying in another language? What if the saying is misspelled or mistranslated?

Louis finds the source of the pulsing music and flashing lights. She sees a small DJ booth to the left of the lit stage. There is one young man wearing large headphones at the controls. He's bald headed and his skin is so white it practically glows. He has thick dark glasses on, what her mother used to call 'birth control glasses'; by wearing them you would look so hideous you weren't going to be fathering (or mothering) any children. The glasses have become much more popular now, even with designer brands that cost into the thousands. Her mother often talked about buying them for their father in 1969, for just two dollars. It was only a year before Louis was born. She probably bought them hoping she could hold off having children a bit longer.

Louis points to the DJ, "Hey, maybe he knows where we can find the Chemistry Bros." They make their way over to the booth; Louis holding out her arms as wide as she can to attempt to hold off the flailing dancers. She comes close to whacking one of the young men in the head, just to keep him from running into her.

They get within a few feet of the DJ booth and a much larger bouncer stops their progress. It's impossible to hear, but Hicks attempts communication with the bouncer anyway. He holds up his badge and the bouncer eyes it warily.

Louis can see that Hicks and the bouncer are engaging in a heated debate from the look on both of their faces, but can't understand a single word being uttered by either. Just as she begins to lose hope, she sees the bouncer making eye contact with someone on the side of the stage. She turns her head to follow his gaze and sees two young Asian men. Both of them are smartly dressed in shiny suits. She turns back to the bouncer just as he is pointing to the men. She looks back at the Asian men as they are bolting.

Hicks finally catches on to the bouncers gaze. He spots the Chemistry Bros running. He pushes past the bouncer. He's focused on the Chemistry Bros.

Louis screams in pain, but she can't even hear her own screaming over the music. She thrusts her arms out pushing away a young man. Dancers fall onto each other like dominoes.

Hicks is slammed from the back by one of the falling dancers. Hicks makes eye contact with Louis, but she waves him away. He takes her meaning and scrambles after the two men. Louis watches Hicks' long strides nearly meet up with the first Chemistry Brother.

He is able to catch up to both of them before they can escape, grabbing the first one by his iridescent blue silk jacket and jabbing his feet out to trip the second man in the process.

Hicks handcuffs one man and puts the other in a hold with his free arm. She meets them halfway, tears running down her face. He sees the tears and looks at her confused. He screams something, but Louis is unable to hear him.

Louis grits her teeth together, "I'm in pain," she rubs her eyes, "I'll be fine, let's just get out of here."

Hicks screams back, but Louis is still unable to hear.

"What?" Louis can't hear anything he's saying through the music and the painful pulsing in her ears. She wants to touch the spot generating such pain on her chest, but doesn't want to touch it because touching it creates an even greater pain.

Hicks' anger shows through in his rough handling of the artificial fraternals. He has both men by their shirt collars, directing their movements and creating a wake for Louis to walk in. He doesn't let go until he reaches the car.

"Damn," Hicks says.

Louis is distracted by her excruciating pain, not paying any attention to Hicks, but manages to look up at him for an explanation.

Hicks opens the back door and shoves in the pair. He starts reciting, or rather shouting, the Miranda warning now that he's in an area where he can be heard. The way he's shouting, he probably can't hear his own voice over the buzzing in his ears.

Louis is so consumed with pain she gets into the passenger seat of the car without thinking.

When Hicks is finished he looks at Louis, "You look terrible."

"I'm fine. You drive."

"I can handle these idiots. Maybe I'll get some help from Quinn. Or Peski. He's been trying to bring these two clowns in forever."

Louis says, "Let's just go book them. Get the paperwork -"

"I hate to break up this soap opera, but what are we under arrest for?" The perps always know their rights, or at least they think they do.

"I'm tempted to haul you in for being an asshole, try not to interrupt a conversation between two detectives and I can lower those charges to general rudeness." Hicks voice reveals that he isn't in the mood for these drug dealers. Louis has heard many stories about his short temper while he was in drug enforcement. He clears his throat, "You were saying?"

Rochester Herald Staff writer David Huang reports:

June 13th 9:09 pm: Rochester Assistant District Attorney Kristine Rocha's case against Dennis Baxter went south today after the medical examiner's office reported the DNA evidence was botched.

Police say back in November Baxter gruesomely killed his step-daughter and stuffed her in a mattress. To cover his tracks he claimed to have received phone calls from her friends saying she was staying with them. Later that evening police found young Mercedes Hewitt's body stuffed in a downstairs mattress.

ADA Rocha was not available for comment on the DNA issue, but a source inside the District Attorney's office commented that further evidence was going to be available at the trial hearing set to begin in two weeks.

Baxter, a famous high school football star from Geneva, has adamantly proclaimed his innocence. His lawyer has been quoted many times saying, "Someone broke into the home and murdered her, not my client." He remains incarcerated without bail in the Rochester County jail.

FRIDAY

CHAPTER 6

As the plane lands at Dulles Airport, Kristine realizes she needs someone to take care of her cat, Houdini. Thinking of him makes her smile during this stressful situation.

The plane taxis. The stewardess welcomes them to Virginia and allows them to use their cell phones. Kristine dials the number for her closest friend, Louis.

"What?" Louis answers the phone.

"Louis, it's Kristine," she shouts.

"It's one a.m.-"

"Yes, well, my sister's been in an accident, I just flew down to D.C."

"Oh my God. Is she okay?" Louis asks.

"I don't know yet. I talked to my mother about an hour ago and she's still in surgery. Ethan didn't make it." She realizes she probably shouldn't have said that so loudly in the plane's cabin.

"Oh no. What about Bryan?"

"Bryan is okay, he was with my mother at the time. So, I hate to ask you this but can you look in on Houdini for the next few days? I know I'm going to be out of town for a little while."

"Sure, I can do that."

"Just don't let him escape!"

"Yes, well he lives up to his name pretty well doesn't he?"

"Yes, he does. Thanks Louis."

"Give Bryan a kiss for me."

"Will do." Kristine hangs up the phone, ready to take on the exhausting day. The plane comes to a complete stop and she unbuckles her seatbelt and jumps up to the aisle with just her gym bag in hand. She is still dressed for her day as a lawyer in her pencil skirt and flowing blouse.

She looks around to see if anyone is staring at her. The plane doesn't have nearly as many passengers as seats, but a grumpy woman two rows back is staring at her. Her flowing blue flowered Muumuu, with pencil thin vertical lines, gives the impression she's a walking wallpaper sample.

The speakers on the plane play Faith Hill's *This Kiss*, forcing Kristine to cringe while waiting for the first class cabin to empty out onto the jet way. The music cuts out, making the annoying song only that much more annoying, as her brain must fill in the gaps. Her jaw clenches.

She rushes to the taxi stand outside the terminal and is amazed by the rush of hot air so late into the night. It's surprisingly even hotter than in Rochester. The earworm started by *This Kiss* is rumbling through her head. She is just moments away from killing the bugger with a good indie band like The Shins, Death Cab for Cutie or The White Stripes.

She steps into a cool taxicab smelling of body odor. The driver turns around. Kristine sees a dark, heavily-lined face, like old weathered leather. "Where to Ma'am?" He asks in a thick Indian accent.

"Fairfax Hospital." She says. She fishes through her little purse for her headphones.

Before she puts her headphones on the taxi's radio announces the weather. "High's tomorrow in the high 90's. It'll be another red flag day out there, and we all know what that means. Stay indoors, air-conditioned if you can. Avoid prolonged exposure outdoors. Jake, do you have an update on the traffic?"

"Yes Stacey, the accident on Fairfax County Parkway involving at least one fatality still has traffic snarling. Just a reminder folks, the Fairfax County Parkway is closed in both directions south of Lee Highway. A white SUV jumped the median into oncoming traffic about six hours ago. Paramedics left the scene a while ago, but investigators are still taking statements and scoping the scene. They estimate having the highway open by six a.m. Please, avoid the area if at all possible."

Kristine's heart sinks. She sucks in a huge gulp of air. Could this be the accident?

***

The hospital has been remodeled since the last time she visited, when Bryan was first born.

Being in such a wealthy community, the hospital has a lot of money to do renovations every decade or so. The hallways have new carpet, the walls are freshly painted, and the artwork appears more modern than during her last visit.

A nice looking older woman, likely a volunteer, works the front desk. She's knitting what looks like a scarf, trailing down to the floor. "Excuse me?" Kristine asks, placing her gym bag on the floor next to the counter.

"How can I help you?" Kristine can see her name tag now, covered with stickers of knitting needles and a ball of yarn, a few hearts and stars, all surrounding the name Evelyn.

"My sister's been in an accident, she was in surgery an hour ago. I'm looking for my mother and nephew."

"Oh my, I'm very sorry. Surgery is in the south wing, dear." Evelyn points toward an opening. "You have to follow that hallway, over there, all the way down until you get to a fork, then turn right. The waiting room is three doors down, on the left. You can't miss it."

"Thank you." Kristine says and hoists her gym bag back on her shoulder.

"You are very welcome young lady. Can I have someone escort you to the area?"

"No. I'm sure that won't be necessary."

"Well, please come back if you need anything." Evelyn doles out what must be her signature 'everything will be okay in the end' smile. It reminds Kristine of her favorite Aunt Sally's smiles. They will melt your heart, even on your cold, dark days.

Kristine follows Evelyn's directions and comes upon the third door on the right, a large glass enclosure. Her nephew is playing with large building block toys, the ones made for three-year-olds. Her mother is busy knitting in her wheelchair.

"Mom?"

"Kristine!" Her mother looks up from her knitting and tucks it in her lap.

Bryan drops his blocks on the floor and runs over, "Aunt Kris!"

"Hey Bryan, how's my man holding up?" she inquires as gently as she can.

"Dad died." Bryan says sadly.

"I know honey, I'm sorry. Do you need anything?" Kristine smiles, but sheds a little tear. She wipes the tear from her eye and straightens Bryan's bangs to get them out of his eyes.

"Grandma H. says that you might take me home to go to bed when you get here, after you talk to grandma," he said. Bryan's sadness flitters away quickly, and his rambling speaking style puts a genuine smile on Kristine's face.

"Sure Bryan, I'll give you a ride back to your place after I'm done talking to Grandma H. If that's what you want." Kristine leans over and kisses her mother on the cheek.

"Go back and play with the blocks for a bit Bryan," her mother's voice sounds choked, and she sends him off.

Bryan gives Kristine a big hug around her belly, the kind that hurts a little as he squeezes on her lower rib cage. "Love you, Bryan."

"Love you, Aunt Kris." He wanders back over to the blocks, picks up a purple one and starts counting under his breath.

Kristine takes a seat next to her mother's wheelchair, "How is she, Mom?"

Her mother speaks in a whisper, "The doctor's were out here fifteen minutes ago. I made Bryan go find me a soda. They say it's not good."

"How bad?" Kristine chokes on the word 'bad'.

"They are doing everything they can, but her injuries are…" her mother sobs quietly, "I can't remember the term they used."

"It's okay, but what happened, Mom?"

"Ethan and Kelly were out on a date; their anniversary was Wednesday. But Ethan had to work." Her mother grabs a tissue from the wadded up wet ones sitting in her lap, next to the knitting, and blows her nose. "The police were here, they said that an oncoming car must have passed over the center line, they are still investigating. Ethan was killed instantly. Kelly was pinned for an hour. She lost a lot of blood." Her mother uses the same tissue, trying to find a dry spot, to wipe her tears. "You're going to have to prepare, Kristine. Your sister might not make it through the night. You have responsibilities."

Kristine looks confused, "What do you mean?"

"You're Bryan's godmother. You promised your sister you would take care of him if anything happened to her. You're the one who chased after her with the paperwork. 'Just in case anything happens', remember?"

The reality of the situation hits Kristine like a brick wall. She did make a solemn promise to her sister that day, ten and a half years ago, while *Law and Order* played on the TV in the background. She promised to take care of little Bryan if anything should happen to her and Ethan. She promised to be his godmother. Even more importantly she's the one that insisted her sister make out a proper will for Bryan's sake. Like every godparent she never actually thought the day would come that she would be needed.

She looks over at Bryan. He has two blocks in his hand and is ramming them together making the little boy sounds of crashing metal and screeching tires.

***

Kristine makes her third circle of the block. It's five a.m. and Bryan fell asleep within a couple minutes of leaving the hospital. The rental car agency dropped off a car for her, a cute little Fiat 500. She had trouble finding the controls, as they seemed to be in odd places. The car runs smoothly though, and the air-conditioning runs perfectly. She's only been to Kelly's house a few times, six months ago, and the houses all look exactly the same in the dark. Technically they all look exactly the same in the daytime as well, but at least in the daytime you can see the house numbers. The streets even have the same names, but slightly different surnames. She can't remember if it was Chicory Place, Chicory Drive or Chicory Close. She gives up on the surnames and concentrates on the numbers but soon discovers that in addition to being difficult to see in the dark, the numbers do not seem to have rhyme or reason from one street to the next. She's tempted to pull over and sleep in the car, but just then a cat darts in front of her car. She slams on the breaks and Bryan is jolted awake. He screams, which scares Kristine. The car comes to a halt.

Kristine slams the car in park, "Bryan? What's wrong?"

"Why did you stop?" Bryan asks semi-coherently, a strange mix of sleepy and terrified.

She starts to explain, calming herself in the process.

"There was a cat -"

"You killed a cat?" He asks, on the verge of tears.

She realizes she's not talking to the real Bryan, but a stressed, sleepy, Bryan. "No, honey, I stopped the car before it hit the cat."

"Are you sure? The cat's okay? I mean, what if you squished him under the car or something?" Bryan asks insistent questions although his voice is calmer than it had been.

"I'm sure. I saw it skitter over there between those two houses." Kristine points to the small space between the two houses. She starts to laugh.

"Why are you laughing?" He asks.

Kristine giggles a bit more; her tired, weary, stressed-out self likes to nervously giggle. "Because I've been driving around for the last hour looking for your mother's house, and it's right there." She points to the familiar green hooded gnome in the front yard holding a fishing pole with a fish on the end. The gnome had been a gag gift from last Christmas. Kelly and Kristine had long given up on giving each other real Christmas gifts and instead tried to one-up each other with the most absurd gifts fitting a theme. Last year Kelly chose 'lawn ornaments'.

Bryan can't help himself and laughs along with her. "Yeah, that's funny Aunt Kris. I thought you knew the way to my house."

"Me too, but these houses all look the same, that is until I saw Ralph." Bryan names everything. During the long, rambling calls with him every week he likes to explain the names he's given to inanimate objects. Kristine can't remember the reason Bryan gave for naming the gnome Ralph, but she remembers it being full of elaborate reasoning and plenty specious.

"Ralph caught a fish." He says with the gentle sound of a boy that has said the same thing everyday for many months.

Kristine takes the car out of park and pulls into the driveway. "Yup, do you remember what kind of fish he caught?" She tests his memory from their conversation months ago.

"Rainbow trout. Dad says that he'll take me fishing sometime soon."

She knows she's in charge of being the strong one, but that last comment nearly pushes her over the edge of tears. She doesn't want to say anything. She takes a deep breath and wipes her eyes.

He frowns and takes his own mimicking deep breath. "Do you know how to fish Aunt Kris?"

"No, honey, but we can learn together." Kristine turns around in the driver's seat to face him with a big smile. It's a 'fake it until you make it' kind of smile, but she doesn't care.

He smiles back at her and unbuckles his seat belt. She thinks about her father cleaning fish by the lake when she was little. The disgust of seeing the fish guts spill out made her quit the hobby before she turned eight. With Ethan gone, she'll need to make more trips here to visit Bryan, and do much more boy stuff with him, like cleaning fish guts. She hopes she can convince Bryan to learn to catch and release, but there's still that sticky situation of getting the hook out.

Kristine is blasted by the muggy hot air of the evening. She's had the air-conditioning on for the last hour in the car and had no idea it is still so hot. The breeze coming off of the lakes keeps the heat in check in Rochester, at least most of the time.

Kristine walks up to the house, pulls out the keys her mother gave her and opens the door. She hears the alarm beeping and is suddenly struck with fear. She can't remember the code to the alarm. Her mother told her before she left the hospital, but she stands there in front of the keypad drawing a blank.

Bryan walks in front of her and types in the code automatically. He takes off his shoes and leaves them in a pile in the middle of the entryway. He marches half way up the flight of stairs, "Good night Aunt Kris."

"Goodnight Bryan." Kristine watches him slog up the last few steps. She knows he'll be asleep by the time his head hits the pillow.

She looks around the room. The house is spotless, as usual. The only mess is Kelly's little pile of knitting in her knitting basket by the couch. She walks over to feel the shiny indigo silk yarn in her hand. The pattern lying on top of the knitting is for a breezy summer tank top with cables and eyelets. Kelly has more time, and much more patience for knitting fanciful projects. Kristine rubs the yarn in her hands and brushes the soft silk on her face. It shimmers in the light from the small lamp next to the couch and she can see that it is actually a blend of indigo and red intertwined.

The couch is soft, like sitting on a cloud. She leans back and it swallows her, surrounding her like a hug.

She thinks about what she's still wearing. The pencil skirt and flowing blouse were perfect for work yesterday, but are feeling a little grungy after so many hours of being worn. Her bra is digging into her shoulders, but wearing the blouse without a bra would be indecent. Her sister Kelly is only a couple sizes smaller and they were the same size until after Kelly had Bryan. Kelly redoubled her efforts at the gym losing the baby weight and more, while Kristine was huddled over her briefs, skipping the gym. Perhaps, she thinks, Kelly would have a nightgown that might fit her.

Kristine shivers, and the hair on her arms stand on end; she rubs them to warm them up. She leans forward to pull her gym bag onto the couch and slowly unzips it. She moves a few things around, including her wet towel and swimsuit. She finds a sweatshirt and sweatpants at the bottom of the bag. She holds them to her face and cringes at the musty, sweat laden smell, but puts the set on anyway.

She pulls out her phone, thinking she'll write Louis a quick update on her sister's condition. As the emails from the evening come in, Kristine's weary eyes scan over them. There are two messages. One is from Mr. Pucket, the district attorney, going over the details of Kristine's departure. The other one is from Marcie, expressing her sympathy and asking for guidance on the paperwork for the Hewitt meeting on Monday. Kristine rattles off some directions for areas of research to Marcie, papers to find, and past trials to review. The email ends up being quite long for one composed on a phone. Kristine hopes Marcie can even read the email through her typos, since she's typing on a tiny keyboard. The exhaustion catches up with her. She leans over onto the soft cloud, her hand still gripping the phone. She pushes her hair out of her face, curls up into a ball and falls asleep almost instantly.

CHAPTER 7

Louis wakes up to find a hand written note on the nightstand. "Dinner at 7. -Will"

She was surprised he got reservations for such an exclusive place. *Passion for Food* was in the paper last month with rave reviews. Even the food critique whined he couldn't get a table for his required second visit. Will told her about the reservations late last week, but has been snappy ever since.

She is stiff when she gets out of bed. The ibuprofen she pops is washed down with cold coffee. Will usually makes a fresh pot while reading the paper, but he must have been in a rush this morning.

Louis wipes a bead of sweat from her brow. She checks the thermometer. It's a balmy 82 degrees outside and 80 degrees inside. She is frustrated with his insistence on fixing the air-conditioner himself, instead of calling a repairman. As a bank information technology director, he wouldn't be her first choice to fix any household appliance.

A few minutes later her cool, mind cleansing shower is interrupted by the phone ringing. She rushes across the room marking her steps with puddles of water.

"Hicks?"

"Good morning gorgeous."

She sighs, "I'm on my way in."

"Yup, just thought you might want to know that the tox analysis came back on those pills we found in the house yesterday."

"And?"

"Absolutely not a match for the junk the Chemistry Bros are slinging. In fact, they don't even look the same at all. I think we are going to have to let them go."

Louis checks her watch, "We can hold them a few hours longer. Or, wait, is their lawyer there yet?"

"Yeah, he's here now. What are you thinking?"

"I'll be there in fifteen minutes. If it isn't their junk, maybe we can sweat them and find out who might be setting them up."

"OK, I'll make sure their lawyer is prepping them for talking."

***

Louis walks into the squad room with a very large cup of coffee.

"Where's mine?" Hicks whines.

"You can get it out front from Yukiko just like I did."

"She doesn't like me."

"Maybe if you order a cup of coffee without asking her out it would help."

"Nah. That can't be it."

Louis shakes her head and smiles. "So, are our suspects ready to talk? Did you scare the pants off of them?"

"They have a lot of experience with being hauled in. Their flunky lawyer actually said he was going to sue us for malicious prosecution."

"Hmm. So we need to tread lightly? My plan may not work."

"I was thinking they could have murdered Tim and Victoria with a different drug."

"Why would they do that? Seems like it would be bad for business to have bogus product out on the street."

"Yeah, I thought of that too, unless they have some sorta grudge against Tim or Victoria? Perhaps, they owed them a lot of money."

"That doesn't make sense either. Why kill someone if they owe you money? You'll certainly never see the money again. Maim them maybe, but not kill. Until we put some sort of connection to Tim and Victoria with the Chemistry Bros, hauling them in here was just for show."

"Quinn hasn't been able to connect Tim and Victoria with anyone."

"What do you mean? And where is he?"

"He went to get me some dinner."

"Where did you send him?"

"Don't worry; I had him pick you something up too. Anyway, he's been calling around to the references that Victoria put in her lease. Some of the numbers are out of service, the rest have never heard of her. The company she put down for her employment doesn't exist."

"The landlord didn't do his homework at all. What about Tim?"

"He wasn't technically on the lease. When Quinn gets back I'll see if he can track down Tim's friends or employer."

"Good. Let's go talk to the brothers."

***

The door opens to the little interrogation room. Hicks must have intentionally confined them to the smallest room. Louis looks at the man in the bright iridescent jacket, "Mr. Lee?"

"He's Ming Lee, I'm Li Chung."

"Mr. Chung, do you know why you're here?" Hicks asks.

Li mumbles, "You think we are selling illegal drugs."

"Actually we think you murdered two people." Hicks says.

"Murdered? No way. You must be mistaken. We have alibis." Ming says.

"We didn't tell you when they were murdered." Louis says calmly.

"Right. But whenever it was, we didn't do it." Li says.

The lawyer clears his throat. "What did I say earlier?"

Both men lean back in their chairs.

"You are right to listen to your lawyer, men. But you listen to what I have to say." Louis says.

Li narrows his yes, "What's that?"

"Take a look at these two." Louis pulls out her tablet and scrolls through the pictures.

"Eww, what's wrong with them?" Li asks.

"They were poisoned by drugs matching the description for 'Lilac Trance'. That's your special brand of junk isn't it?" Hicks asks.

"It's not junk." Ming says.

"We don't know them." Li says. "Anyone could make a drug look like ours."

"The way I see it, if someone tried to make a drug that looked like yours, they'd need a reason." Louis says.

The men exchange looks.

Louis continues on, "I'm thinking you might have an idea of who would want to discredit your drugs. Is there anyone that has been particularly interested in your recipe?"

"No, man. No." Li says. "People wanted to know what it was six months ago, but now everyone is real cool. I mean, it's just a concentrated cough syrup and some other stuff."

Ming makes a face staring at the picture of Victoria in the tub, "You need to put that picture away, it's gross."

"Yes, it is. I need to find who did this to these people. You need to be my eyes and ears, if you hear about anyone other than yourself selling these drugs you need to contact us."

"Does that mean you're letting us go?" Ming asks.

Hicks pounds his fist on the table, everyone jumps except Louis. "She asked you to contact us. Do we have a deal gentlemen?"

"Yes." The men reply in sync.

Someone pounds on the one-way mirror with three short knocks.

As the door closes Lieutenant Olsen barks at Louis, "There's another couple with those fevers. Paramedics are at the scene. 623 East Blossom Avenue. You guys get on this one before it becomes the front pages."

"Yes, ma'am." Louis replies. Everyone seems to stop and stare, including Lieutenant Olsen, as Louis slips on her blazer. Her face turns flush when she notices her little painful grunt.

Hicks gets in the passenger's seat, "Seriously, what is wrong with you?"

"It's a heat rash. Will hasn't fixed the A/C and I wake up in a cold sweat. I just need to pop some more ibuprofen."

CHAPTER 8

"Mom says you'll never get it," she taunts. "She says you have fingers like a moose." Kelly laughs her high-pitched seven-year-old hyena laugh.

"I'll get it." Kristine snarls back. She pushes in the right needle, mouthing the poem her Aunt Sally taught her.

In through the front door,
Run around the back,
Hop through the window,
Off jumps Jack.

"That silly poem doesn't help. You put the needle in the wrong place."

"No I don't."

"Yes you do."

"I don't." Kristine knows better than to escalate her voice and get her mother's attention, but she can't help but to fight back.

"You do."

"I don't."

"Do so."

"That's how Aunt Sally taught me. I fix it on the way back."

"Then your stitches are all twirly."

"So?"

"So, mom says it's wrong. Mom says Aunt Sally doesn't knit right."

"I don't care. I'm doing it her way." A silence grows between the sisters. Kristine tries hard not to mouth the words to the poem, but she's still saying them in her mind.

At least her Aunt Sally was patient enough to teach her how to knit, her mother wasn't.

Kristine finishes her row. She looks over to see that Kelly's scarf has grown even faster than a weed. Kristine's cheeks turn red. Her palms are sweaty. "Why are you here?"

"What do you mean?"

"Why don't you knit somewhere else?"

"I like it here; mom says that this room has the best natural light."

Kristine looks out the early evening window to the large moon reflecting off the new snow. "Do you even know what natural light is?"

"Yes." The little girl protests.

"No you don't."

"Yes I do!" She screeches.

"What in the devil is going on in there?" Their mother shouts from the next room.

"Nothing, Mom," the girls singsong in unison.

"Can you girls do nothing a little quieter?"

"Yes, Mom," the girls singsong again.

"Fifteen minutes until bed time."

Kelly puts down her knitting on the coffee table, in the middle of the row. She bounds off to her mother's bedroom, half skipping and half jumping with the full force of a hurricane. Surely she'll ask for more time, she always does. She'll get it too, she always does. She'll make some excuse about needing to work on her perfect scarf, or needing hot chocolate, or wanting water, or not liking her pajamas, or it being too quiet, or worse, complaining about Kristine's snoring. Kristine is sure she doesn't snore. It's all just a game for Kelly, a way to stay up longer.

Kelly hardly sleeps at night, not since their father left. His departure was swift, loud, and furious. There was shouting. Her father pulling the leather suitcase out of the closet, so big that Kelly and Kristine would take turns zipping each other up inside. His pressed shirts were thrown out of the bedroom door, then the ties. Her mother was shouting about the receptionist ironing his shirts, doing his laundry and listening to the endless revisions of his closing arguments. Then her father was yelling about proof. Once the expensive leather shoes started flying, Kristine ducked her head back into their room. Kelly was fast asleep, and Kristine knew not to wake her, but couldn't help it and shook her anyway. "Kelly, wake up."

"What? What is it?" She asked groggily.

"Mom and Dad are fighting."

"So?" Kelly rubbed her eyes.

"I think she's kicking him out." Kristine whispered.

"Why is she kicking him?"

"Not kicking him, kicking him *out*."

"Why?"

"Because the receptionist ironed his shirts? Or maybe the receptionist has to iron his shirts?"

"You don't know what you're talking about." Kelly rolled over and tucked her blanket over her shoulders.

"Yes I do. She said he has to leave." Kristine talked a little louder over the shouts and banging shoes coming from the hallway.

"Leave?" Kelly rolled back over to stare at her sister with piercing eyes.

"Yes, that's what kicking out means."

There was another round of shouting. Kristine heard her mother stomping down the hallway, screaming. She couldn't make out the words; it was like listening to a screaming match under water.

Kelly sat up and stared at the door. "He'll be back, you'll see."

"Maybe."

"I'm going back to sleep." Kelly pulled the blanket over her head.

Weeks later Kelly hadn't slept much, except at school, in class. Their father had not returned. Kelly asked about him everyday, sometimes multiple times a day. She pleaded with their mother to ask him to come back.

The muffled sounds of sock covered pattering feet come closer. "Mom says we can stay up until nine thirty." Kelly beams.

"Can we watch TV?" Kristine asks, hopeful.

"I didn't ask, but I don't think so." She shakes her head for extra emphasis and picks up the knitting from the coffee table. Far from being the straight garter stitch scarf Kristine is working on, Kelly is knitting a scarf with a twisting cable down the middle. Kristine couldn't understand why it took her so long to get the simple knitting stitches and Kelly picked that up, and more, in such a short time. Kelly was always praised for her neat, perfectly even stitches. Her mother often clicked her tongue and told Kristine not to pull so tight, not to put such a death grip on the needles.

Done with another row, Kristine puts her knitting on the coffee table.

"Where are you going?"

"I'm going to bed."

"You don't want to stay up and knit with me?"

"No, I don't."

"Why not?" Kelly's face contorts into a frown.

"Because I'm tired."

Kelly puts her knitting down, again in the middle of the row. Kristine shakes her head in disgust. She couldn't possibly put her knitting down in the middle of the row. Surely she would bump the knitting and drop stitches.

"Just stay up a little longer?" Kelly pleads.

"No, I'm going to bed," Kristine hisses, so as not to attract their mother's attention.

"But Kris!"

"Don't call me that! My name is Kristine."

Kelly's voice is much louder than Kristine's whispers, "Okay, okay, *Kristine*. Please?"

"Shh! You're going to get mom in here and we'll both be in trouble."

Kelly opens her mouth to shout and Kristine reaches out her hand to cover her sister's mouth. "Shh! I'll stay, just be quiet!" She hisses.

Kelly smiles with her eyes behind Kristine's hand.

***

Kristine wakes up to the sound of Bryan's laughter, a quiet ring and her hand vibrating. It takes her a few moments to realize the giggling is coming from her ringing phone, still gripped tightly in her hand. It's her mother's special ring. She fumbles the phone, trying to find the slider for unlocking. In her haste she nearly knocks it on the floor, but manages, just barely, to answer the phone.

"Mom? How's Kelly?" Her mother is sobbing. Kristine feels like all the air from the room is gone. Her head spins. She takes a deep breath, holding back her own tears as she listens to her mother's wails. "Mom?" She asks softly, hesitantly.

"She's out of surgery. She's alive."

"Oh thank God." Kristine exhales.

"You need to come. Bring Bryan." Her mother's voice strained in a way Kristine cannot recognize.

"Yes, of course." She blinks her eyes willing them to get back into focus. "We'll be there as soon as we can."

CHAPTER 9

There is a patrol car and an ambulance at the scene when Hicks and Louis park in front of the little blue house. Louis lets out an audible yelp as she takes off her seatbelt. Hicks looks over at Louis, but a young blonde woman exiting the house snaps his head the other way. Her paramedic's uniform is neatly pressed.

"She's new." Hicks raises his eyebrows and grins.

"How do you know?" Louis asks.

"I've got a memory for blondes, and I've never seen her before." Hicks steps out of the car. He meets the young paramedic on the walkway to the house as she is removing her latex gloves with a snap of each hand. "What's going on in there?"

The woman's hands shake violently. She shakes her head, "Two dead bodies, we tried to save the wife, but she was too far gone. We did everything we could, but a fever like that-"

"How high was the fever?" Louis interrupts.

"One hundred and seven. Even if we were able to get that fever down, she could have had brain damage at that temperature." She dry heaves a little.

Louis looks puzzled, "Did she say anything Masterson?" She asks, reading off of the young paramedic's nametag.

"Nothing, she was unconscious." Masterson chokes on the word 'unconscious'. Her hands reach up to her face. She looks as though she's seen a ghost in the house.

It must be her first dead body. She taps Masterson on the back, "Don't leave yet, we may have some more questions."

Hicks opens the wooden door, "Whoa".

Masterson's partner, only slightly older than Masterson herself, is laying out the details to two uniform cops. "We got the call about twenty minutes ago. The wife called, said her husband was in distress. When we arrived no one answered the door. We could see the wife here, on the floor," he points to the woman, "through the side window. We called for backup, but we figured we needed to get in here quick. We punched through the window, unlocked the door. We did the assessment, she had a fever and her BP was through the roof. I started pumping her with fluids and I told Masterson to look around for the husband. She found him, dead, in the kitchen. As I was readying the wife for transport, she expired. Not much we could have done for her with a fever that high anyway."

Hicks pipes up, "Did you find any pills?"

"Pills? No, we didn't find any, but we really weren't looking." Douglas, the paramedic, looks around as though he missed something. "What makes you think pills, Detective…?"

"Hicks, and," he points at his partner, standing over the woman's body, "this is Detective Baker." There is an IV line extending from the dead woman's arm and assorted medical debris scattered across the floor. "I'm asking about pills because we were just at a scene yesterday. Boyfriend and girlfriend, both with fevers, were dead at the scene. We found some pills, little purple ones with 'L' and 'T' etched in them."

"I'm surprised that wasn't sent out as a general announcement." Douglas says.

"Me too." Louis groans.

"So you're talking about, 'Lilac Trance'." Douglas says with certainty.

"Yes, we have the Chemistry Bros in custody. What do you know about the drug?" Louis asks.

"It's a designer drug, a little cough syrup, a little erectile dysfunction and some other 'herbs'. Doesn't do this though." Douglas says surveying the scene.

"What makes you say that, Douglas?" Louis inquires.

"I've been working the club area downtown for the last year. Lilac Trance has been a real favorite in that crowd recently. It showed up maybe six months ago. I've never seen anyone develop a fever or die from it."

"I see." Hicks says, "Then we need to find something else that Tim and Victoria had in common with this couple..."

"Neil and Sara Kitt" One of the uniform cops reads from his notebook.

"Mr. and Mrs. Kitt," Hicks repeats.

Louis finds the husband in the den, "Well, he's dressed."

"It's almost eleven a.m., I would hope so." Hicks shrugs.

"But he's home, on a Friday, at eleven a.m." Louis says.

"Yeah, if I was home sick I wouldn't be dressed."

"Right. So, we need to find out why he is home, and where he went this morning."

Hicks starts walking toward the garage, "Maybe the car has GPS?"

"Go check. I'll look in the living room." Louis walks through the living room. Pictures of the happy couple and their twenty- something daughter appear on every wall, and nearly every flat surface. There are pictures of them riding horseback, on the beach, posing in front of abstract art, and Italian fountains. Books and magazines take up the rest of the room.

Hicks comes back, "There's GPS and the last place he searched was a house address in Marketview Heights."

"Marketview Heights? What's a guy like this doing going to a house in Marketview?"

"I don't know."

"Look upstairs, see if you can find anything."

Louis picks through the books, looking at the titles. The shelves have lots of travel books, a few memoirs and tons of romance novels. She picks out a few of them and each cover supplied with a gorgeous male specimen, sometimes with a helpless female hanging around his neck. Louis pulls out "The Scottish Lover". This particular male specimen has a bare muscular male torso wearing a kilt. Louis laughs.

She hears Hicks making his way to the living room, "Something funny?"

"Yeah, Mrs. Kitt had an interesting taste in books." Louis holds up the "The Scottish Lover" for Hicks to see.

"I coudn' afford da' shirt!" Hicks says in a fake Scottish accent.

Louis shakes her head and smiles. "Nothing unusual in the living room. What did you find upstairs?"

"The usual. A few marital aids, a dusty exercise bike, more books, no pills, other than a couple prescriptions." Hicks' voice seems defeated, four dead bodies and nothing to show for it. "Baker, I hope this isn't some disease we are picking up?"

"Me too. Let's look in the kitchen. The techs should be here any minute to do a more thorough job." Louis walks toward the kitchen and spots what she's been looking for the whole time, a small baggie, just like the one in the first crime scene. "Bingo," she says and leans over to pick up the baggie. She holds it up and waves it in front of Hicks.

"That could be for anything, you know. It doesn't have any pills in it."

"Yes, but I'll put a quarter down that trace is going to find whatever was in Tim and Victoria's baggy was in here." Louis puts the baggie back where she found it. She thinks to herself, maybe the Kitt's knew Tim and Victoria? If they did take the same drug maybe they got it from the same person. She walks over to the phone in the kitchen. She goes through the same procedure as she did with Victoria's fake rotary phone. The beeping continues until she finds what she's looking for, "Ah ha!"

Hicks peeks through the refrigerator. He pulls out a carton and looks at Louis while examining the expiration date on the skim milk, "What?"

"There's a number from nine a.m., same as the one from Victoria's yesterday."

"Out-going or in-coming?"

"Out-going for both of them."

"Huh, call it." Hicks sniffs at a plastic container.

Louis pulls out her cell phone and dials the number. She lets the phone ring eight times. "Nothing."

"No machine? Nothing?"

"Nope, I wonder if he only takes calls from numbers he recognizes? Maybe we should use the Kitt's phone?" She puts down her cell phone and dials the number again from the Kitt's phone. She listens to another eight rings, "Again, nothing."

Hicks holds an aluminum swan he's been digging at. "They ate at Chez Marin last night. She had the special."

Louis smiles, "Okay, how do you know that?"

"Because Chez Marin always has Chicken Marengo on Thursday nights."

"How do you know it was that restaurant and not some other restaurant?"

"Because no one else around here serves this dish, it's a Chez Marin specialty. It's a French dish of chicken, garlic, tomatoes, olives, white wine garnished with a crayfish and a fried egg. It was served to the victorious Napoleon army after the battle of Marengo. They used whatever they could find to feed the ravenous soldiers."

"How do you know it was last night and not a week ago?"

"There's not a single piece of food in this fridge more than a week old, the milk is from yesterday, at most."

"Huh, and how do you know it was hers and not his?"

"Because men always finish their dinners, they don't take home doggy bags that look like swans."

CHAPTER 10

Kristine can see her sister through the glass. Only, it isn't her sister, it's a hollow shell of a woman that looks like her sister. She looks around, but cannot see her mother.

"Is my mom in there?" Bryan asks. He stands on his tip-toes to see above the glass.

"Yes." Kristine says softly. Before she opens the door she bends down to talk to him. "Bryan. I want you to be prepared. Your mom went through a rough surgery last night."

"Okay."

"If you want to leave, you just tell me. Okay?"

"Okay." He repeats.

Kristine squeezes his little hand. Bryan squeezes her hand right back.

She watches his face grow scared at the site of his mother. "What are all those things?"

"They are life support machines." Kristine says. "They are helping your mom breath, and making sure her heart beat and blood pressure are okay." She pulls up a chair next to her sister's bed and sits down.

"Oh." He wipes a tear from his eyes. "Is she going to be alright?" He sits on her lap.

"I don't know, Bryan. I hope so."

Kristine leans over to hold her sister's hand. It's warm. *Kelly, what happened last night?*

***

"But I love him." Kelly sits, doodling on her jeans.

"You barely know him." Kristine slams her ethics book closed. This conversation will take too long. It will feel like three hours, but probably take an hour. "When exactly did you meet this guy?"

"I've known him for *weeks*." Kelly looks at her older sister. Kristine sees the eyes are not quite in focus.

"You've known him for weeks, and you had a date with him when?" She methodically places each book back in her bag.

"I haven't really had a date with him." She admits, but then adds, "We had coffee."

"Oh coffee. Well that explains it. Love at first bean." Kristine is now at a loss of things to fiddle with.

"How do you know I don't love him?"

"Because you're too young. You're only nineteen."

"What are you talking about? You're only two years older than I am."

"Yes, I know."

"So what makes you the authority on love and age requirements?"

"I'm not an authority. I'm just realistic. You don't really know him. You can't know him enough to love him. You like him superficially."

"I don't know how you can possibly judge my love for someone you haven't even met."

"Well, you haven't really met him either. What's his favorite food?"

Kelly looks at Kristine then back at her doodling, "I don't know."

"Every man I've ever dated loved to eat. I always tried to find out early what their favorite dish was and try to make it for them."

"Is that why every man you ever dated has dumped you?" Kelly mocks. "Your food is so horrible?"

"No." Kristine thinks about the simple failures she's had in these attempts to impress: the way too salty spaghetti, the lumpy gravy on biscuits, the small kitchen fire and the broken glass from a roasted chicken. Why would she pick a guy's favorite dish to destroy? "What's his major?"

"He hasn't declared one yet. He's taking general studies."

Kristine rolls her eyes. General studies is like declaring your major as 'underwater basket weaving', but not as focused.

"Not everyone has their entire life mapped out like little miss Krissy."

"Don't start with the nicknames. I don't have to be here."

"Yes you do. You have to drive me home and I have class in an hour."

"No I don't, you can take the bus."

"Mom says that she can only afford one car, and after the accident she never taught me to drive."

"Wow, you really can't stop bringing up the accident. You don't think mom punishes me enough about that? I thought we agreed to never bring that up again. Anyway, you're just scared to drive. I've offered to teach you a dozen times."

"I'm not scared."

"Lazy then? It's too easy always getting a ride from your older sister? Maybe I don't want to stay here for an extra two hours for your evening courses?"

"You always study anyway."

"I could study at home."

"You always say you can't because mom distracts you."

"You're doing a fine job of distracting me now. I was studying, you know." Kristine huffs and pulls her English textbook out of her bag. "Okay, what kind of relationship does he have with his parents?"

"I don't know okay?"

Kristine watches her sister draw on her jeans harder with more angular lines. Perhaps she's gone too far. Perhaps it will only make her think she loves him more.

She stares at her sister. "Okay, tell me what makes him so wonderful."

Kelly stops doodling and looks up at her sister. "He talks passionately."

Kristine smiles, but doesn't interrupt her.

"He's funny, but not like a jerk. He says funny things that make you think about what he's saying. He… I don't know. We have chemistry. He cares about people. He cares about me. He cares about what happens to me." Kelly looks like she's going to burst into tears, but tucks her legs up to her face instead. She sits on the little cafeteria stool, occupying the smallest possible space.

"Well, I guess that's good." Kristine smiles.

***

"Kristine?" Her mother's voice pulls her back out of her daydream.

"Mom?" Her mother is sitting in her wheel chair on the other side of her sister. "What did the doctor's say?"

"Bryan, honey, can you go get me a soda?"

"No. I don't want to." He whines.

"I don't think you should be here for the conversation." Her mother says holding out a wad of change. "Please. Get me a soda."

"Alright." He hops off of Kristine's lap. He shuffles out of the room, barely lifting his feet off of the ground to set it back down again. Just before he opens the door he turns to look at Kristine. She feels her heart crush in her chest.

"What is it, Mom?" Kristine still holds her sister's hand in her own.

"There was a lot of damage. Kelly had to be resuscitated twice this morning. She hasn't woken up from the coma."

"Did they say what her chances were?"

"They wouldn't say."

CHAPTER 11

The detectives arrive at the address to find a skeleton of a house. Weeds and greasy truck parts hold the pieces of cinderblock and timber together.

The gravel driveway is well used. "Someone's been here recently," Hicks points down to the oil stain in the driveway. "And look, there's a path to the door." He points to the door. It's barely hanging by its broken hinges.

Louis steps toward the house. She peeks around the open door. Dark shades cover the windows. Her eyes struggle to adjust. She listens for any sounds, but all she can hear are the traffic noises coming from the interstate a few blocks away. She places her right hand on her sidearm, peeking through the doorway around the corner. Her eyes begin to adjust. Louis sees a dingy, dark walled room, filled with musty, brown furniture. The mold smells bring back memories of digging through treasures in her great-grandmother's house in Saratoga. A small beam of light is coming from across the room, but it's not sunlight. The light is strong, but florescent green. She looks back at Hicks and whispers, "There's a room lit up behind the living room."

Hicks takes a few steps forward. A board in the porch gives way with a loud crack. His body tumbles to the ground through a hole in the porch with an even louder thud. "Damn." He winces and grabs his shin.

Louis turns her attention back to the house. She sees the light beam turn off and her pulse turns up a few notches. She pulls her gun out of the holster. She crouches down to where her partner is still rubbing his leg from the pain. Louis whispers, "Hicks? There's someone in there, he turned off the light."

59

Hicks pulls himself together, almost silently, but he struggles to break his foot free from under the porch. She always said that his six foot tall, two hundred and fifty pound frame could be ninja-like when he wanted it to, but not today. He brushes the dust he gathered from the fall out of his eyes. He grabs his gun, pointing it toward the darkness. "Rochester Police Department, come out with your hands up." He commands in a loud, clear, bellowing voice.

There's a short shuffle of feet, then a large crash of shattering glass and a whisper, "Shit."

She makes her way through the living room, one step at a time. Her eyes are completely adjusted to the dim light. A small ashtray in the shape of an ant hides amongst an army of empty cheap beer cans. The beer cans are all crushed from the center. She takes a few more careful steps on the threadbare carpet. She attempts to make it between the armchair and the end table, to the hallway. The hallway must lead to the previously lit room she saw behind the living room. She hears more shuffling feet, then a doorknob slowly turning. She readies her gun toward the hallway, but clips one of the beer cans she didn't see hanging just over the edge. She looks down just as a cascade of beer cans fall from the end table. A louder sound comes from the first door in the hallway. The door bursts open. The detectives see a flash of a person leap from one room, and crash into the next room.

"Hold it right there!" Hicks demands.

Louis rushes after the small, dark figure. She watches his sneakers disappear out of the far corner window. "Hicks, he's going out the window!"

Hicks runs out of the living room, finding the same hole he created just moments ago. This time he crashes the same leg straight through the hole. "Damn it."

Louis leaps over Hicks and snakes her way through the tall weeds and random car parts toward the back of the house. The sneakers she saw are no longer in sight. She makes her way through the junk in the backyard to look over the decrepit fence. There is a sea of other houses down a hillside, all in similar dilapidated condition. She looks down the row of houses that look like carbon copies of this house. It's like a scene from Mad Max. She makes her way back to her partner. She passes by the frame of an old chopper motorcycle, burned and bent into a nearly unrecognizable shape. Hicks is no longer stuck, cartoon-style in the porch. The beam of light she saw earlier from the living room is back. Beautiful specks of dust seem to dance in the beam of light. She notices that the door the dark figure came out from is also generating light in the room. She wonders if the dark figure returned for something, but unburdens her worry with a quick question, "Hicks?"

"Back here." Grumbling loudly.

Louis works her way past the beer cans again, nearly stepping on another can, but this time kicking it out of her way. She turns to look into the brilliantly lit room to see Hicks standing in the middle of a bathroom. The bathroom is full of chemistry beakers, bags of powder, a small stainless steel scale and a dozen different pots and burners.

"What is this?" She holds her nose against the acrid smell.

"Well, this, Detective Baker, is what we used to call a fifth grade birthday present." Hicks chuckles.

"A what?" Louis looks around the room, confused.

"Olivieri, in drug enforcement, got a chemistry set when he was in fifth grade. Said he loved it, played with it constantly for weeks. He did all of the experiments that were spelled out in the book, right down to the letter. But then he got bored. He mixed his chemicals with household stuff to find out what happens. He started with pop and then worked himself up to cleaning supplies. One of the chemicals he mixed with the cleaning supplies melted the Formica countertop in the bathroom. His mother took

61

away the chemistry set and he was grounded for a month. So, when we found bathroom, kitchen, or closet chemistry labs for creating drugs we called them 'fifth grade birthday presents'."

"I see, and this lab is for creating what exactly?"

He looks around the room cataloging the supplies, "I can't know for sure, but it doesn't look like meth, maybe ecstasy? Or maybe a poison?" He shakes his head, "What am I saying? All drugs are poison. Some of them give you a pleasure before they kill you, but in the end, they all kill you."

Louis takes a moment to think about the rare, profound comment from Hicks. She shakes her head, "I think we are looking for a more immediate killer."

She wanders toward the room that the dark figure used to escape. She finds no less than five full ashtrays and even more beer cans. The beer cans have the same crushed centers as the ones in the living room. The bed is bare, no sheets, no blankets, no pillows, just little mouse droppings. She notices stuffing coming out of part of the bed. The mice are either using the bed as a home, or for insulation. On the floor, near the window, she spots what she's been looking for. "Hicks," she calls out to her partner, "come in here for a second."

He makes his way through the detritus and walks over to her from the doorway, "This guy likes his beer and cigarettes."

"Yeah, I imagine he lived off of them for a while." She points down to her find, "There's a footprint on the floor."

"Great, I just called the cavalry; let's see what else we can find out about this place before the techs get here. I found some bills on the counter in the kitchen, all past due."

"What's the name on the bills?"

"A nice anonymous name, Jane Smith. She's the same one on the title. I looked it up when I filled out the warrant."

"When was it bought by Miss Anonymous? You never know though, it could be her real name. I have two friends, Jeremy Smith and Mike Smith, no relation."

"Sure you do." Hicks snickers, "The house was bought three months ago."

She thinks about the yard, "For how much?"

"Three grand at an auction."

"Well, I'm pretty sure Miss Anonymous doesn't actually live here. That bed is gross, and there's no clothes, no food and hygiene products."

"If someone did live here, you think they'd care about hygiene products?"

"I hope the cavalry arrives soon." Louis looks at her watch. "Or I'm going to be late for dinner."

"Don't tell me you're going like that." Hicks says.

She looks at her clothes. Little bits of dust and ash cover her blazer and pants.

"You take the car, and you're going to need a shower. I'll call Quinn and get a ride back." Hicks smiles.

"Thanks." Louis runs to the car.

"Don't worry. I'll do all the paperwork too." Hicks groans.

CHAPTER 12

Louis runs into the restaurant, but the maître d' politely, but firmly, blocks her way. She's late. She searches the packed room, full of colorful dresses, and men in dark suits. The hand blown glass sculpture hanging from the ceiling is a huge presence. It looks like a brighter, glossier version of a stalactite. She spots him at a small round table, near the kitchen door. She is amazed that her husband Will is able to get a reservation at all at such an exclusive place.

"Ma'am, I can direct you to your table," the maître d' whispers.

"Yes, my husband is over there" she says waving her hand over her shoulder, wincing in pain.

Will looks up from his phone. He stands up as Louis approaches.

"Sorry I'm late." She says, leaning over to kiss him. The taste of his salty lips and the smell of his cologne is an elixir only Will can produce. She practically falls into her chair. "Caught a weird case this afternoon," she remarks as she looks around the room and contemplates taking her shoes off. She can feel the blood suddenly rush to her toes.

"You always catch the weird cases." Will says automatically, following their years of well-established scripts.

"Speaking of weird cases, you made these reservations, and you've been elusive for a couple weeks now. Are you going to tell me what's going on?" Louis leans in over the large fresh flower centerpiece. She calculates in her mind what fresh cut flower centerpieces must cost the restaurant on a daily basis.

"Yes, well." His voice trails off. "I talked to my manager yesterday and…"

His sour face and mumbling do not match the news he's just revealed. Louis looks at him puzzled, why on earth would he be so evasive about talking to his manager? "What am I missing?"

"There's a situation…" Will looks down at his wine.

She knows it's a Chardonnay, Louis' summer favorite. She refuses to drink red wine once the outside temperature hits eighty degrees, only white. Just one strange rule of hers amongst many more he's had to learn over their fifteen years of marriage.

As he opens his mouth the waitress appears at their table.

"Good evening ma'am. My name is Sheri. I'll be serving you. May I pour you a glass of wine from the bottle, or would you like to order another wine perhaps?" The short brunette waitress has a long white cloth apron, neatly pressed as if reflecting her perfect posture, yet her weary smile gives away her exhaustion.

"Yes, the wine from the bottle would be nice. Thank you, Sheri." Louis watches as the waitress deftly maneuvers her glass around the centerpiece, picks up the bottle from the wine stand and pours the wine. This glass finishes the bottle. She looks confused and checks her watch. She thought that she is just a half hour late, but she is actually closer to an hour.

It is often hard for anyone to tell when Will is drunk, since he has such a calm and mellow personality. She suspects this is why his face didn't match the news about the manager.

"Ma'am, the specials for today are Hong Kong crab cakes served on a bed of sautéed baby bok choy. We also have a lamb salad with fregola. The lamb and greens are locally sourced. If you have any questions about the menu I'd be more than happy to help." A short silence follows the speech. Louis and Will are staring at each other.

Sheri bites her lower lip and raises her eyebrows expectantly.

Louis breaks the silence. She knows the waitress wants to put in the orders before the late evening rush. "I'm sure you're ready to order, Will?" She looks up at the waitress, "The crab cakes sound fine Sheri."

"I'll have the steak. And please bring another bottle of this wine." Will says flatly, still staring at Louis.

"Certainly, sir. Is medium rare -"

Will interrupts, "Yes, that's fine."

The waitress backs away and races toward the kitchen.

Will thumps the table with his fingers, his other hand rubbing his temples. Louis knows this is not a good sign. Her curiosity is getting the best of her, but she knows she can't rush him to get his story out. Her patience will be rewarded in the end. All of his stories take patience; patience she doesn't always have in abundance, but the stories are always worth it.

Will takes a deep breath, "So … I … well, at work …"

Louis' phone rings. A few people nearby, including an older woman with tanned leather skin, bright pink lipstick, and enough bling to feed a small impoverished nation for a month, stare at her as she fishes for the phone. She sees the caller-id, 'Robert Hicks' and silences the ringing. She knows he's probably calling to update her on the status of the investigation. Perhaps he's found something, but either way she needs to participate in this moment with her husband. "Sorry, babe, please continue."

"Yes, well, the Director of Oper-"

Louis' phone beeps loudly indicating a text message has arrived.

"Operations." Will's voice is louder, and she can hear the slur of the wine affecting his speech.

Louis' phone beeps again and she lifts it up to see the message "911" from Hicks rolling across the screen.

"Shit. I'm sorry Will. It's an emergency from Hicks. I have to take this. I'll be right back." She picks up her phone from the table. Will rolls his eyes. The older woman again stares in disgust at her. She walks briskly toward the restrooms.

Just before Louis makes it to the small alcove outside the restrooms, the phone rings again. "What's going on Hicks?"

"Baker, we got another one. The wife is dead. The husband is being rushed to the hospital. The wife is hot as hell. Not the kind of hot you want to take out on a date."

"Damn. When did it come in?"

"Fifteen minutes ago, the paramedics were spooked by the heat, called it in. Husband's going to Memorial. How soon can you meet me there?" Louis can hear the siren from his car. "I'm about twenty minutes away now."

"I'll be there soon. I just need to talk to Will." Louis hangs up the phone and hustles back to the table. She grabs the blazer from the back of the chair. She looks into her husband's eyes and frowns, "I'm sorry honey. I -"

"Have to go." Will says mocking her and finishing a sentence he's heard hundreds of times.

"I'm really sorry. Another case, but the husband is alive, perhaps we can get something out of him. Do you want me to wake you when I get home? We can talk then?" Louis winces in pain as she puts her blazer on. She leans over the table to give her obviously annoyed husband a kiss.

"Yes, we need to talk. We really do."

"Okay, I'll see you soon. I love you." Louis turns swiftly.

She hears him mumble, but doesn't turn around.

CHAPTER 13

Kristine's call to Mr. Pucket had not gone well. Marcie didn't show up for work today and the Hewitt case was going sideways. She tried to call Marcie herself a few times. Mr. Pucket wanted to know when this mysterious evidence was going to be presented to him. Kristine didn't know what he was talking about, of course.

Mr. Pucket ended by saying, "If you don't get this case back on track, it'll be both our jobs. I have a press conference in an hour. I better have something to report."

"Kristine, why are you so sweaty?" Her mother asks.

"I was outside on the phone with Mr. Pucket." Kristine collapses into the chair next to her sister's bed.

"Who's that again? I can never keep your friends straight."

"First of all, he's not a friend, he's my boss. Second of all -"

Her mother cuts her off, "Shh!"

"Mom, she's in a coma. The doctor said we should talk to her, not whisper around like ghosts."

"Don't say ghosts!"

"Fine." She crosses her arms and lets the whirring and beeping sounds from the life support machines fill the room.

"Mom, I have to go back to Rochester tomorrow."

"What do you mean?"

"I mean, I have to go back to Rochester tomorrow."

"I heard what you said." Her mother growls, "I want to know what you mean."

"I mean I need to go back to work. I mean that my case is in trouble, and so is my job."

"Like I've told your father a thousand times, you aren't the only lawyer in the office."

"I know that mom, but I'm responsible for this case and my paralegal disappeared. I bought a ticket back for eight a.m."

The little black nurse walks into the room and interrupts their conversation before her mother has a chance to explode.

Her mother chats up the nurse again. "Kelly is such a good mother. She stays home with my grandson, you know. She has a law degree, but she chose to take care of Bryan. It's a full time job, I should know. I stayed home and raised my two daughters while my bastard ex-husband was off gallivanting with the receptionist."

"Is that right?" The nurse says. Kristine thinks it must be a conversational reflex, since the nurse hasn't even turned to look at her mother since the last visit.

"Yes, the man can't keep it in his pants. Although, that new wife of his sure seems to keep tabs on him."

That's because she's co-dependent, Kristine thinks, but wouldn't dare say. She has no interest in getting involved in any conversations about her father right now. He stopped by, between cases, this afternoon. Her mother was barely able to speak the entire length of his visit. It's funny how the two had been married for twelve years, and divorced for almost twenty-five, but still couldn't stand each other long enough to hold a polite conversation.

"Do you have any children?" Her mother asks the nurse.

"Yes. Two daughters, both of them are in college. My youngest, Madeline, wants to be a nurse, like me. But I told her to be a doctor. God knows she's smart enough."

"That's wonderful." Her mother beams over at Kristine.

Kristine looks down at Bryan. He is lying on the floor. His concentration is laser focused on the video game he's been playing for the last two hours. She could hardly pull him away to say 'hi' to his grandfather during his brief appearance.

All at once the machines above Kelly start beeping. "What's that?" Kristine asks.

The nurse doesn't reply. She presses a button on the wall. "I need doctor Trepman in here now. Code blue."

"What's going on?" Kristine pleads.

Another nurse busts into the room.

"What's happening?" Kristine asks.

Bryan takes off his headphones.

"What is it?" Kristine asks again.

A woman in a white doctor's coat rushes into the room. "What's going on?"

"She's in cardiac arrest." The second nurse says.

"What does that mean?" Kristine asks.

"BP's down." The first nurse says.

An orderly runs into the room, "What can I do?"

"Get them out of here." The doctor says, pointing to Kristine and Bryan.

"No." Kristine shakes her head.

"I'm losing a pulse." The second nurse says.

"Ma'am. Please come with me." The orderly blocks her way.

"No. I'm not leaving her." Kristine protests.

"Ma'am, let them do their jobs."

Bryan starts to cry.

Kristine picks him up.

The orderly directs her toward the door.

"Is mom okay?" Bryan whines.

"I don't know, honey." Kristine pulls his hair from his face. They sit on the hard plastic chairs outside the room.

Her mother wheels herself over to them. She's sobbing.

"Did they say anything?" Kristine asks.

Her mother shakes her head.

CHAPTER 14

Louis looks around the mostly empty emergency room. One man holds his hand over a bleeding head wound and a few people look like they are there for the air-conditioning and a young couple are hovered over their infant son. People are dying this weekend, instead of just getting sick. What if there is some disease killing these couples? What if it was air borne and her life is also in danger, but she doesn't know it yet? She reaches over to her sore right shoulder and peeks at the tiny bumps forming. She's had heat rash before. Why on earth would this burn so much?

She finds Detective Hicks feeding change into the coffee machine in the far corner of the room. He pulls out the coffee from the machine. The cup's cover has a poker hand, but she can only see the ace of hearts. "Hey Hicks."

"Baker, I'll buy you a cup of coffee, see if I win the hand."

"Sure, no milk though," Louis grabs her stomach with feigned cramps.

Hicks starts feeding the machine more money, one coin at a time. "We're going to be pulling an all-nighter, I'm sure of it. I'm just waiting for the next set of bodies, you know?"

"Yes, I know. We're behind the eight ball on this one." Louis grabs the coffee from the machine and moves to cover the hand. She also has an ace, a three, a king and two tens. "A quarter."

Hicks rechecks his hand. He stares down Louis, "Raise you a quarter."

Louis returns Hicks' stare, "Call."

Hicks holds up his hand. He's got that ace Louis could see, but also two kings. "Damn." She reaches down to her pockets, "Sorry, I don't have any change on me."

"No problem, I'll add it to your mounting debts." Hicks mimes pulling out a bookie's notebook, licking a pencil and marking down her debt.

"Funny. So, what's this guy's name?" Louis sips the hot coffee and it burns her tongue a little. She can't remember the last time she had cheap vending machine coffee. At least it is hot, and caffeinated, even if it does taste a little like chicken soup.

Hicks sips his coffee, "Mm, burning hot and sweet. Just like I like my women." Hicks winks at Louis. "His name is Charles Mahoney."

"Wait, *the* Charles Mahoney? I've seen him a dozen times in the paper." Louis read an article just last week about his local bio-plastics business winning some award. His business employs hundreds of people, and is just short of an entrepreneurial miracle in 'these tough economic times'.

"One and the same. You've seen him in the paper, and I've seen him at the OTB more than a few times." Hicks smiles.

"Fellow gambler, huh? Have you asked the front desk yet about him?"

"Yeah, they're currently moving him from the ER to his own private room. That red-head over there," Hicks points to the tiny red-head woman manning the ER front desk, "says she'll tell me when his majesty is settled in his new room."

Louis sips her coffee, contemplating their crazy case. How on earth did Charles escape this plague? If the tiny pills at Tim and Victoria's are 'Lilac Trance', is it possible that's what killed them? Does the baggie in the Kitt's house contain traces of the same drug? If the paramedic has seen this drug for a while, why would it suddenly start killing people with a fever?

"I see that look in your eyes, Detective Baker." Hicks elbows Louis.

"What look?" Louis backs away from his elbow before he accidentally rubs her shoulder, and her real pain is revealed.

"That look that you get, when you are putting all the pieces together, pieces that don't fit yet." Before Hicks has a chance to explain further the tiny red-head from the front desk marches over to the detectives.

She stands a little too close and stares up at Hicks, "Mr. Mahoney is resting now in his private room. Dr. Slemp said he would like to speak to you before you speak to Mr. Mahoney. He'll meet you upstairs on the third floor outside room 312." Her squeaky voice sounds like wet rubber shoes marching across a newly waxed floor.

"Thank you, Liza." Hicks winks.

"Oh, you can call me Lizzy." She flirts back and pats her hand against his arm, subtly feeling his bicep.

Louis thinks she's going to be sick. She grabs Hicks' blazer and leads him along to the elevator. "Bert, she's tiny, and squeaking, really?"

"Hey, it never hurts to flirt." Hicks grins.

The elevator doors open up and instantly Louis wishes she had taken the stairs. An instrumental version of "MMMBop" is playing in the elevator, not that the song even had words to begin with. Louis nearly jumps back out, but realizes it's too late. The song will be playing in her head for the next hour, at least, even if she did escape. Hicks knows about her private hell with elevator music and hums along for fun.

Louis tries to shake off the annoying song of the day, trying to think of any other song, but only other annoying songs come to mind. She shakes her head and marches toward the only doctor in the hallway, obviously waiting for them. He's a burly man with gray hair, but no wrinkles to match. Men always age so much more gracefully.

"Dr. Slemp, I presume?" The joke Hicks never fails to tell at every opportunity.

"Yes, and you are?" Dr. Slemp says. His weariness comes through in his voice, sonorous with a short sigh at the end.

"This is Detective Baker," Hicks points to Louis, "and I'm Detective Hicks, we are from Rochester Homicide."

"Homicide; well Mr. Mahoney is alive and well," Dr. Slemp clears his throat.

"Yes, sir, but his wife has passed, and many other people have died in the last two days with the same symptoms as his wife." Louis points out.

"Same symptoms? How might you have the medical training to establish that?" Dr. Slemp says indignantly.

"Sir, they all had fevers. Really high fevers at the scene." Louis is careful to keep her tone even.

"I see. Well, Mr. Mahoney did not have a fever." Dr. Slemp clears his throat again in what must be a personal tick.

"What were his symptoms?" Hicks asks.

"I'm not at liberty to discuss that, I'm afraid." Dr. Slemp sniffs the air.

"That's okay, I already know he was puking at the scene." Hicks gives the doctor a grin.

"Yes, well, why ask me then?" he clears his throat again. Louis rolls her eyes.

"Curiosity. It's my job, Doc." Hicks smiles again. "We'll be talking to Mr. Mahoney now, thanks." He walks away leaving the doctor clearing his throat, once again.

Louis leans in to whisper to Hicks, "I thought I was going to have to slap him if he cleared his throat one more time. What a waste of time."

"Well, when was the last time we got good info out of a hospital doctor?" Hicks says in a booming voice loud enough for everyone on the hospital's third floor to hear.

Charles Mahoney lay on his bed looking ashen. Liquids are being pumped into his body and fresh cut flowers already sit by his bedside. A young woman, with long straight brown hair sits by his side holding a pink water pitcher. As the detectives walk into the room she moves to stand in their way. "Sorry, no press! Mr. Mahoney needs his privacy." Her voice has the kind of grating pitch that shouldn't be heard outside of a kindergarten classroom.

Louis winces and corrects the young woman, "We aren't press. We're from the Rochester Police Department, Homicide."

"Oh, ah, sorry." The young woman steps aside to let the detectives in.

"Mr. Mahoney?" Hicks asks.

"Please, you can call me Charles."

"Yes, well, Charles." Hicks emphasizes the formality of his name, "I'm Detective Hicks, this is Detective Baker. We need to talk to you about your wife, sir. I'd like to start by saying, I'm sorry for your loss."

"Yes, well, it hasn't really sunk in yet?" Charles looks down at the tissue in his hand. His eyes blur a little, he lets out a cough and the young woman rushes to his side with a small pink plastic basin. He takes a few long breaths, a few hard swallows, then heaves.

Louis knows Hicks is a sympathetic puker and has to turn around to keep himself from becoming nauseous. Charles' heaves and the sound of vomit splashing into the basin echoes in the room. Hicks holds his nose from the smell. A few agonizing minutes tick by. He whispers to Louis, "Is he done yet?"

"Not quite." Louis can't help but to smile. Looking after her little sisters, Jo and Bobbi, involved plenty of vomit. She earned herself an iron stomach after Bobbi learned to puke on command to avoid middle school exams. Louis' mother was unable to handle Bobbi's newfound talent, so Louis often had to clean up the mess. Her other sister Jo got sick easily, as if she spent the day in elementary school licking the hand rails.

Louis takes the time to observe Charles and the young woman. It takes a certain amount of love, or at least close friendship, to hold someone's vomit basin. The woman seems unusually dressed for the occasion in a tight pin striped blouse, an even tighter gray skirt and shoes that scream "sexy career woman ready to trounce out the competition." This hardly seems like an appropriate time to ask the woman questions, but when has Louis ever waited for an appropriate time for anything? "So, who might you be?" Louis looks directly at the young woman.

She knows she's the only one in the room that hasn't been introduced and she looks up from taking care of Charles. "I'm Mr. Mahoney's personal assistant, Holly Tuft."

"I see, and where were you this evening, Miss Tuft, while Mr. Mahoney and his wife were experiencing medical issues?" Louis tries to put a delicate spin on the tough situation.

"I was at home. He called me and said he and Mrs. Mahoney weren't feeling well and that I should come over right away."

Her voice's mixture of high pitch and lip smack makes Louis cringe again. "Did you?"

Charles' heaves continue unabated.

"Well, I got there as soon as I could, but the ambulance was there first."

"Okay, so you were not at the scene before Mrs. Mahoney passed away?"

"No, I told that cute cop all this at Mr. Mahoney's house."

Hick's back is still turned, but he manages to inject himself into the conversation. "Do you happen to remember the name of this cute cop?"

"Ah, no, but he had red hair, and freckles."

Hicks and Louis say in unison, "Quinn?"

"Oh yeah. That's his name, Quinn." For some reason she puts a dreamy emphasis on the name. She grins like a teenage schoolgirl, but her smile fades quickly. She has to adjust the basin she's holding to keep the puke from hurling toward her blouse.

Hicks laughs a little under his breath, but stops during a very long heave from Charles.

"Did Mr. Mahoney often ask you to come over to his house?" Louis asks.

"Not, like, everyday, but once or twice a week. It's weird actually, because Mrs. Mahoney was supposed to be out of town, she must have come back early?"

Charles tries to get on top of the heaving, "She called me this afternoon and said she was home."

"Where did she go?" Hicks asks.

"She," He stops for a moment to catch his breath, "was in Germany, looking to acquire a painting for her gallery."

Louis is confused, "Her gallery?"

"Yes she," Charles' look worries Hicks, "has a gallery downtown, it's called the Clean Slate Gallery."

The name sparks a memory in Louis' mind, "I've seen that, they hire graffiti artists to paint the gallery every few months."

"Yes, she is the curator. She called because she wanted me to pick up something on the way home."

"And what would that be Mr. Mahoney?" Louis looks into his eyes, trying to spot a lie. His information seems a little too forthcoming, making her suspicious.

Charles seems to hesitate before answering, possibly out of nausea. "I asked you to call me Charles," he hesitates further, but this time showing the classic signs of deception by averting Louis' eyes and glancing up at the ceiling. "I don't know how to say this exactly, but," his eyes meet Louis', "she wanted drugs."

"Drugs?" Hicks turns around, no longer hearing signs of heaving.

"Yes, she likes to partake in…" Charles hesitates again. Louis begins to think that perhaps he has a thing for drama? "Well, she and her friends sometimes use party drugs. Not like hard drugs."

"What kind of party drugs, Charles?" Louis makes sure to use the name he's asked them to use, so as to avoid more drama.

"Well, her friends have been taking a drug called 'Lilac Trance'." Charles reaches for his stomach and Holly is quick to grab a new plastic basin from a pile on the floor next to Charles' bed.

"Lilac Trance? How often does she take this party drug?" Louis plunges on. She is beginning to think the heaving is part of Charles' drama.

Charles clutches his stomach then looks up at Louis, "About once a week?"

"You said you were supposed to pick some up? Where do you get it?"

Charles hesitates once more, but there are no signs of heaving. He glances back and forth to each of the detectives.

Louis begins to get impatient. Either the body count, the stress of the evening, or the lack of time spent with her husband is catching up with her. While she knows she is generally an impatient person, she is usually able to get it under control during duty hours. At this rate she'll be ripping the heads off of witnesses soon. "Charles, we are with the Homicide division, we don't care about you and your wife's illicit drug use, except for how it pertains to our case."

"It's not me doing the drugs."

"No, you said she does these drugs with her friends?"
"Yes."
"Which friends?"
"Ah… you know just friends."
"People from her gallery?"
"No -"
"Anyone specific?"
"Yes… no. Not really… I don't know their names."

"You don't know your wife's friends?" Louis tries hard to keep her rolling, doubting eyes in check.

"No, I don't really know them."

"Other people died the same way as your wife. We need to find out why and if your wife had a connection."

Charles seems unnerved when Louis brings up the other victims. His surprise is unmistakable. "What other people?"

"Tim Sherman, Victoria Teague, and Neil and Sara Kitt. Do you know any of those people?" Louis moves in closer to his hospital bed.

Her lunge frightens him further and he heaves again, although this time he misses the small pink basin and vomits into Holly's lap. She looks up at Charles in shock and horror. "I'm so sorry, Holly." Louis notices that this is the first time he even acknowledged her presence, other than vomiting into the little basin she held.

"It's okay Mr. Mahoney, I just need to, ah, change. I'll call the nurse. I'll be right back." She gathers up the vomit in her tight pin striped blouse and scurries out of the room.

Hicks is holding his nose and breathing heavily to try and keep from heaving himself.

Louis is sympathetic to Hicks' condition, "Why don't you wait outside, I think we only have a few more questions."

Hicks isn't one to argue in these situations, "Yes, I think I will duck out." He leaves Louis to finish the interview.

Louis doesn't hesitate to jump right in as soon as the door closes, "So, you didn't know any of the other victims? That is, besides your wife?"

Charles looks down. Louis senses that something isn't quite right. "No, I didn't know any of-"

Louis interjects, "What about this drug dealer?"

Charles looks back up at Louis, his illness is mysteriously gone, not a heave in sight. "Black man, missing a front tooth. He keeps saying he's going to get

79

that fixed someday with all his 'monies'. He goes by 'The Jamaican'. I don't know his real name."

"How do you contact him?" Louis writes down notes in her notebook, not bothering to look up at Charles, who is obviously lying.

"I text him that I'm looking to score, he gives me a location."

Louis continues to look down, hiding her rolling eyes. How hard could it be to find an imaginary drug dealer? "Great, we're going to need your phone."

"Ah, it's back at the house. I didn't take it off the charger."

"Charles, don't leave the city. If we need to get in touch with you how shall we do that?"

"You can call Holly. Her number is 585-555-3786."

"Thank you." Louis hands him her card from her blazer pocket, "If you think of anything you haven't told us," *like more description for your imaginary drug dealer*, "please don't hesitate to call. Feel better soon. We'll be in touch." She walks out of the hospital room just as Holly walks back, her top replaced with a gym bag loose fitting T-shirt, so wrinkled it looks like someone ironed them in.

"So, you're finally done then?" Holly's grating voice makes Louis cringe again.

"Yes, Mr. Mahoney gave us your number, please don't leave town in case we have more questions."

Holly looks concerned. "But, Mr. Mahoney has a flight to the city next week for a big trade show. I hope you'll be done with this investigation by then."

Hicks pipes up, "So do I, Holly, so do I."

Holly pushes the door open to the room with a bump of her hip, giving Hicks a small swoon.

The door shuts and Louis grabs Hicks' arm. The two advance toward the stair well. "Get on the phone as soon as you can to your buddies in drug enforcement. We are looking for a drug dealer named 'The Jamaican.' He's a black man, missing a front tooth. He sold Charles the Lilac

Trance. Although I think he's about as real as the Easter Bunny, we need to follow up."

Louis' rushes down the three flights of stairs.

Hicks huffs out a question, "Great, what else?"

"His cell phone is back at the house. He used that earlier today to contact the 'Easter Bunny', I mean 'The Jamaican.' I think we need to get there next." Just as Louis finishes the sentence her phone rings, "What?"

"Detective Baker?"

"Yes?" Louis continues to rush down the stairs taking them two at a time.

"This is Officer Quinn."

"Quinn?"

"You need to get over here, to the Mahoney residence."

"We're actually on our way now. Can you find Mr. Mahoney's cell phone? He said he left it on the charger." Louis stops in her tracks when she sees the crowd of reporters outside the hospital doors. Quinn yammers on but she has stopped listening, only hearing the word 'paint'. She blocks Hicks' way, and motions toward the door.

Hicks sees the cameras, "Uh oh."

"Yeah, let's go around back."

"What?" Quinn is confused.

"Nothing Quinn, talking to Detective Hicks. We'll be right there." Louis doesn't wait for a reply and hangs up the phone. It's as if the press can smell blood in the water. The detectives dash to Louis' car. They arrive to see a young Asian man, smartly dressed, is waiting there. She tries to place him. She's sure she's never seen him before.

"Is it true that Charles Mahoney is in the hospital?" His voice is soft, but insistent. To Louis it is a welcome change from Holly's grating pitch.

"Who are you?" Louis looks at him confused.

"I'm with the Rochester Herald." Louis thinks at this time of year with his youthful looks, he's likely an intern or freshly graduated from the university.

Louis' training in press negotiations comes in handy, "No comment." Five hour training session came down to an easy sentence, "If you were not told to talk to the press your only answer is, 'No comment'" The trainers went through dozens of combinations, but really the rule is pretty simple. Just say "No comment" and you can't go wrong.

"Is it true that his wife died?" He moves to step in front of Louis when she grabs the car door.

Hicks' clutches the guy by the back of his shirt. "Perhaps you missed it when she said 'No comment'?"

The reporter is a little startled. "Ah, sorry. I just need something for the blog roll. I heard a lot of people died in the last two days. I want to find out what's going on."

Louis' exhaustion begins to show, "You and me both." She hesitates and smiles, "Look, give me your card. I'll call you and give you a quote, even if it's a little one, tomorrow morning. Perhaps before the nine-to-fiver's wake up for their morning coffee."

The reporter reaches inside his back pocket and hands Louis his card. She reads the card, 'David Huang, crime blogger, Rochester Herald.'

"David, I'll call you later." Louis gets into the car and Hicks walks around to the passenger's side. "Why don't you take your own car?" Louis looks curiously at Hicks. She flinches at the pain putting on her seat belt.

"I'll get Quinn to drive me back to my car. What the hell is going on with you Baker?"

"Nothing. Just a heat rash."

The crowd of reporters block her exit from the hospital's parking lot. "Crap."

"Let's go lights and sirens. Ten points if you hit the cameraman." Hicks smiles and plops the siren on top of the roof.

***

Louis turns the corner a few blocks from the Mahoney's address and is stopped by a roadblock. She rolls down the window and notices the air has finally cooled down from today's blistering heat, but the humidity is still high. The uniformed officer from the roadblock shines a light in her face.

"Detective Baker?" He asks.

"Yes," Louis replies, annoyed, "and you are?" She is blinking and squinting up at the man behind the flashlight.

"Oh, sorry detective." The man brings down the flashlight and Louis' eyes take a moment to adjust.

Hicks' however recognizes the officer right away, "Sergeant Walsh. It's been a long time, how's your wife?"

"We're divorced." Walsh grumbles.

"Oh, good for you, see you at Frank's bachelor party, then?" Hicks has a way of finding the silver lining of any dark cloud.

"Yeah, you're on, Hicks!" Walsh smiles.

"May we proceed to the crime scene now, gentlemen?" Louis isn't in the mood for Hicks' sociability tonight.

Sergeant Walsh is still grinning widely, "Yes, Ma'am. You'll see it's the last house in the cul-de-sac. It's the one that looks out of place."

Louis crinkles her brow, wondering what qualifies as looking out of place. "Thank you, Sergeant." Louis puts the car in drive. She leaves the window down, enjoying the newly cooled fresh air she's missed the rest of the day.

Several Colonial style houses are lit up in a disco mix of flashing lights at the end of the drive. When she spots the out of place house, the comment Sergeant Walsh made makes more sense. One ultra modern looking blocky house sits at the end. While the rest of the houses are crowded together, the Mahoney's must have purchased the lots adjacent to their house, as it stands alone. Louis can't make out the different levels of the house, as the windows are at random heights. The exterior is a mix of dark wood, polished metal and smooth white stone.

Louis parks in the circular driveway, already holding three other police cars. The garage door is open. A few crime scene techs walk in and out of the house through the garage.

Hicks jumps out of the car, "Do you know what this is?" He slams the door to Louis' car and strides quickly over to the black sedan.

"Should I?" Louis walks into the spotless garage. There are no tools, no hardware, no supplies, just two cars, one white, and one black. Hicks is drooling over the black car and Louis recognizes the white car as a Mercedes. Even in the low light the white paint gives off a pearly glow.

"This is a Continental GT Bentley 4 Liter V8. Zero to sixty in four point six seconds." Hicks stands back and admires the car with a little whistle.

Louis smiles, feeling her sense of humor come back. She leans over the car and takes a snooty look over at him, "Pardon me, do you happen to have any Grey Poupon?" Her voice is full of proper English pomp.

"Ha. Ha. Very funny Baker." He shrugs and mocks her fake accent, "Some people just can't appreciate a fine automobile like this. Did you know this car comes in seventeen shades of black?"

"Why would you need more than one?" Louis laughs, "Let's find Quinn." They make their way through the garage, following a few techs to the gleaming polished stainless steel kitchen, with white marble countertops. She finds Quinn standing on the last step leading from the kitchen to the enormous living room.

Louis stands behind Quinn. Before she is able to say anything to him she is struck by the living room's minimalist furniture and maximum scale paintings. The paintings are all abstract; one is just white with subtle tints of blue forming a square in the center. Her tired brain struggles to comprehend the painting. It's the same feeling she had as an elementary school student, the first time she saw a painting like this at the museum.

Hicks elbows her in the side, causing her to grunt in pain, "Don't worry, I don't get it either."

Quinn whips his body around to face them. "Oh, detectives …."

"What kind of situation do we have here?" Hicks raises an eyebrow.

"Ah well. It's another fever." Quinn points to the woman on the bright white carpet.

"Yes, well, we know that. What else do you have? Did you find any Lilac Trance?" Louis asks impatiently.

"No. But we did find a few weird things?" He looks down at his notebook.

"What kind of weird things?" Louis looks around, not noticing anything out of the ordinary, except sparse furniture and strange art.

"Well, Mrs. Julie Mahoney has paint on her fingers." Quinn points over to the body again, indicating Mrs. Mahoney.

Louis follows Quinn's pointing finger, "If she's over there, why are you over here?"

"I don't want to mess up the carpet."

Helms grins, "I think it's a little late now to worry about her carpet."

Louis looks down to see a trail of scuffed footprints across the white carpet and shrugs. "You said weird 'things'. What else have you found?"

"The paintings are fake and -"

"Fake? How do you know that?" Hicks interrupts.

A small bald man pops his head in from the other room. "Because I told him they were."

Louis strides across the lush carpet toward the man, "And you are?" The carpet is so plush and white it feels like walking across fresh snow on a warmly lit winter day.

The man reaches out his hand to shake Louis' hand, "James Henry." He fishes around in his small satchel for his card, and then hands it to Louis.

She reads the card, 'James Henry Esq. Executive Insurance Adjuster, Cloak Insurance Agency'. "I don't believe you should be here, Mr. Henry. This is an active crime scene." Louis scolds.

"Yes, well. I know that. This Reinhardt piece is a criminal reproduction." Mr. Henry clicks his tongue and his pen at the same time. He adds a few notes in the notebook he's holding, shaking his head in disgust.

"Yes, well, regardless of the paintings, you may have noticed that you are standing over a dead body?" Louis points down to the woman on the floor. Her sheer white blouse blends in with the white carpet. Louis can see the sweat has matted down her hair, hair that was not so long ago pinned back neatly in a tight low bun like hers. In fact, her hair is the same color. Were it not for the beauty mark on her cheek Louis would think she was looking into a mirror.

"Yes, well." Mr. Henry tucks his notebook back in his leather satchel. "Mrs. Mahoney asked me to come here. I was here when Mr. Mahoney was hauled away in the ambulance."

"Why exactly did Mrs. Mahoney ask you to come? And how do you know these paintings are fake?" Louis points to the nearest immense painting.

"Mrs. Mahoney called me a few hours ago. She said that I needed to get here right away, that something was wrong with her paintings. Of course, I came right over. Well, as soon as I was able to break free from one of my other clients that is." Mr. Henry smiles at Louis, but his eyes break from hers. He leans his head to the left to look around her. He sees something in the gold-flecked painting behind her. He clucks his tongue again and pulls his notebook back out of the satchel. He makes a long hand written note in his notebook and rubs his forehead as though he were brushing his non-existent hair out of his face. When he finishes with his note he looks up at the confused detective. He points at the painting. "You see this here?" He points to the bottom left corner of the painting.

"See what?" Louis moves in closer to the painting, not seeing anything obvious.

"This! This!" He points hard at the corner. He clucks his tongue again, a sound annoying her as much as the doctor earlier. After a moment she shakes her head. "Seriously, you don't see that?" He lifts his arms in disgust, "I can spot it from at least ten feet away. I can't believe anyone would think they could pass this shoddy fake past Mrs. Mahoney. Honestly, given fifteen minutes I could train even you to spot fakes like these."

She winces at the insult, "I'm afraid Mr. Henry, if you aren't going to answer my questions, I'm going to have to take you to a nice room where you can admire the gray paint on the walls."

"Gray? Sounds horrid." He looks confused for a moment and the look of shock on his face makes it apparent that he gets her meaning. "Detective, if you would just look at this corner of the painting very carefully."

Louis moves in even closer, her face nearly touching the five-foot plain black painting. In the endless sea of black she sees a small fleck of gold. "The gold?"

Mr. Henry shakes his head, "No, no, the corner. Do you see that small bit of bare canvas? Every painting here has a small clue."

"So the bare canvas wasn't part of the original?" Louis' asks with an apparent lack of confidence after her incorrect guess about the gold paint.

"No, John Morris doesn't leave bald spots in his series on bleak plumber's lives, detective." Mr. Henry's emphasis on the word bald makes Hicks expel a little laugh. Mr. Henry turns to frown at Hicks, who quickly looks down to examine his notebook. He then turns to Louis and sees her grinning. He pushes on, "Every piece in this house has a small clue to its falsehood. The painting in the dining room is so newly painted you can smell it. The ones upstairs however, are harder to identify."

"Are you saying every painting is fake?"

"I can't be sure until I get them all to the lab. We'll need to do a thorough analysis, for insurance purposes." His voice trails off. He walks toward another painting as though he is touring a museum exhibition.

"Mr. Henry, right now this is a crime scene. If you were here when Mr. Mahoney was taken to the hospital you need to go with Quinn and give him your statement."

"So I guess I get to examine those gray walls after all." Mr. Henry sighs.

Louis smiles, "Yes, the city employees think of it as their masterpiece."

"Detective Baker, the walls are a statement on municipal disgruntlement." Hicks says, never one to miss joining in on the fun.

Louis waves Quinn over, "Please escort Mr. Henry back to the station."

Quinn charges over from his small spot near the kitchen, "Yes ma'am."

Louis watches the little insurance adjuster leave the room, quietly angry. "I don't know about you but I'm sick of talking about paintings. What have you found out about Julie Mahoney?"

"Well, as Quinn pointed out, she's got paint on her fingers." Hicks takes his gloved hands and picks up her hand to show Louis.

Louis scratches the back of her neck, "She works at a gallery, that can't be too unusual."

"But it's, just on her right index finger. Nothing on her clothes."

Louis takes another look at her clothes, thinking her friend Cece probably knows the designer, "Yes, look at them, you wouldn't paint in an outfit like that. Of course, I wouldn't paint in any clothes."

Hicks grins, "You prefer to paint in the nude?"

"Funny." Louis says sarcastically, "What else?"

"Mike found a wine glass on the, I don't know, what would you call that? A coffee table maybe?" Hicks points to a short table a few feet away. "It's sorta like an octopus was cast in bronze and smashed with a hammer, wouldn't you say?"

"Sure. Possibly a statement on the commercial fishing industry." Louis mimics Mr. Henry's voice.

Hicks laughs and holds his nose to make an even more snobbish sound, "Actually, it's a normative statement on aquatic ecology."

Louis shakes her head in bewilderment. There is no way to out-Hicks him, better to give up now. "What else?"

"A martini glass in the kitchen. Techs have bagged both glasses and their contents for the lab. There's no sign of forced entry. There's no baggie of drugs anywhere." Hicks looks down at his notes to make sure he hasn't missed anything.

"Okay, what about Mr. Mahoney's phone? That's what we came here for."

"Mrs. Mahoney's phone was in her purse." Hicks points to the tech carefully examining the contents of Mrs. Mahoney's purse a few feet away. "But we didn't find Mr. Mahoney's phone."

"He said it was on the charger." Louis recalls the conversation from earlier.

"Yes, but it's not. The charger is on his desk. There's no phone attached to it." Hicks walks past a large wall, with an equally large painting hanging on the wall in the den. He leads Louis to the floor to ceiling glass office with two desks. "See, here's the charger, but no phone."

"Damn. I was hoping we could get a bead on the drug dealer he mentioned. Why would Mr. Mahoney lie? Unless of course he was lying about the drug dealer, and with a description like 'The Jamaican,' how could he not be lying?"

"Perhaps he forgot he actually took the phone with him?" Hicks gives Mr. Mahoney the benefit of the doubt.

"Maybe Aria can do some magic and track down Mr. Mahoney's phone. We also need her to track down that number from both of the other scenes today. Maybe that number belongs to 'The Jamaican'?"

"I don't remember any 'Jamaican' from my time in drug enforcement."

Louis knows the pace of drug enforcement is fierce. The dirt bags selling poison come and go constantly, like a revolving door installed in the jail.

Hicks sighs, "I'm going to make that call now. Peski should be just about getting into the squad. Who knows, maybe we'll get lucky and he'll know this 'Jamaican'."

Louis thinks about her abrupt departure from dinner and checks her watch, eleven p.m. Her husband must be asleep by now, considering how early he usually wakes up. She thinks about the conversation she had with Will, before her phone rang. She wonders what happened at work that it required a fancy dinner and a private conversation. A raise perhaps, but why would he get a raise but be upset by it? What is bothering him so much? She knows as sure as the sun rises that he won't want to discuss it on the phone. The temptation is pretty high to work it out with him now. Louis and Hicks might be driving around for hours trying to find 'The Jamaican'.

Louis can hear Hicks' conversation coming to an end. This is the part where he cracks a smile and a joke with one of his 'drug buddies' as she calls them. Over the last year, Hicks' 'drug buddies' have come in handy, but they love to have long conversations. They are always pestering Hicks to find out how he got out of drug enforcement and into such a sweet deal in homicide.

"Yeah, Peski, so I'll see you at Frank's bachelor party?" There's a short silence, "Well of course there are

going to be strippers, it's a bachelor party, dumbass."
Hicks laughs hard. He hangs up the phone. "Peski says he's
never heard of 'The Jamaican', he knows a guy that's
missing a tooth, but that guy is white as a sheet."

Louis looks down, and winces in pain as she lifts her
hands to her forehead to rub her temples, "Great, now
what?"

"We drive!"

Chapter 15

Kristine lies on the couch in her sister's house, staring up at the ceiling fan. Her mind is troubled by the thought of taking care of Bryan on her own. Should she move back to Virginia? Let him stay with his friends? Perhaps she should move him up to live with her in Rochester? Where will he go during the day, while she's at work? Work. It will be so difficult to get a job here, in Northern Virginia. It's lawyer central. The reason she moved away to begin with. She likes it in Rochester; her friends are there, and her life. Maybe Bryan can try living in Rochester for the summer? Then, at the end of the summer, before school starts, they can negotiate if he wants to stay. Schools. What schools would he go to? Would he get along with the kids there? She never liked starting in a new school, or making new friends.

As if she didn't have enough to think about, the Hewitt case pops into her mind. How can a bastard like Dennis Baxter have done such an evil thing to a young woman? He was her stepfather. If he is able to get away with raping and murdering his own step-daughter on a technicality, because of some incompetent young doctor from the medical examiner's office, she'll scream. She's going to do everything she can to make sure the bastard is found guilty. If his DNA wasn't in the young girl's vaginal swab, there must be some explanation. Perhaps he used a condom. If he used a condom, the crime must have been premeditated. He planned it. If he planned it, he must have made a mistake. Who plans a murder by burying the body between the mattress and the box springs? The more Kristine goes through the evidence in her head, the less it seems to make any sense.

After a particularly frustrating round of thinking, she pounds her fist into the couch. She hears a small voice from the top of the stairs, "What's wrong Aunt Kris?"

Kristine is transported back to the here and now. She wonders how long Bryan has been watching her. She's lost her only sister, and her nephew's only mother. "Come over here." She whispers, careful not to talk too loudly and wake her mother from her nap.

Bryan makes his way slowly down the stairs, step by painful step. Kristine knows from her talks with Louis that kids know, almost instinctively, when something terrible is going on in the adult world. Her talks with Louis started early in their relationship. They sat in stifling heat, in the attic rooms in the Old Inn at Letchworth Park. They shared an ornate Victorian room, lit by a little red brocade lamp with black fringe. On the third night, after Kristine bore her soul, confessing her confused relationship with a much older man in the town she left, Louis described her parent's tremulous relationship. Their conversation lasted well into the early morning. Louis described their fights, and how she always knew, just from the smell in the air when she walked in the door that her father had been on another bender. The benders didn't often get physical, but Louis' mother always shouted, always nit picked, always pushed her father to the brink in order to wear down her husband.

Bryan reaches the last step, he's been concentrating on the stairs and he looks up, almost as if he needs something else to concentrate on. He focuses on his aunt. He meets her eye.

Kristine decides to be honest, "Come sit with me. I'll tell you a story."

Bryan walks over to his aunt and is sucked into the plush couch by the dent that Kristine makes.

"When you were born there were complications."

Bryan smiles repeating what he's heard dozens of times, "Yeah, Mom says that I'm always late, even when I was born."

"Yes, that day she made me promise that if anything ever happened to her and your dad, I would take care of you."

"Mom says you are my god-mom."

"That's right," Kristine chokes on the words. "Do you understand what I'm saying Bryan?"

"Yeah. You are my god-mom." Tears fall down his cheek.

"Yes, Bryan. I'm your god-mom. We need to talk about you moving to my house. We need to talk about our future together."

Bryan thinks about this for a moment. She tries to imagine what he's thinking about. Kristine can see the worried look on his face, but she hasn't figured out what exactly he's worrying about. She decides to be patient and let him lead.

"Where will I sleep?" Bryan finally asks.

Kristine hadn't really thought that issue through, but comes up with a plan on the spot. "Downstairs. I'll take out the bookshelf. I can put all those old dusty law books in storage."

"But, what about Pete?" Bryan whines.

Kristine wracks her brain trying to remember who Pete is. She hasn't had much sleep, but she's sure she doesn't have another nephew. A stuffed animal? A pet? She honestly cannot remember. "Who's Pete?"

"My gecko. Mom got him for me last week. She wants me to be responsible. Responsible and take care of something for the summer."

Kristine laughs and smiles at Bryan, "Pete can hang out right next to you. And you can take care of him all summer long."

"Okay." Bryan scratches the back of his head, "I'm hungry." He whines, "What's for dinner?"

"Good question, let's go raid the fridge and see what we can find." Kristine gets up from the couch. Bryan sinks into the valley left behind.

***

Kristine can hear the muffled sounds of her phone ringing just as she finishes making the last chocolate chip pancake. She flips a few of the pancakes onto Bryan's plate quickly. She runs to the living room, searching for her phone. The muffled sound of the phone ringing ends and she cannot find the phone. She searches the coffee table, removing every men's magazine, gardening magazine and knitting magazine to look underneath them. She searches the end table, moving the knitting. Finally, she thinks to look between the couch cushions. She fishes it out from between the cushions just as the little bell rings to indicate she has a voice mail.

She stands in the middle of the living room, listening to the message, staring at her sister's clock, calculating in her mind. After listening to the message she searches the room for a pen and paper.

"Bryan?"

He walks into the living room. Chocolate covers his mouth. "What?" He asks with a full mouth.

"Where does your mom keep her scratch paper?"

"Her what?"

"Paper for writing down messages, scratch paper."

"Oh." Bryan walks over to a little old-fashioned telephone stand, and then pulls on the little drawer. It doesn't budge. He pulls a little harder and the drawer handle comes off in his hand. He's stunned, holding the little brass handle in his hand. His face puffs up, his eyes squint tightly, and his chin works his way towards his nose, creating an exaggerated frown.

Kristine watches his reaction in slow motion until he starts to cry. "Oh, Bryan, it's okay honey." Kristine walks over to comfort him.

"I broke it." Bryan sobs, his mouth still half full of chocolate pancake.

"I know. It's okay. I can fix it." She wipes his bangs out of his eyes. She wipes his tears with her shirt. She notices little chocolate pancake stains he's left on her shirt and smiles.

"Can you fix it?" He sobs.

"Yes, of course I can." She grabs the handle from his hand. She holds it up to the drawer and notices that the little antique loop holding the handle in is slightly bent. "Where does your dad keep his tools?"

He wipes the snot from his face with his robot pajama sleeve, "In the garage."

"Great. All I need is a pair of pliers. Do you know what those look like?"

"Um," He wipes the tears from his eyes with the other sleeve, creating good chocolate stain symmetry, "I think so."

"If you get me a pair of pliers I can show you how to fix this drawer handle and we can get to the goodies inside."

"Okay" Bryan trots off to the garage, sniffling.

A few moments go by and Kristine goes back to thinking about her message. It is almost too unbelievable. There just isn't enough time. Her wandering mind is brought back by the sound of metal tools hitting the floor of the garage. She leaps over the steps in the entry way and busts open the garage door. "Bryan?"

"Yes?" He looks up from a sea of metal tools. He's standing in the middle holding a very large set of pliers, like the kind used for plumbing. "I have the pliers." He smiles while struggling to hold up the two-foot long pliers.

"Excellent." She smiles back, "Hopefully you didn't wake up Grandma H. in the process." She picks up the tools, placing each one back inside the toolbox. She finds the little pair she really needs, "I think these ones will work a little better don't you?"

"Oh, yeah. Those ones will work better because they're the right size." He points out.

"Right, let's go fix that drawer." They walk back to the tiny telephone stand. Kristine sits down in front of the drawer. Bryan watches eagerly as she places the little brass antique handle inside the left loop. She uses pliers with her right hand to work the handle into the tiny right loop. She smiles at Bryan and he beams right back at the job well done. She pulls at the handle but it still doesn't budge. Maybe looking around somewhere else for a piece of paper might be a good idea. Just as she's about to give up hope the drawer breaks free. She can hear a piece of paper crumple as if it is stuck in the back of the drawer. She pulls out the drawer fully. She peeks into the back of the drawer and spots a dark purple folder, crumpled and taped to the top of the underside of the drawer.

"What is it Aunt Kris?"

"I don't know, honey." She uses her fingernails to remove the tape from the folder. She pulls it out and opens it up and skims through the first few lines and flips through a few pages. The look on her shocked face, the second time in less than fifteen minutes, is tough to hide from Bryan.

"What is it?" Bryan whines.

Kristine shuffles through a few more pages, she shakes her head.

"Aunt Kris?" Bryan whines.

Kristine shuts the folder. "Ah, it's nothing, just some insurance papers." She lies.

"Oh"

"Why don't you go back to eating the rest of your pancakes, before they get cold?"

" Okay." Bryan shuffles back to the kitchen slowly.

Kristine pulls a little note card out of the drawer. She carefully closes the drawer back into the telephone stand. It goes in much easier this time, without the offending purple folder blocking the way. She takes her phone out of her sister's sweat pants pocket and dials the number again for her voicemail. She takes careful notes, while listening to the message. She paces back and forth in the living room. The room is quiet, except for the sound of Bryan humming along to his own tune, while finishing his pancakes. Her mind fixes on one idea. She knows she was a fool to think that she could drop everything and there would be no consequences. *Why can't he wait a few days? Just until after the funeral?*

She closes herself up into the tiny bathroom to make a few phone calls. When she comes out she can hear faint noises coming from down the hallway. She strains to identify the sound. She finally understands she is hearing her mother's hushed sobs. She wonders which bit of additional bad news to tell her first, but she can't bring herself to decide. She walks back into the kitchen.

She smiles at Bryan's messy face, "Hey, why don't you wash your face and change into some clothes. I'm going to take a quick shower. Meet me down here in fifteen minutes. We'll walk to the park."

"Cool!" He races up the stairs. She forgot to tell him to do it quietly while Grandma H. is still sleeping.

Kristine walks toward her mother's special room. Kelly always mockingly called it 'The Pepto Bismal room'. She adorned it with every shade of pink she could find, her mother's favorite color. There are two pink ceramic lamps with bright pink lamp shades, pictures of pink roses in pink tinted frames, pink lace curtains, pink Depression glass candy jars with little pink candies inside, little pink pigs frolicking on the bookshelf that is lined with antique books, each with a pink spine. The sheets are pink and the comforter is tied together with copious pink ribbons.

Kristine knocks on the door. "Mom?" She whispers.

Her mother sniffles, "Yes?"

She cracks open the door, "I need to talk to you..." Kristine looks around the room, spotting a new pink bunny sporting a pink-polka dotted ribbon, "... and take a shower." She picks up the bunny, turning it over in her hand.

"She found that just last week," her mother sobs, "at the antique show, the one they have at the fairgrounds every year?"

"I know the one. I'm going to shower, Mom. There's some chocolate chip pancakes keeping warm in the oven for you."

"His favorite. I make them on Sunday's when he comes to visit me after church."

Kristine smiles and unzips her gym bag. She pulls out her running shirt and shorts.

"My God, that stinks. You can't go out in public like that."

"Yeah, I forgot how much they smelled."

"Your sister has to have something from a couple years ago you can wear. Why don't you go upstairs and look through her closet?"

Kristine tries to push past her mother's slight. She can almost feel the sting. She knows not to respond, it would only make things worse. She puts her sweaty clothes back in her gym bag. She walks out of the room and up the stairs. She runs into Bryan as he clomps down the stairs.

"Where ya going, Aunt Kris?"

"I need to borrow some of your mom's clothes," she hesitates for a second, "if that's okay?"

"Sure, Mom's not going to need them anymore, except maybe..." Bryan's mood turns quickly. Kristine can see the thunderstorm racing through his mind.

She takes a deep breath, waiting to let Bryan's thought complete, ready for a big hug he's going to require. He surprises her, however and doesn't finish the sentence. He hums to himself for a second. He rushes downstairs, crosses the living room wood floor in three steps and a long slide into the couch. He picks up the remote, turns on the TV and dials in the cartoon channel just as Wile E. Coyote smacks into a large brown desert rock. She laughs. It must have been what he was thinking of doing before she interrupted him.

***

She grabs hold of her ponytail, breathing in her sister's shampoo, rosemary and mint, the perfect aromatherapy. When she walks back down the stairs, her head clearer, Daffy Duck is convincing the naïve Elmer Fudd that it is, in fact, wabbit season.

Bryan turns around on the couch, "Can we go to the park?"

She smiles, "It's getting late and, I need to talk to Grandma H."

"Oh, okay. Then we can go to the park, right?"

"Yes, but just for a short while." Kristine escapes the conversation, opening the door to the kitchen.

Her mother is parked at her spot at the kitchen table, eating one of the chocolate chip pancakes. "I don't really like these, you know. I usually just make them for Bryan and have an egg sandwich or something."

"I'm sorry Mom, do you want me to make you something else?"

"No. But can you pour me a glass of water? This is so sweet. Did you eat?"

"No. I'm not hungry."

"You should eat something, skipping meals can cause weight gain."

Kristine turns her body, looking around for a piece of fruit and shaking her head, but not enough for her mother to see. "When were you going to tell me about Kelly and Ethan?"

"What about them?"

Kristine opens the breadbox, thinking, *maybe she doesn't know*.

"What about them?"

Kristine pulls out a croissant, "Nothing, never mind." She takes a bite of the croissant; it's stale but still melts in her mouth. She knows, just from the taste, that it came from the 'Little French Bakery'. "Mom, I still have to go back to Rochester."

"What? What do you mean you have to go back to Rochester?"

"My case -"

"Your sister just died. You have responsibilities Kristine Anita Rocha. You have responsibilities to your sister. You have responsibilities to Bryan." Every sentence is emphasized with the butt of the fork on the hard antique table.

Kristine is shocked at hearing her full name spoken in anger for the first time in several years. She mentally goes back to her childhood days, as if she were trying to talk her way out of some trouble. Even her voice turns to a pleading whine, "I know, it'll just be for a couple of days."

"What could possibly be more important than Bryan?"

"Shhh!" she holds up her fingers to her mouth and looks toward the living room.

Her mother lowers her voice, but not by much, "Kristine, I mean it. What?"

"The D.A. called. The case I was working on, the lawyer for the defense found out about some DNA evidence that was botched. He wrote a motion to dismiss the case. Somehow it went before a judge this afternoon. The judge says that we have until Monday afternoon at one o'clock to find some other evidence in the case, or her killer is going to be set free."

"Okay, why does it have to be you?" This sentence is emphasized with the fork cast onto the porcelain plate.

"It's my case, Mom."

"Well then, why can't someone else do it?"

"Everyone else is busy too, Mom."

"I don't believe that for a second, you just think you are irreplaceable. Just like your fa-"

Kristine interrupts, "Fine, I can't trust that my paralegal can handle it, she's too new. At least two other lawyers refused to take the case because they said it was hopeless."

"Hopeless?"

"Juries watch too much TV. They insist on DNA evidence, or some other magical scientific evidence that points to the defense." Kristine rolls her eyes, "The more obscure the better, in fact."

Her mother sits, steaming. "You have to take him with you."

"What?"

"I said, you have to take him with you."

"But -"

"Kristine, you are his mother now. You have to learn that your job isn't first, Bryan is. He is for the rest of your life."

"You're *my* mother, why can't you help *me*?"

A stare down starts between the two bull-headed women. But Kristine knows the heated conversation is over when her mother speaks the next line very softly, "You have no idea how much I am helping you."

Knowing she's lost the argument before it's really even started, she too takes a softer tone, "Fine, are you coming too?"

"No, I'm not. I'm not going to fly. You have to be back here by Tuesday afternoon. I'll arrange the funeral. By myself." Her mother pushes the wheelchair away from the table.

Kristine feels the shame and guilt that is directed her way with her mother's gray-blue eyes, "I'm sorry, Mom."

"Don't be sorry, be here on Tuesday."

CHAPTER 16

"Haven't we seen this block before?" Louis asks.

"Yup, but these roaches scurry so fast you have to double back." Hicks eyes scan the back alley.

"I don't think this guy even exists." Louis grits her teeth.

"Yeah, he's not here. This used to be a good place to find the scum bags." Hicks blows air out like a leaky tire. "Okay, I give up. I'm tired."

"We need to go back to headquarters for your car and then I need to go to Kristine's and check on her cat." Louis deftly turns the car around.

"She lives only a few blocks from here, why don't I drop you off?"

Louis thinks. She should go home and talk to Will, but he'd be long asleep by now. She needs to get some sleep as well. She could go to Kristine's and take a quick nap and be home before Will wakes up.

She makes a turn toward Kristine's house. She squints to hold back the pain, "I hope Kristine has some ibuprofen or something. My arm is killing me."

Louis pulls up to Kristine's tiny, freshly painted yellow house with lacy curtains in the kitchen. Houdini, the cat, jumps up to the bay window a few feet from the front door. His fluffy tan tail swipes back and forth wildly. In cat language this is an obvious display of anger at being left at home while his owner is out having a good time.

Louis gets out of the car in a daze. She walks up the stepping stone walkway to the front door. She stumbles over a weed sticking out between the stones like a tuft of hair from an eighties troll doll. She fiddles with the key, always a tight fit. Kristine has talked about getting it fixed for as long as she's owned the tiny house. She opens the front door and without thinking allows the door to swing open just a bit too widely. Houdini is more than ready for his great escape.

Hicks jumps out of the car. Louis chases the fluffy cat from one direction, but the cat flips over unsure of what to do now that he's finally escaped. Hicks approaches from the other side. Together they corner him near the chain link fence. Louis wishes that pulling a gun on the suspect would have that effect, but it rarely does. The detectives move in slowly. Houdini stares them down and flips back over onto his paws. Hicks fakes a move toward Louis. The sandy colored, fluffy Persian takes off. Hicks manages to snag the escape artist's tail. Houdini will have none of this and counter attacks Hicks with a swipe of his paw and a sharp chomp. Hicks takes the opportunity to grab the scruff of the cat's neck with his free hand.

"Nice catch, Hicks." Louis can't help but laugh.

"Yes, this cat needs to find a better hobby. Basket weaving, perhaps." He hands the cat over to Louis. She grabs him securely, while making sure to hold him well away from her chest.

Hicks gets back into the car as Louis steps into Kristine's house. She closes the door and sets the cat down on the floor. He races off, running in a flash up the stairs. After she's done with the kitty chores for the ungrateful escape artist, Louis forages in the pantry for something to eat. She finds some chips and salsa and proceeds to think about the long day, crunching each chip loudly. If Lilac Trance has been selling for months, why would it suddenly start killing people? Killing people with drugs doesn't seem like a good idea for the drug dealers, wouldn't they just lose clientele? Perhaps it is just a bad batch of designer drugs? If that's the case then 'The Jamaican' is a real drug dealer. So, who is 'The Jamaican' and why has drug enforcement never heard of him? Her mind drifts a bit more thinking about how Charles Mahoney described 'The Jamaican' and her mind takes a left turn. Why was the insurance adjuster at the scene? If he's right, why are all those paintings forgeries?

Louis takes out her phone and writes a quick email off to Carlos Alvarez, the squad's forensic accountant and Aria Park, the technology expert. Aria's fake cell phone tower was able to pin point their suspect this winter. It was a huge break in the case that likely saved the life of the victim the suspect was going to torture a few miles away.

The room is warm, but she feels cold. Louis is sure she turned off the A/C to save on Kristine's electricity when she walked in, but she starts to shiver. She grabs a blanket from the back of the couch and lays down, her feet propped up against the arm of the tiny love seat.

SATURDAY

Rochester Herald Staff writer David Huang reports:

June 14th 5:00am: A new hearing has been set for Dennis Baxter, the man accused of murdering his step-daughter, Mercedes Hewitt, says his attorney. The DNA evidence Mr. Baxter was indicted on was found to be improperly tested by the city's forensic lab. The judge in the case, Schultz, said he was disappointed in the lack of other evidence against Baxter. The new hearing will be set for one o'clock on Monday.

In other news, Julie Mahoney, wife of Charles Mahoney, the pharmaceutical manufacturer, was found dead in her home last night. This is the fifth reported death related to extreme fevers. The medical examiner's office refused to comment on the case, but a source inside the examiner's office says that they have been unable to rule out the cause from a disease.

CHAPTER 17

Louis looks around the room, her eyes trying to adjust to the darkness. She's curled up into a ball, trying to remember where she is, when it is. The itchy warm blanket envelops her like she's an egg roll. It's soaking wet and sticking her body. She shivers and knows something isn't right. Her hands are clammy. She tries to swallow, but her mouth feels like cotton, she has no saliva. Instinctively she touches the back of her hand to her forehead. She feels the warmth of her fever and leaps off of the couch. She paces around the room, still forgetting where she is. Her brain finally kicks into gear. She thinks about the previous day, all those deaths, all from a fever. She remembers she is in Kristine's house when she sees Houdini's glowing cat eyes gazing at her from across the room. She runs to the bathroom. She flips the switch and the harsh light causes her to cringe in pain. She slowly opens her eyes only to face a stranger. The face looking back at her is unfamiliar. Her eyes are blood shot. Her face looks bruised. Her hair is matted against her face. She turns on the cold tap and her hand brushes against her chest. A fiery pain she has never felt before runs through her entire body. She cries out in agony.

She hears the doorknob jangle and gets a hold of herself. Her mind is racing. How is it possible someone would be invading this home? Why now of all times? She searches the room for a weapon. In the corner of the room she spots a table lamp. She grabs the lamp with both hands, grunting through the pain.

There's a loud knock on the door and a muffled voice, a voice Louis is unable to understand. Her heart is beating so fast she can't hear anything but the blood pumping through her. She shouts loudly, her voice shaking "I have a weapon!" She hears a frantic pounding on the door. She tightens her grip on the table lamp.

Louis' heart is racing. She takes deep breaths. She tries to control her heartbeat, to slow it down even a notch. She knows the brief meditation works when she can just make out the voice on the other side of the door, "Louis? Are you okay?"

She's confused for a moment, trying to place the familiar voice. The doorknob jiggles a bit more. The knob finally turns. The low light from the street lamp outside creates a silhouette she recognizes. She puts the jigsaw pieces together. The voice. The shadowy form, "Will?" She exhales deeply and loosens her grip on the lamp.

He slams the door, "Louis? What's going on?" He searches the room, trying to follow the sound of her voice and breathing.

"Oh Will." She drops the lamp. Shards of the ceramic skitter across the floor.

He finally finds the light switch. Will looks around to the horrid scene. "Louis, what happened?"

"I dropped the lamp." She says guiltily.

"Yes, I mean, why are you defending yourself with a lamp? Why do you look like crap?"

"I don't feel well. I have a fever." Louis speaks calmly, but at the word 'fever' a wave of panic courses through her spine. "Call 911."

"What?" Will is further confused by her sudden panic. He rushes toward his wife.

"Call 911, don't come near me!" She screams.

"Okay, okay. I'm dialing." Will pulls out his phone and makes the call. He gives the operator the information he knows, and makes sure to tell them that Louis is an active police officer. This is something she taught him to do years ago, if anything ever happened to her that required a paramedic. Will stares at her in disbelief.

She slumps down to the floor and lets out a short scream. Louis calms herself to listen to Will's conversation.

"Fine," He says, "but I need to ask my wife a few questions." He looks down at her, "Louis, the paramedics are on their way. Can you tell me what the hell is going on?"

"I have a fever."

"Okay, what else?"

"Those people today, they all died of fevers, all of them before the paramedics could arrive." Louis sobs.

"Oh shit, what can I do?" Will drops the phone on the counter and runs over to his wife's side.

"I don't know." Louis sobs.

CHAPTER 18

Louis wakes up to a bright light and a dull pain in her chest. She blinks her eyes trying to focus on anything. She smells the harsh chemicals of disinfectant and an intoxicating elixir that brings her eyes back into focus.

"Louis?" Will's tranquil voice is a perfect match to the smell of his light cologne, fighting through those harsh chemical smells. She can hardly believe his smell is so powerful.

She meets his eyes. Her mind is full of questions as she remembers the broken lamp and the fever. "What -"

Will cuts her off, diving directly into the most important part, "You have shingles."

Louis is confused, "Shingles?" She blinks a few times, still trying to get her eyes to focus clearly. "Don't old people get shingles?"

"Well, you are no spring chicken, my dear." Will grins at his unintended pun. "Anyone can get it, anyone that's had chicken pox."

"Is that why I've been in excruciating pain?" Louis grits her teeth at the thought of the pain, but realizes that she isn't actually feeling any discomfort at the moment.

"Yes, the doctor gave you something for the pain, and a strong anti-viral. He was here an hour ago and said he'd be back soon." Will smiles. He looks down at the novel in his hand.

Louis' detective mind, while feeling fuzzy at the moment, works through a few issues from yesterday, "Will?"

Will looks up from the novel. The cover reads *You've Got Mystery* in large loopy red letters, "Yes?"

Louis carefully phrases her next question, "You said yesterday, you talked to your manager?" She smiles, knowing there is more to it.

"Yes, well, I ..." Will opens his mouth further, but no more information pours out. He tries to tuck his nose back into his book.

Louis waits for the end of the sentence, at least until he goes back to reading.

Will looks up from his book, "We don't need to talk about it right now. I…" he avoids eye contact, choosing to look out over the tops of the trees from the hospital's window.

"You what?" After fifteen years of marriage she knows his delay tactics, as if they were her own.

"I think we can talk about it later, it's not important." He takes a deep breath. "I thought it was, but it's not."

Louis doesn't pounce right away. They've had these conversations before, and she knows that he knows what's coming. She just can't help but to continue on with the scripted conversation anyway. "If it's not important, then why don't you tell me what's going on?"

"Louis, drop it okay? I don't want to talk about it right now."

Mercy comes in the form of a tall blonde, wearing fancy shoes that reflect Cece's bright neon floral wrap dress as she bounds into the room.

Louis' eyes still haven't come into focus and the brightly colored dress makes her squint, "Cece, I can see you coming from a mile away."

"Louis, how can you joke at a time like this? You didn't show up for coffee this morning, I called your cell and no one answered." She frets and adjusts her skirt.

"Yes, I'm sorry. I've been a little busy." Louis teases.

"What in the hell happened to you?"

"I've got shingles."

Cece cringes and backs up a foot. "Shingles? Old people get shingles. We aren't *old*."

"You say that as though it were a crime, Cece." Louis is having the most fun she can while lying in her hospital bed, certainly more fun than arguing with Will.

"It is a crime. We are not old." She pulls up the tiny doctor's swivel chair and sits down demurely.

Will says, "It doesn't just affect old people, Cece."

Louis thinks for a moment, "How did you even find out I was here?"

"When you didn't answer your cell, I tried Will. When he didn't answer, I tried Kristine. When she didn't answer, well, I was forced to call Bert. I swear if he asks me on one more date…" If finding Louis was a matter of life and death, speaking to Detective Hicks was her last resort before death.

"I'm so sorry you had to go through that. I'm fine. Really, I'm sorry I didn't call." Her sincerity isn't fully appreciated by Cece however, since it is accompanied by a smirk.

"Well, while I was on the phone with Bert he asked me to pass along some information on your case."

"Oh?"

"Yes," Cece pulls out her little floral and paisley notebook. "He says, 'Can't find 'The Jamaican'. And…" she pauses and stares at her notebook, pulling it further away from her face. "I can't read my handwriting. I think it says, 'call that insurance guy'." She looks up from her notebook, "Does any of this make sense to you?"

"Yes, thank you." Louis wonders why she needs to call the insurance guy, and not Hicks. Quinn must have taken his information last night. Most likely he isn't in the mood to talk to a snotty insurance adjuster. She wonders what she's even supposed to call about? She also wonders when the hell she'll be able to get back to work. It'll be something she'll have to ask the doctor, whenever he decides to show up.

"Why in the hell did Bert know that you were in the hospital and not me? I'm your best friend." Cece's jealousy is notorious.

"I have no idea, I just woke up. The last I remember, I had a fever, I broke Kristine's lamp, and told Will to call 911."

"Are you in pain?"

"It was excruciating. They've given me something for the pain though."

"Do you still have a fever?"

Will looks up to the monitor attached to Louis' left finger, "Nope, came down about an hour ago."

Louis wonders how long she's been out and looks around for a clock. She just spots one out the open door and across the hall. She squints still trying to get her eyes to focus.

Will fills in her silent question, "It's nine a.m."

Louis stares at him in amazement, then it strikes her. "Nine a.m.? I need to get to work!" She jolts upright and throws off her blankets, but the sudden movement makes her feel ill. Her head feels like it's stuffed with spiky marbles.

"Louis, stop." He stands up and pushes her back into the hospital bed, careful not to touch her right shoulder. "It's Saturday, the police force will be fine without you." He throws the blankets back on top of her. "About this message from Hicks," Louis is very familiar with Will's tone. It is the voice he takes when he's laying down the law. The tone of voice that says he very much means business. "He can handle the investigation for a few days."

"I know that." Louis says, again following their established conversation pattern. "But I can make phone calls, follow up on a few leads from here."

Cece's cell phone sings K.C. and the Sunshine Band's, *Boogie Shoes*. She waltzes out of the room to take the call.

Will shakes his head and goes back to reading his book.

Louis, however, isn't done being a detective, "Wait, how did you even know that I was at Kristine's?"

He puts his book down in frustration. "Hicks. When you didn't show up at the house I called your phone. You didn't answer, so I called Hicks. He told me he dropped you off at Kristine's."

"Yes, I haven't heard from her since Thursday. Last I heard she flew to D.C."

Cece walks back into the room, "Kristine's in D.C.? What happened?"

"I don't know yet. Her sister was in an accident." Louis says flatly.

"Why am I always the last person to find out what's going on?"

"You aren't. I don't know either. She called to ask me to take care of her cat."

"I can take care of the cat too. Why didn't she call me?"

"I don't know Cece, why don't you ask her?"

"I would, but she's not answering her phone."

Louis wonders why Kristine isn't answering her phone. Maybe she's on the phone? Or maybe she's in the hospital also, watching over Kelly.

Cece smiles and changes the subject. "I wanted to tell you about my big date tonight." She bats her eyes Louis.

"Oh, with whom?" Louis raises her eyebrows.

"A customer. I put him into a pair of Fiorentini and Baker's." Cece describes every customer by what shoes they wear, or bought. "Then he wanted me to pick out a shirt for him. By the time I was picking out his tie, well, he asked me if I was doing anything on Saturday night."

"Where are you going?"

"He said it's a surprise, but that I should bring my overnight bag."

"Cece, you don't even know this guy."

"Oh, I know him. Anyone who can afford Fiorentini and Baker's…" She winks.

"Cece, you should be careful. You haven't even dated anyone in a while, you should take it easy." Louis chides.

Cece huffs. "Well, I spent so much time tracking you down, now I have to go to work." She hefts her bag over her shoulder. She takes a moment to look at Louis. She sighs and leans in to kiss her friend on the forehead. "You get better, that's an order." She saunters out of the room, her hips swaying in their usual attempt to attract all the attention she can.

"Be careful!" Louis shouts just before the door closes. Cece turns her head and smiles.

The phone next to Louis' bed rings. She looks at Will, and he looks at her. He shakes his head nearly imperceptibly. She bites her lower lip. She doesn't like defying him, but she has an idea of who is calling. She picks up the phone. Will rolls his eyes and puts the book back in front of his face, as if playing a toddler game.

"Detective Baker." She says with authority as if she were answering her desk phone in the squad room.

"Well, seems you're doing much better." The soothing voice of Detective Hicks comes through the hospital's phone.

"Got your messages."

"Yeah? Did you talk to that insurance geek yet?"

"No. I was -"

"Okay, but now there's a new lead."

"A new lead?"

"Yes, and a new problem." The line goes silent but she can hear Hicks hen-pecking at the keyboard.

"Well? Do I have to beg for them?"

Hicks chuckles and the hen-pecking stops. "One of them is from your boyfriend."

"What are you talking about Hicks?" She says with genuine confusion.

"You know, a certain muscular, tanned -" He lets the silence build, "accountant? You don't remember the last time you two collaborated on a case?"

"Yes, I do. We caught the hit man, as I recall."

"Yeah, and I remember you drooling all over him."

"I was not drooling." She says in a whisper.

Will looks at her confused. Her cheeks redden and she breaks eye contact, "What did he say?"

"He said that there are some mysterious deposits and withdrawals from Mr. Mahoney's private account."

"Mysterious how?"

"I should let him tell you, he used a lot of mumbo jumbo words that get you all weak at the knees."

"I have no idea what you're talking about."

"Yeah right."

"What's the problem?"

"The Mahoney's house was broken into last night."

"What do you mean broken into?"

"The upstairs is ransacked. Someone unsuccessfully tried to open the safe in the basement."

"How did that not set off the alarm?"

"Someone typed in the code."

"We should go check that out."

Will looks up from his novel with a scowl.

"Yeah, I'm taking Quinn and we are going to go check it out, that is, as soon as he's done with his laundry."

"His laundry?"

"Yeah, he had some sorta incident last night after he left the Mahoney's house."

"What kind of incident?" She laughs, anticipating the story to cheer her up.

"He was writing up the reports from last night. The one remaining operating printer on the second floor wouldn't print. So, being the technical guy he is," Hicks says sarcastically, "he starts investigating. He looks at the little help screen. It has some incomprehensible message, 'chickens in the forward deck' or something. So he checks the paper, and there's plenty of paper. He pulls out the toner, which he's done a few times down in 'bike squad', but this time he does it wrong. He ends up dumping what was left of the toner onto himself."

"Oh, I guess that's what happened to his clothes." Louis affirms, disappointed by the story's lack of climax.

"Yeah, but that's not the best part. He finds a new toner in the supply closet, gets that one all installed, the printer still won't print. This time the message says something like the secret to cutting up blowfish. Well anyway, it was some message he was sure he recognized as a paper jam. The damn copier jams on a daily basis, and he's used to that, so he goes through all the nooks and crannies, getting his inky fingerprints all over the machine. Finally, he finds this little, tiny sliver of a piece of paper. But then this morning," Hicks lowers his voice a little, "Lieutenant Olsen comes storming in. 'Who the hell molested the printer?' She's storming around the squad room, looking for the culprit. She's spitting fire and has everyone show their hands."

Louis laughs, "She didn't!"

Will looks at her and asks, "What's he on about now?"

Louis laughs a bit more, "Hold on, Hicks." She looks at Will, "The new guy, Quinn, was molesting the printer and Erica Kane is on a witch hunt." Will has nicknames for everyone Louis works with. Erica Kane got her nickname from her fight to the top through cunning wile, crafty conduct, smooth-talking management and good old-fashioned ass kissing.

Will smiles, "Nice."

She lifts the receiver back up, "Go on Hicks."

"So, I'm sitting at my desk smiling, because I know who it was, since he called me to tell me he was going to be late. He told me exactly what happened. So, she's on to me, thinks I did it. I even made a show of hiding my hands for extra effect."

"Did she accuse you?"

"No, she didn't want to ask me directly, so I'm certainly not going to tell her otherwise."

"Hicks, you're a huge trouble maker."

"So, how long until I can break you out of there?"

Louis lets out an exasperated sigh, "I don't know, I haven't even talked to the doctor yet." She furrows her brow, covers her hand over the microphone and looks back at Will, "Who is my doctor anyway?"

He looks up from his book again, searching his memory for the name, "Ah, Dr. Slemp."

She uncovers the phone, "Pick me up in an hour." She can hear him laughing, "And don't go to the house without me."

"Aye, Aye, captain."

She hangs up the phone.

Will is hot under the collar, "What the hell?"

She throws off her covers, "Tell the good Dr. Slemp that I'm leaving."

"Seriously? I rescued you last night from a total panic, you passed out, and now you think you're just going to walk out of here?"

"Well, actually I'm going to get cleaned up first. Is my overnight bag still in the car?"

"Yes." He says shaking his head, pursing his lips.

"Can you get it?" She asks impatiently.

"HELL NO!"

"Will?" She asks, staring him down.

"No, you're going to lay back down and let the doctor's do their work." He points to the bed, pulling back the covers.

She defends her position, "Dr. Slemp is a quack. I met him yesterday. His throat clearing is irritating."

Will shakes his head, "Yeah, it was nauseating. I'm glad you were asleep, he's got the bedside manner of a troll. But that doesn't mean you are going to go traipsing out of here."

CHAPTER 19

Kristine stands at the office door, hoping someone else is inside. She tries the door. It's locked, so she digs through her purse looking for her office key chain.

Bryan's large eyes register amazement, "All those are for you?"

"Yeah, I don't remember what half of them do, anymore. I only use a few of them." She shuffles through the key ring. She's looking for the one with 9643 etched into the head of the key.

"Then why do you have all of those?" Bryan asks, adjusting his heavy backpack. When he was told he was flying off to Rochester for the weekend, he packed four heavy books, his video game player, a few movies, three full sized board games, ten movies, a peanut butter fluff sandwich, and two pairs of socks. Thankfully Kristine examined the contents of his pack and asked him to also include shirts, pants and underwear.

"Well, some of them are for filing cabinets, some of them are for the office rooms, there's one for my desk and," Kristine finally finds the right key, "this one is for the front door."

"How do you know which one is which?" Bryan asks.

"They all have number codes," she shows him the front door key, "the front door has 9643 etched in it."

Bryan looks around for that number and points to it, decorating the door's handle.

She leads him through the door, shuts it and locks the door behind her. A loud, sustained beep comes from a little panel on the wall. Kristine walks over to it, punches in the four-digit code and the beeping stops. "Whew. For some reason I always think I'm going to type in the wrong number and have the cavalry here in a few minutes. But I made a little poem to remember."

"What kind of poem Aunt Kris?"

"It goes: Five feasts on the fourth of July, seven salads on one big checker table."

"I thought poems rhyme?"

Kristine shrugs, "They don't have to."

She listens to him chanting the poem a few times out loud.

They walk through a set of double doors and Bryan stands in front of the short marble staircase leading up to a grand archway, his mouth agape. "This is just like the time we went to the Museum of Natural History."

"This way." She says. They walk down a long hallway. Each door has a small brass and wood sign with a name. Bryan counts aloud each one of the urns with fake flowers adorning the hallway, "Seven."

She unlocks another door. This door has a sign, 'Kristine Rocha, Assistant District Attorney.' She takes a deep breath and opens the door wide for him, "Get comfortable, we're going to be here for a while." She sets her bag and briefcase on her desk, "You can take that desk over there, at least for now." She points to the smaller desk, on the other side of the room.

"Who sits here?" Bryan asks.

"It's Marcie's desk."

"Who's Marcie?"

"She's my paralegal."

"What's a paralegal?"

"It's a person that helps a lawyer with her case."

"Oh." The pictures on Marcie's desk make tinny noises knocking together when he places his heavy backpack on the desk. "Where is she?"

"I don't know, she isn't answering her phone." She pulls out her laptop, pushes it into the port replicator with a loud clank. The laptop fan whirs to life and makes chime noises.

"So Marcie will be here later?" Bryan perks up.

"Maybe, why don't you try calling her? Maybe you'll have better luck." She's only been her paralegal for two weeks, and it's already time to start filling out the paperwork to get her fired.

"Okay, what's her number?"

Kristine reads the number slowly, "Ah, 585-555-3323"

Bryan dials the number. He looks at his aunt, confused.

"Oh, sorry, you have to dial nine first."

He dials the number again, "It just rings and rings."

"Yeah, that's what I have too. You can try again anytime you want." Kristine smiles. She'll let him do the psycho dialing.

She watches Bryan as he looks at her desk, trying to recognize anyone from the picture frames. She notices he picks one up, examining it closely.

Kristine rifles through her briefcase. She unlocks the filing cabinet and files the purple folder.

Bryan takes out his Nintendo DS and pokes in a little game cartridge. The game plays its cute theme music, making Kristine smile. He hunches over and starts clicking away at the buttons.

"Bryan, I'll be right back."

"Huh?" He asks, but doesn't look up.

"I said, I'll be right back." She repeats.

Bryan makes a grunting sound that she takes as an answer.

She walks out of the room and down the hall a few doors. The room she walks into, the room she dreads, has all of the current files in large lockers. She shuffles through her key ring again, looking for the right key. She starts pulling out the three boxes of files on the Hewitt case and placing them on the floor. She signs the logbook with her special lawyer's signature.

While in graduate school, she decided to make a pretty, fast and flourishing signature, just for work. One of her more fascinating and engaging professors waxed on for a full class over adopting a special signature for lawyering. The signature should be able to be written quickly, he said, and at the same time difficult to replicate.

She starts stacking together two boxes, holding them with just one hand and leaning them up against her head. The third box is lighter, and she carries it with her spare hand. She struggles down the short distance back to her office. The top box makes a sound like sand paper rubbing together. She's sure the top box will slide off if she leans over to put the light box down. She ends up using her hip to hold the light box against the door and turns the knob very slowly.

She hears the thumps of Bryan's footsteps and expects him to be standing at the door helping her, but when she peeks around the door, Bryan is busily playing his video game.

He looks up. "Hi," he says casually.

"Hey, can you help me with these boxes?" She grunts.

He leaps up from the desk and she hears the thumping sound of his footsteps coming toward her. He grabs the box from her left hand and she grabs the top box just before it topples onto the floor.

CHAPTER 20

Hicks strides into the hospital room mischievously. "I'm here to bust you out of this joint."

Will shakes his head in disgust.

Louis smiles brightly, she's already dressed and ready to go, she has been for the last hour. Will started by arguing with her, but is now giving her the steaming silent treatment. She finally bargained for her clothes by promising to stay until she talked to the annoying doctor about her condition and treatment.

Her smile turns into a dramatic frown, "What took you so long?"

"The Mahoney's wasn't the only place broken into last night." Hicks licks his lips and smiles with his eyebrows.

"Oh?" Louis smiles again thinking, perhaps the case is a wrap?

"Someone used the code to get into Clean Slate Gallery last night. The only place disturbed is Julie Mahoney's back office."

"What do you suppose he is looking for?" Louis swings her feet off the bed, onto the floor.

"He? How do you know the burglar is a 'he'?" Hicks smiles.

"Just a guess. Did anyone at the Clean Slate Gallery notice anything missing?" Louis asks.

"Nothing, but we should talk to Julie's assistant again. She was hot. I could totally get over her weird tattoos." Hicks grabs Louis' overnight bag.

"We don't have time to talk to any more of your chicks." She leans over and kisses Will, just a polite kiss in front of Hicks.

Will shakes his head and rolls his eyes. "You should be going home." He grumbles.

Louis ignores him. She pushes the door open with a small grimace on her face, "Okay, let's check out the house."

Will follows the two of them out of the hospital room, "Honey, please be careful."

"Yes, I'll be careful."

Hicks presses the button for the elevator. The elevator door opens and an instrumental version of 'Another Brick in the Wall' is playing in the background. Hicks hums along to a few bars to annoy Louis. "What did the doctor say?" He asks.

"He said, you're driving." She tries to ignore the song, and Hicks' humming. "Do we know if anything is missing from the house?"

Hicks shrugs, "Nothing obvious."

"Did the techs find any fingerprints in the house yesterday that shouldn't have been there?"

"Not that we've found yet."

Louis huffs and shakes her head.

"Hey, there's a lot to process, and," he checks his watch, "it's only just after eleven now. It hasn't even been twenty-four hours."

"Right, it just seems like it has." The elevator opens. Louis tries to think of any other song, but Pink Floyd is stuck there now. "Another brick in the wall, all right," she mumbles.

CHAPTER 21

"I'm bored." Bryan sighs, weighing down his fists with his chin. His face looks like it has been manipulated by that fancy software that makes you look like you're looking into a fun house mirror.

Kristine spent the last two and a half hours digging through the files. She's not quite half way through. She's been interrupted a number of times, each interruption causing her brain to inefficiently cycle through the same information. The frustration wells up inside her, but she puts great effort into calming her voice, "Why don't you switch to a book then?"

"I've already read a book," he frowns. Slowly a smile appears on his face, "What about one of those books?" He points to the three-inch books on the shelf under the window.

"You want to read law books?" She laughs.

"Have you read them?"

"Yes, most of them."

"What's in them?"

"Books about the law."

"What does that mean?"

Kristine is at a loss for words. She really can't image, right now, how to describe books about the law to a ten year old. She goes for a laugh, "That it's boring."

Undaunted he walks over to the bookshelf and pulls out 'New York Zoning Law and Practice' and reads the title out loud. He plops the three-inch first volume on the floor, opens to a random page and starts to read the words, not quite out loud, but not silently either. He stops, furrows his brow, "What does 'I-N-D-E-M-N-I-F-I-C-A-T-I-O-N' mean?"

"The word is 'indemnification'. They are reparations for something lost or suffered." She repeats from her memory bank for the definitions of lawyer's words, looking down at a report to see a few more of the special lawyer words on the page she's reading.

A silence takes over the room. He bursts out, "But, what does 'reparations' mean?"

"Bryan, if you let me work, we'll get out of here sooner." Her frustration bubbles to the surface again.

"Oh, okay." He closes the book with a loud smack. "Aunt Kris?"

"Yes honey?" She asks with an exasperated sigh.

"Can I make a fort out of these books about 'inn-i-dem-fi-cation'?" Bryan mispronounces the word, scrambling and emphasizing the wrong syllables.

Kristine decides to ignore the mispronunciation. She smiles, "Absolutely, they might as well be useful somehow."

She looks down again and sees something she previously missed. She writes the name 'Katy Bowden' down on her legal pad. She scans the report for more information. There appears to be none at all except the name, date and a brief summary of the call, saying nothing more than she has information on the case. The date catches her eye, November eighteenth. She shuffles through the last five pages of her hand written notes and spots the date she's looking for. The botched DNA evidence, the one clearly pointing at the stepfather, came through on November seventeenth. The call was never followed up on. It wouldn't have been because of the iron clad DNA evidence.

She picks up the phone and dials the number from the report. She lets the phone ring eight times. There's no answer, not even an answering machine. Her mind races, the number could have been written down wrong. Maybe Katy Bowden moved? Maybe she changed her number?

She dials the number for the operator. The advertisement and recorded message plays asking her for the listing, "Katy Bowden" she says.

There's a short wait with clicking noises until the operator rattles through her scripted message ending with "Sorry, there's no listing for Katy Bowden in Rochester or in Monroe County. I have an Anthony and Janet Bowden in Greece, and Sherry Bowden in Edgerton."

Kristine thinks, perhaps Katy lives with one of these other Bowden families, or maybe they know her? "Can I get both of the listings, please?" The operator rattles out both of the numbers and she writes them down. Neither listing matches the phone number on the report.

She dials both numbers. No one answers, so she leaves messages on each the machines. Why would they answer the phone on such a beautiful Saturday? The weather brought a cool breeze this morning. A welcome change when she and Bryan stepped out of the plane. There are only a few more days until summer and then the days and nights will be hotter. Anyone smarter than Kristine would be happily enjoying themselves outside while they still can. She should be on beach maybe, by the lake. It would be a perfect day for that. She looks up at the small window. She watches people walk by and sighs deeply. She cannot afford to wait, she needs to find Katy Bowden, but she shouldn't bring Bryan in tow. Edgerton isn't the best neighborhood. And furthermore, he shouldn't be there when she's talking to strangers about rape and murder.

She picks up her phone again and dials her best friend Louis. No one answers. Strange, she thinks, Louis always answers her phone. She can't imagine a scenario where Louis doesn't answer her phone. The message beeps, but Kristine doesn't leave a message.

Kristine dials Louis' phone again. "Damn."

"What's wrong Aunt Kris?"

"Nothing, I just can't get a hold of anyone!" She decides to call Cece, in a last ditch effort to find someone to watch Bryan. The phone rings four times. Kristine wracks her brain for anyone else she might call when Cece finally picks up.

"Oh, if it isn't my good friend." Cece answers the phone sarcastically.

From Cece's tone she knows this isn't going to be an easy conversation, "Hey, sorry I didn't call sooner. I need you to look after Bryan for a couple hours."

"So, I'm good enough to take care of your nephew, but not your cat?" Cece whines.

"Houdini doesn't like you." Kristine answers back directly.

"And your nephew?"

"He doesn't know you yet. Can I drop him off?"

"What in the heck are you doing back in town anyway? I thought you were looking after your sister?"

"Kelly …" She chokes up, not ready to tell people, but needing to explain, "died." There's a silence while Kristine composes herself. "D.A. Pickett called to tell me that I have until Monday morning to find any other evidence in the Hewitt case, implicating Dennis Baxter, or he's going to drop the case."

"Oh my God! I'm sorry. I'm at work. You can drop him off here for a couple hours, tops. I'll just say he's a private shopping customer. You know how Marc is." Marc, her manager, has been paranoid since Cece's grand mental breakdown in the shoe department. Only a long talk with Detective Louis Baker and the solemn promise that nothing dramatic would ever happen again in the shoe department allowed Cece to keep her job. That and the fact that Cece can sell anyone shoes, specifically expensive, designer shoes.

"A couple hours should be fine. Where is Louis? I could use her help, too."

"Wait, you don't know where Louis is? I know something you don't?" She singsongs the reply, the way Kristine's sister used to do, when they were little.

"No, Cece, if you think I'm in the mood -"

"She's in the hospital."

"What?"

"Yeah, she's got an old people disease. A big rash."

"You mean shingles?"

"Yeah, shingles, it's from chicken pox."

"I know."

"How do you know?"

"My mom's had it twice."

"See what I mean? Old people. Do you think it's contagious?"

"It's not communicable, you'll be fine."

"Good." She exhales into the phone.

"Cece, I'll be there in ten minutes."

CHAPTER 22

The techs are still combing through the Mahoney's house when Louis and Hicks arrive. She looks down at the doorknob, "There's no sign of forced entry."

"Yeah, whoever broke in here had a key and knew the code." Hicks says.

"He could have been here for hours looking through the house."

"There you go with 'he' again."

"Okay, 'the burglar' could have been here for hours. More likely Charles Mahoney faked a break-in."

"One thing doesn't fit that theory, though."

"What's that?"

"The safe. Let's go look at it."

The detectives walk through the living room. The large paintings that were mounted on the wall only yesterday have been yanked forcefully off the wall and lie in a pile on the floor. "Isn't that odd?" Louis asks.

"Yeah, but they were fake, so why steal them?"

"Good point. Maybe who ever broke in here knew they were fakes? Maybe the burglar was looking for something behind the paintings?"

"Could be. I think the stairs to the basement are over here." Hicks points to the smallest door in the room.

The basement is unlike any other part of the house. The ceiling is a normal height and the shelves lining the walls are packed with various knick-knacks. There's a metal-on-metal grinding sound and there is a course metallic smell in the air.

"What's that smell?" Louis shouts. As they turn a corner in the room she sees the eight-foot tall safe. There's a tech in front of it, wearing a heat protective suit. Bits of metal fly in random directions.

"The techs are trying to break into the safe." Hicks shouts.

The tech stops drilling momentarily. He reaches for a bit in his toolbox.

"Why didn't they just ask Charles Mahoney for the combination?"

"That's the funny part. They did. He doesn't know it."

"Wait, you're saying, someone broke into this house using a key for the door, a combination for the alarm and tried to break into the safe that Charles Mahoney doesn't know the combination for?"

Hicks says, "I know what you're thinking -"

"Yeah, it's a pretty strange coincidence."

"You don't believe in coincidences." Hicks shouts over the renewed drilling.

"Exactly." Louis shouts back. "How do we know the burglar didn't get into the safe?"

"We can't be sure, but there were signs of drilling but the door wouldn't open. The lock wouldn't even turn anymore."

"Does Charles even know what is in there?"

"He has no idea." Hicks shouts back.

There's a loud crack and the drilling stops. "Damn, that's a tough one." The tech wipes his brow.

"Will it open?" Louis asks.

"Sure just hold on a minute." The tech takes off his protective mask.

"Mike?" Hicks recognizes the tech, "I thought it was your day off?"

"It is but -"

"Open the safe already." Louis groans impatiently.

Mike turns the handle to the safe. Louis gets into position to be the first person to see what's inside. Louis thinks of what could be in there, jewels or money. Even better, some clue as to what killed Julie Mahoney. Mike strains, pulling hard on the door.

Louis jumps when Hicks' phone rings.

Hicks pulls out his phone. He stares at the caller-id, "Huh, that's weird."

CHAPTER 23

Kristine rolls her eyes at 'Wendell', the name Bryan had given her GPS last summer. As usual, Wendell is as lost as she is. She's not even sure why Wendell took her down this way. She knows she's seen this same gas station at least one other time on this route, and the dash through the small alleyway isn't something she wants to repeat. She pulls over to a formerly beautiful Tudor style house with dark timberlines and wrought iron lamps. The white picket fence is missing many of its slats, looking more like an eight year old pushing out his baby teeth. The remaining ones look rotten. The house still has all of its windows, which is more than you can say for most of the other houses she's passed by on Wendell's tour. She pulls the GPS down from its stuck-on perch. She pushes the map around, looking at Wendell's route to her destination. When she finally finds the house, she realizes that she must have passed by the small street, probably about the time Wendell said he was recalculating.

She puts the car back in gear and then pulls out of the parking spot. A large, multicolored old truck turns the corner and makes a screeching sound as the cars bump together. He blares the horn at her. In her frustration she beeps back, but her horn sounds like a toy horn compared to the old truck's. The young man at the wheel turns and gives her the finger. Almost instinctively she memorizes the license plate number and writes it down in her notebook. She gets out to examine the damage. There isn't much. She's shocked how he just drove off. She pulls her small digital camera from her briefcase, and takes a picture of the damage. Fearing another car making a matching dent in her own body, she gets out of the street and back into the car.

She follows Wendell's directions to the letter this time, slowing down near intersections to make sure she doesn't miss the turn. Halfway down "Blossom Avenue", a name as common as "Peach Street" in Atlanta, Wendell tells her she's arrived at her destination on the right. A few houses up the street she parallel parks between two circa 1980's luxury Lincolns. One is silver and the other dark blue. The silver Lincoln looks like it hasn't moved an inch since the eighties. All four tires are flattened to the ground. As she passes by the dark blue Lincoln, she peeks into the windows to see the backseat is full of boxes of brightly labeled vegetable peelers.

She walks up the sidewalk, scanning the odd numbered houses and finds 813. The houses are bungalow style, but 813 has manicured grass and a nice garden of blue hydrangeas, surrounded by small, carefully mortared, cement blocks. Each of the clusters of blue hydrangeas is a different tint from an almost white to a sky blue, and one a shade of light purple.

Kristine pushes the doorbell and waits. She doesn't hear anyone. She knocks on the door until her knuckles ache, and still no one answers. What was she expecting exactly? The woman hadn't answered her phone. She decides to walk the worn pathway over to the neighbor's house. She rings the doorbell and she hears a woman's voice call back, "Hold on a moment, I'm on my way." She waits for a few minutes that seem like an eternity, when a cute, wrinkled old woman answers the door, still clutching onto her walker.

"You here for the peeler?" She asks, struggling to look up at Kristine. She manages to meet her eye by turning her head slightly sideways as she looks up. Kristine notices a single curler hanging from the back of her head.

"No ma'am. My name is Kristine Rocha. I'm looking for your neighbor, Sherry Bowden."

"Sherry. Yes, she bought a case of peelers, around Christmas time. She gave them out to her family, she said."

"Oh."

"I can show you how they work, if you're interested." The woman shuffles her walker away from the door, standing up straighter with each shuffle. "What am I thinking? Of course you're interested, you're here for a peeler."

"Well I -"

The woman interrupts, likely not even hearing Kristine. "These peelers are really the best in the industry." She drags the little tennis balls on the bottom of her walker down the short entryway, toward the kitchen. She makes a three point turn, her neck cranes up a few inches, "Honey, were you born in a barn? Shut the door. It's hot out there and you're going to let all the A/C out." She makes another turn with her walker and mutters loudly, "Damn kids. I'm on a fixed income, you know? Can't afford to cool the whole state of New York."

Kristine decides to settle in for the peeler demonstration, perhaps then she can get some information out of the neighbor.

She walks into the kitchen and the woman is still muttering, but now it's all about the peeler, "They're made in Sweden. The Swedes know good design."

Kristine looks around the kitchen. It's not like a normal house kitchen, more like a chef's palace. The appliances, large and small, are gleaming stainless steel, and the countertops are polished pink granite. On one wall there are only pots, a huge variety of pots. Each of the pots is outlined with permanent marker. The stove has six burners, Kristine can't remember ever seeing a stove with six burners, only in magazines. The kitchen, she thinks, really looks like it came straight out of a magazine.

The woman makes an effort to open the massive refrigerator door. Her arthritic hands pull out a few carrots and English cucumbers from the massive, well stocked refrigerator. She takes out a large acrylic cutting board from a stash of a dozen in a specially designed cubby just for cutting boards. She places the cutting board and the vegetables on the large center island. She begins her lecture on the peeler. Kristine isn't listening anymore, just watching the master at work. She lays out each of the long straight carrots and effortlessly peels them. Kristine catches a few words here and there, but she's already sold. She knows for a fact that she'll be walking out of this beautiful gourmet kitchen, with a new peeler.

Kristine finally thinks of a good question, "Does it come in different colors?" She noticed that the peeler's handle is bright orange, a color that will surely clash with her own black and red kitchen. She's had fun finding and collecting bright red appliances.

The woman takes a deep sigh, as though the question had no merit, "Well, yes it does. I said earlier that it comes in five colors: Orangesicle, which is the one I have here, Apple Green, French Blue, Eggplant, that's purple, and Fire Engine Red."

"Perfect, I'll take one in Fire Engine Red."

"One? Don't you have relatives? Friends? These little peelers make the perfect Christmas present, you could really get your Christmas shopping done early." The old woman uses her crooked pointy finger to emphasize each of the last few words.

"How much are they again?" *This woman will not be satisfied until I've purchased a case*, she thinks.

"They're fifteen dollars each, or one-fifty for a case. The case comes with a dozen." The old woman says with a smirk.

Kristine knows she didn't come here for a peeler, but she also knows she'll be walking out with twelve of them. "Do you take credit cards?" *Sayonara vacation fund!*

"We take Visa, MasterCard and American Express, but I'd prefer Visa or MasterCard if you don't mind. What colors do you want sweetheart?"

Kristine digs through her purse. "Two of each," She says disappointed, "surprise me with the other two in the case."

The old woman leaves her walker behind and uses the counter top to work her way over to a large closet; one that Kristine had thought was a pantry. As the doors open she sees thousands of peelers, floor to ceiling, stuffed in each of the shelves of the pantry. To the left a small cubby with the woman's receipts and credit card processing machine. She pulls out the machine, a paper receipt, a flattened small box and twelve peelers and places them all on the island. She puts the box together and places each of the peelers inside. She then writes out the receipt and then holds out her hand expectantly for the credit card. Kristine reluctantly hands her the card. The woman swipes the card through the machine. It makes little beeping, then a buzzing noise. They both stare at it like children watching a jack-in-the-box. The magic words appear on the screen that the woman is waiting for. She hands back the card and a strip of paper for Kristine to sign. The woman digs into a large marble cup holding a handy set of pens Kristine hadn't noticed before, and hands her a pen with 'McKinley Bank of New York' neatly etched into it.

She signs her name on the slip of paper, as she thinks about her fantasy vacation to Mount Fuji. Her heart thumps a little harder when she thinks about how she's going to pay for Bryan's college. What if he wants to become a lawyer like his mother, aunt and grandfather? How could she ever begin to pay for all that schooling on her current salary? Maybe she needs to start putting her efforts into the defense business?

She looks at the receipt, "Mrs. Kennedy?"

"Yes Miss -"

"Kristine Rocha." She says.

"Rocha? You know my favorite candy growing up was Almond Roca? The drugstore in Edgerton used to sell it to me for a nickel. This guy in Lake George fancies himself a historical candy maker and I tried it up there. The recipe is all wrong though, too sweet. I told him so, but young men have this habit of not listening."

"Yes, I am aware." Kristine isn't going to hand back the receipt until this old woman answers a few questions, questions not about peelers. "Do you know when your neighbor might be home?"

"Dan would be at work. He works at the airport."

"No, ma'am, not Dan, your other neighbor, Sherry Bowden."

"Oh, she went to drop her daughter off at summer camp. She'll be here for dinner though," the woman turns her head again to take a look at the clock. "Oh my, I better move dinner along."

"Her daughter? What is her daughter's name?"

"Well -" The old woman hesitates. "Who did you say you were again?"

"I'm Kristine Rocha, from the district attorney's office in Rochester. I need to speak with Sherry Bowden concerning a homicide case."

"A homicide?" Mrs. Kennedy's eyes look frightened at the thought.

"Yes, her daughters name?" Kristine knows she should have done the research ahead. But research takes time, time she doesn't have.

"It's Katy. Little Katy Bowden, she's got her mother's eyes."

"You said she'll be here for dinner?" Kristine says, even then knowing that she can't possibly wait for Sherry.

"Well, yes, and I really must get to working on dinner. I imagine she'll be famished after the drive to -" the woman hesitates.

"Ma'am, you don't have to tell me anything more, but I really need to talk to Sherry and her daughter as soon as possible." Kristine's phone rings. *Not now.*

She reaches in to silence the phone, but peeks at the screen first. The caller-id reads 'Cece' and her heart races

to the bottom of her stomach, *something happened to Bryan.*
"What's wrong with Bryan?"

"Nothing. I just, well Marc came in for his shift early.
You have to come get him."

"I thought you said two hours?" Her voice is a
conspiratorial whisper, her hands covering her mouth. She
leaves the kitchen and walks down the hallway toward the
front door.

"It's been almost two hours."

"Oh." *Where has the time gone? Is this house some sort of
temporal twilight zone?* "Let me call you right back."

"You need to come get him, soon. He's adorable by
the way."

"Yes, I know."

"He helped me make this killer sale on these
Mezlan's."

"He's selling shoes now? I'll be there as soon as I
humanly can." She hangs up the phone and walks into the
kitchen. She grabs a pen from the marble holder and pulls
a piece of paper from her legal pad. She writes a note.
"Mrs. Kennedy, when Sherry gets in I need you to have her
call me as soon as possible at this number. It is extremely
important."

"Yes, I see." Yet, she isn't looking. Mrs. Kennedy
stands over a pot of boiling water and places a large
tomato in it with a wire basket.

"Ma'am, really, it's important, tremendously urgent."

"Yes, well so are these blanched tomatoes. Seems like
everything in this world is urgent nowadays. I'd appreciate
it if you leave me to my business. I'll make sure Sherry calls
you."

"As soon as possible."

"Yes, as soon as possible." She lifts the basket back
up and with slightly more force plunges the tomato into a
different pot. Kristine can hear the ice swirl around and
watches as the old woman methodically starts peeling the

tomato. Almost as an after thought Mrs. Kennedy adds, "You could always call her on her cell phone."

"You have Sherry's cell number?"

"Of course I do. Neighbors have to look after each other, even in this day and age."

Kristine pulls her notebook back out, ready to write the number down.

"See she gave me her number when little Katy started staying home by herself after school. I only needed to use it once. That was the time that Katy had a boy over, well I thought it was a boy. You know you really can't tell these days. I was just appalled when Joyce, do you know Joyce?"

"No." She says quickly, impatiently.

"Oh, well she lives a couple blocks over. Well she -"

"Can I please get the number?"

"What number? Joyce's?"

"No, Sherry's, your neighbor. You said you had her cell."

"Oh yes, for when little Katy is home by herself."

"Right. Please. It's urgent, I need that number."

"Fine. I'll be right back." The old woman huffs, grabs her walker and shuffles out of the kitchen. She returns in a few minutes, but to Kristine it feels like hours. She hands Kristine a white slip of paper, brown from age around the sides. Scrawled in clear elaborate blue cursive pen is 'Sherry Bowden 518-555-9856'.

"Thank you, I'll see my way out." She gathers her things and marches out the door.

"Don't forget to shut the door!" Mrs. Kennedy shouts down the hallway.

Kristine slams the door shut.

She calls Louis, again. There's no answer. She hangs up the phone and dials the number for Sherry Bowden's cell.

"Hello?"

"Hello, is this Sherry Bowden?"

"Speaking."

"Hello Mrs. Bowden. My name is Kristine Rocha."

"Yes?"

"I'm from the district attorney's office in Rochester."

"How did you get this number?"

"From your neighbor, Mrs. Kennedy."

"And how many peelers did you end up buying for that information?"

"Ma'am I'm calling because your daughter called the police a few months ago concerning the case I'm working on."

"I'm really very busy right now. I -"

"Mrs. Bowden, -"

"It's Miss Bowden." She says with disgust, emphasizing 'Miss', "I haven't been married in fifteen years."

"Miss Bowden, I'm investigating the Mercedes Hewitt murder. Our prime suspect is about to go free on a technicality if I don't find some hard evidence very quickly."

"Girls tell lies, I'm sure my daughter didn't know anything about that. Anyway, I don't want my daughter involved in what happened years ago."

"Years ago? Mercedes died last fall, it hasn't even been a year."

"I know that. I -" her voice trails off.

"You what?" Kristine asks impatiently.

"I just don't want to dig up what happened in the past. Katy and I, we left all that behind. I don't want to get involved. I can't imagine why she called the police."

"What happened in the past?" she asks, but the line falls silent. Kristine pleads, "It's very important that I talk to your daughter."

"She's in summer camp. Horseback riding."

"Yes but if she has informa-"

"She's doing what little girls should do. They shouldn't be getting involved with murder investigations."

"Ma'am, if you don't talk to me now I'll have to get a subpoena and you and your daughter will be talking to me in court." Kristine knows it's a bluff. She wouldn't have enough information, or time, to haul her into court for this case.

"Fine. Get your subpoena, but if you really want to know what's going on you should talk to his mother."

"Who's mother?"

"Dennis' mother. She lives in Geneva."

The phone goes dead. She types 'Geneva' into Wendell. The GPS beeps and calculates her drive, fifty-seven minutes. She still has to rescue Bryan.

She dials the number for Louis again, and again she listens to half a dozen rings before Louis' cheerless message is played. She groans, nearly a scream, in frustration. She's hit a desperate level and tries calling Will. He picks up on the second ring.

"Kristine?" She can barely hear his voice over loud music in the background.

"Will, is Louis still in the hospital?" She shouts into her phone. She thinks for a moment about the neighbors, or even Mrs. Kennedy watching her shout in her car.

"No, she's not."

Is he slurring? He doesn't even slur when he's had more than anyone at the party. "Will, are you okay?"

"I'm perfectly fine. Time of my life. Why do you ask?"

He's definitely drunk. "Where are you?"

"A bar, I heard it's quite happening. Beth here has been very… loquacious."

"Beth?"

"Yeah, Beth, I told her about my little situation."

"What situation is that?"

"Oh, nothing. Doesn't matter."

"Okay." Kristine knows that she should really dig further, but Will is not her problem. She's got many problems right now, and Will is definitely not one of them.

"I need to get a hold of Louis, do you know where she is?"

"Well, it's Saturday, her day off. So she's chasing bad guys with Dick Hicks."

Kristine is at a loss for words. Her one shining example of how a relationship might work, crumbling in her ears. They say that you don't want to know how the sausage is made, could marriage be like that too?

"Will, I'm sorry something is troubling you, but I have to go. Go home before you do something you'll regret."

"Nice to talk to you too, Krissy." The nickname makes her cringe. Her mother tried out a dozen nicknames when she was growing up, but none of them stuck. She was determined as a child to be Kristine, not Kris, not Krissy, and certainly not Kandy - she screamed the first time her mother uttered this nickname.

She hangs up the phone and regrettably searches through her phone's contact list.

Chapter 24

Hicks grabs for the phone holstered on his belt. He looks down at the screen and grins ear-to-ear looking at the message displayed on the caller-id. "Why, ADA. Rocha, to what do I owe the pleasure?"

Louis smiles, his formal tone with her best friend Kristine has always got on her nerves, which is why he does it, continues to do it, and will never stop doing it.

She listens to the sounds of her best friend talking to her frustrating partner on the phone and pulls out her own phone. *Damn*, she thinks, *my phone is dead, no wonder she called Hicks.*

"Why yes ma'am. She is currently standing right in front of me impatiently waiting to find out what's inside of this safe."

Louis reaches for the phone, but Hicks pulls away playfully.

"Yes ma'am." Hicks hands the phone to Louis.

"Kristine? I just noticed my phone is off, I'm sorry."

"That partner of yours is a complete ass, you know that?" Kristine's exasperated voice seems on edge, tenser than just dealing with her aggravating partner.

"Yeah, I'm well aware of that information. How's your sister doing?"

Louis hears her choke up a little, "She passed away yesterday."

"Oh, God, I'm so sorry."

"Thank you." She sniffles.

There's a short silence and Louis can hear Kristine's muffled sobs. "Is there anything I can do?"

"Yes," there's a deep sigh on the other end of the line, Louis can hear her wiping her nose. "Can you pick up Bryan from Cece's work?"

"Bryan? Bryan who?" Louis racks her brain for someone named Bryan, but can only think of Kristine's nephew. Why would he be at Cece's work?

"My nephew."

"What is he doing in town?"

"He came with me." She sighs again.

"What are *you* doing in town?"

"The Hewitt case fell apart. Someone leaked information to the defense attorney about the DNA issues. D.A. Pucket gave me until Monday to come up with other evidence against Baxter, or he's dropping the case."

"Oh, no."

"Oh, yes."

"But, why is Bryan with you?"

"I'm his legal guardian now. I wanted to leave him with my mother, but she won't take him, not even for the weekend. She's trying to teach me a lesson, I suppose."

"Oh, honey, I'm sorry to ask you so many questions. I can get him, but we've got a lot going on with this case. We need to get out ahead of it. Would it be okay if I asked Aria to watch him? She's in the office today, thankfully working on the case."

The silence grows again. "Yes, Aria would be wonderful, can you arrange it?" Louis knows the words are positive, but the stress and hesitation in her voice is unmistakable.

"I'm sure Aria will be alright with it. She's great with kids you know."

"I'm sure she is. Thanks."

"No problem. Keep in touch."

Louis nearly hangs up, but hears Kristine's voice, "Louis?"

"Yes?"

"Not that it's any of my business, but I just talked to Will."

Louis lets out an exasperated sigh.

"I think you need to talk to him, he sounded, well he sounded... drunk. He never sounds drunk."

"Thanks. Yeah, I'll talk to him soon." Louis hangs up the phone and hands it back to her partner. She picks up her own phone and dials Aria. She explains the whole situation to the computer technician, who is more than willing to help out. She hangs up quickly, noticing the Mike has finally cracked the safe. He and Hicks are poking around the inside.

"So, what is it?"

"Not much." Mike says.

"What do you mean, not much?"

"I mean, there are just some tubes and a little USB stick." Mike stands aside.

"We need to find out what's on that USB stick." Louis says. "What's in the tubes?"

Hicks opens one, "What else? Paintings."

***

"Take a right here." Louis says.

"Baker, I know the way to the mall." Hicks laughs.

"Oh, yeah."

"So, let's rehash," Hicks says.

Louis smiles, Hicks loves to rehash, and re-re-hash. The more he talks out loud the closer they both get to the bottom of every case. Louis is sure he likes to hear the sound of his own voice more than anything in the world.

"So there were break-ins at the Mahoney's house and her gallery." Hicks starts off.

"Whoever broke in couldn't open the safe." Louis says.

"Maybe it was multiple people and one of them found what they were looking for before the other one was able finish with the safe?" He asks rhetorically.

"We also know that whoever broke into the house had a key and knew the code to the door."

"But didn't know the code for the safe; her safe."

"Charles is the only survivor so far with all those other couples dying together. The evidence points to him." Louis says.

"He was in the hospital last night, do you think after losing all those fluids he could break into his wife's office and try and break into a safe?"

"He's rich, he could hire someone. Or maybe he could talk his personal assistant, Holly, into doing it for him? She was willing to hold his vomit basin. I'm sure she would do a lot more for his affection."

"Don't say vomit." Hicks makes a noise.

"Barf is your kryptonite, Hicks." Louis laughs.

"So, what next?" Hicks glances over to her at the red light.

"We have a serious lack of evidence with Julie Mahoney's death. We can't find the phones. Aria said those are all off too. What did Aria say about Tim and Victoria's computer?"

"She said there was a large encrypted file she's working on decrypting. She said some mumbo jumbo about circumventing something or other." Hicks stops talking

The light goes green and she's overwhelmed with a thought. "Speaking of mumbo jumbo, didn't you say Carlos had a lead as well?"

"The well-built, tanned, forensic accountant 'Carlos', you mean?" Hicks grins.

"Yes, that 'Carlos'." She shakes her head.

"Yeah, like I said on the phone he found some mysterious deposits and withdrawals from Mr. Mahoney's personal account. Specifically, a withdrawal last week for over two hundred and fifty thousand dollars."

"Whoa, mysterious is right. I think we need to talk to Mr. Mahoney. I'll call Holly Tuft and arrange another meeting." Louis flips through her tablet for the number.

"Wait, not yet. I think we should find out a little more. Right now he's suspect number one in my book, and I don't think we need to show our cards just yet." Hicks leans over the steering wheel, like a hunter spotting deer. Only, he's a mall patron hunting a free spot.

"There." Louis points to a car pulling out of a spot.

Hicks makes a tight turn and stops, allowing the little silver Volvo enough room to pull out. From the other direction a little red convertible pulls up. Louis watches a little gray haired lady, barely tall enough to see over the steering wheel, pull out of the parking spot. Just as she clears the spot, the little red convertible zips into the space between two SUV's.

"There's a reason red cars get all the tickets. It's not because they are bright and attract attention, it's because they're driven by little-red-convertible-driving ass holes." Hicks snarls.

"That's actually an urban myth." Louis corrects him, laughing and unbuckling her seat belt. "Why don't you just stay here and I'll get Bryan?"

Walking into the mall she heads up the escalator. A tall woman in front of her, with miniature bee-hive hair doo, cow print blouse, and wearing a short pink leather skirt turns her head to look at Louis. Her bright pink lipstick face turns instantly alarmed, like Louis is some sort of horror to be seen. Louis stares back at the woman as if to say, "What the hell are you looking at?"

The mystery is revealed as she passes by a ten-foot mirror and is startled by her own horrid reflection. She's been sweating profusely. Even worse, her hair is wind swept making her look like she spent the last few hours in a hurricane.

"What in the hell happened to you? You look like …" Cece's voice calls out from the shoe department.

Louis notices she didn't finish the sentence since she's still on the clock. She hurries over to Cece, "It's nothing. I've been at a crime scene."

"I thought you were in the hospital?"

"I was. Then I was at a crime scene."

Cece looks at her watch, "I don't know what's keeping Kristine so long. She said she'd be here soon."

"Yeah, I'm here to get Bryan."

"Oh? She didn't bother telling me that." Cece's jealousy bubbles up again, this time manifesting itself in a quick toe tap of her brilliantly colored shoes.

"Where is Bryan anyway?" Louis isn't going to get into another conversation over their three-way friendship and who likes who better.

"He's with Annette. She's teaching him how to tie a tie. He's so adorable!" Cece rolls her eyes up to the ceiling in delight, "You know he sold three pairs of shoes today? He's going to be such a lady killer when he grows up."

"I can't wait to see him. It's been since last summer. Where's Annette?"

"They're over there in Children's." She points to the area.

Louis looks in the direction she's pointing to see a kid mannequin playing hopscotch and little Bryan playing along. "Bryan!"

He looks up, curious at who called him. He half skips, half runs toward Louis. She starts walking his direction.

"Wait Louis, let me get you his backpack." Cece ambles over to the shoe department's stock room. She comes back carrying a little orange backpack as though it were full of bricks.

Louis grabs the backpack and groans at the weight. "What have you got in here Bryan?"

"Clothes, books, games. Three games. My DS, and…" Bryan puts a finger to his forehead, "… and some movies. I ate the peanut butter fluff sandwich."

"I see." Louis laughs. "Do you remember me?"

"You're Aunt Kris' best friend."

Cece huffs at the slight and shakes her head.

Bryan continues unabated, "The woman with the boy's name, Louis."

Cece looks at her watch again, "Well, I'm almost off work now, time for my hot date. It was nice meeting you, Bryan." She bends down and holds out her hand to shake.

"It was nice meeting you too, Cece. Maybe I can do the register stuff next time?"

"Maybe." Cece laughs.

"What's his name Cece?" Louis asks with a wink.

"I'm not telling you. You'll just look him up in your computer and tell me all the horrible speeding tickets he's got."

"Why are you so worried, does he drive a fast car?"

"Maybe, or maybe you'll tell me he was a suspect in a rash of stolen lipstick crimes. Forget it. I'll do fine learning about people the way normal people do."

"Fine." Louis looks down at the boy, "Let's go Bryan. Your aunt asked me to pick you up and take you to the police station."

"Is Aunt Kris there?" He beams.

"She has to take a little trip, but she'll be back soon."

"Oh, okay." Bryan looks down at his shoes.

"Do you like computers?"

"Yeah. Doesn't everybody?"

"No, not everybody. I'm going to take you to the smartest computer person on the planet."

Bryan's face lights up, "You know Bill Gates?"

Louis laughs, "No, my friend Aria. She uses computers to help track down criminals."

"Oh, cool." He says a little less enthusiastically.

Louis helps him into the back of the car. His backpack hits the floorboards with a resounding thud.

Hicks turns around in his seat, "What have you got in there? Bricks?"

"No. I've got clothes, books, four books. Three games, my DS and some movies. I already ate my peanut butter fluff sandwich."

"I see." Hicks chuckles, "Are you hungry?"

"Yeah."

"Bryan, this is Detective Bert Hicks, my partner."

"You can call me Bert."

"Are you guys married?"

Louis and Hicks laugh hard. Louis explains, "No, he's my co-worker. We work together to track down bad guys."

"Oh, cause the partner's in that show 'Cross & Cross' are married."

"That's TV. In real life police partners aren't married. They just -" Louis flashes Hicks a look before he's able to finish the sentence.

"They just what?" Bryan asks as the car pulls out of the mall.

"Not important." Hick shakes his head. "What do you want to eat?"

"Pizza!"

"Well, my man, you're in luck. I know this place right next to the station. They sell real New York City style pizza."

"What's that?"

"Well, an authentic New York City style pizza has a thin crust, but it isn't crisp. It's foldable. The pizza is cooked in a really hot oven, giving the dough a perfect texture. It has sauce, but not too much. It has mozzarella cheese, never any other blends of cheese. But not too much cheese. You can order it from the street, fold it up and eat it without all the toppings falling on the ground."

"Wow, you know a lot about pizza."

151

Louis laughs, "Yeah, he knows a lot about all kinds of food."

***

Louis walks Bryan into the squad's computer lab. She looks down at him to see the stacks of blinking computers suitably impress him. A large bun of hair points toward the ceiling and Louis can hear the gunfire-rapid tap of keys at the keyboard. Aria is the smartest and prettiest computer technician Louis has ever met. Her Korean parents can't understand why she would waste her time on such a frivolous job, but Aria loves helping the police solve crimes. She spends her evenings sharpening her forensic computer skills. Aria has unearthed many of the key pieces of electronic evidence in their past cases.

"Aria?" Louis calls out.

Aria peeks her head over the pile of computers like a gopher out of a hole. "Louis?"

"Hey," She looks around the stack to see Tim and Victoria's Pepto Bismol pink laptop on Aria's desk. "This is Bryan, Kristine's nephew."

"Pleased to meet you, Bryan." Aria smiles.

Bryan smiles back silently.

"I've got something new for you."

"What's that?" She asks perking up.

Louis fishes the USB stick in an evidence bag out of her pocket. "We found this in Mrs. Mahoney's safe. Someone tried to break into her house and her office, maybe they were looking for whatever is on this drive?"

"Could be ; let's see what's on it." Aria takes the drive and plugs it into her government issued laptop. "Hm. Looks like 3GP files."

"What's that?"

"They are video files saved by newer camcorders."

"Oh, so there are videos?"

"Like movies?" Bryan asks.

"Yes, like movies, home-movies." Aria says. "They are quite long, this one is four hours, this one is five hours, and this one is two hours." Aria makes a few clicks on the screen, "This one is shorter, just seven minutes."

"Let's look at the seven minute one." Louis leans in.

Hicks clears his throat, and points to Bryan.

"Oh." Louis scratches her head, and then reaches into her pocket. "Bryan, why don't you take Hicks and go get a soda."

"I don't want a soda." He whines.

"Can you get one for me?" Louis pleads.

"I guess." He frowns, grabs the money from her hand and stomps away.

"Hurry, play that video."

The video starts with a barely lit room. When the lights come on the camera shifts from being out of focus to focusing on the Mahoney's living room. "That's where we found Mrs. Mahoney." Louis points to the floor in the video.

A few seconds later a woman comes into the picture. She's wearing heels, a flowing flowery dress, and is carrying a large painting. The painting looks exactly like the one in the background of the video. Over the course of the seven minutes Louis and Aria watch as the woman painstakingly replaces the painting she's brought in with the one on the wall.

"Can you zoom in?" Louis asks.

"I can, but I doubt you'll be able to see any better. As you zoom the pixels will get larger and less distinct."

"Can you sharpen it up at all?" Louis asks.

"It's not like the movies, Louis." Aria sighs, "I can sharpen it up some, but it'll take time, and I doubt you'll be impressed with the results."

"Nonetheless, email me the best still you have. I'll show the picture to Charles Mahoney, maybe he'll recognize her."

Hicks bounds into the lab, "Anything good?"

"I'm sure it wasn't anything you would have hoped for. It's a video of a woman replacing one of the paintings with a fake."

Bryan walks in and hands Louis a soda.

"Did it look like Victoria or Mrs. Kitt?" Hicks asks.

"No, not to me. Way too scrawny for either of them." Louis says. "I think we should have a tech team go over the green painting in the living room for finger prints."

"Sounds like a good idea." Hicks sighs, "Hm. Have you had any luck tracking down those phones, Aria?"

"Well, as I said over the phone I still can't get a line on any of the phone numbers you sent me. I think it's too much of a coincidence to have that many phones go dead at the same time. The warrant for the phone records hasn't come through yet."

Hicks pulls out his phone, "If I have to track down a judge at the golf course I will." He spins around and steps toward the hallway.

"Wait. There is one thing." Aria stops him before he leaves.

"What?"

"Both Tim and Victoria's cell phone and that phone number you found in their land line all come from the same group of burner cell phones."

"Oh?"

"Yeah, I have the list right here." Aria points to a piece of paper on her desk just in front of Bryan.

Bryan looks down at the paper.

"Interesting," Hicks looks back at his phone, "That might help me heat things up."

Louis rolls her eyes at the pun.

"I'll be right back." He swaggers out the door.

Aria points at the shiny little pink laptop, "I wasn't able to get started on getting into the encrypted disk on Victoria's laptop until this morning."

"This morning? I thought you had the laptop two days ago?"

"Nope, just got it."

Damn Quinn, Louis grinds her teeth.

"Well it turns out that she was one of the users affected by the leak of millions of passwords by that new site, eyesocial.com, a few months ago. The hackers in that case sent out a list of leaked emails and passwords. I looked up her email address on that list. She used the password 'M-i-5-t-a-k-3-n-I-d-3-n-t-i-t-y' on the eyesocial.com website."

"M-i-5… what? Does that spell something?" Louis tries to work out the letters in her mind.

"Oh, yeah it's 'MistakenIdentity' with the 's' as a '5' and the 'e' as '3'."

"Mistaken identity? Interesting."

"That password didn't work for the encrypted disk, but people don't usually vary their passwords too much so I wrote a script to try different variations, like switching the 'i's to '1's, adding a bang and so forth."

"Your techno babble always confuses me. What's a 'bang'?"

Bryan blurts out the answer, "It's an exclamation point!"

Aria beams at the boy, "Very good Bryan. Where did you learn that?"

"I'm taking a computer class in school. Our teacher, Mr. Goldstein, he calls it a bang. He talked about when he was growing up and learning Unix, something about a comma line."

"You mean a command line?" Aria giggles.

Bryan blushes, "Yeah, command line."

"Great," Louis says, "now there are two of you."

"Yup, I heard you were going to come help me out?" Aria directs her question at Bryan.

"I can help?"

"Of course you can. I've got a few tasks lined up for you already."

"Well, if there's nothing else I'll leave you two smarty pants to your computer forensics." Louis musses up Bryan's hair. She turns toward the door and Hicks bursts into the room.

"The warrant is ten or fifteen minutes away. How long will it take you to get the call list from the phone company?"

Aria plays with her hair, "Well, for this particular burner phone company I usually have to sit on the phone with them for a half hour to get through to the right person. Once I get the phone records I'll punch them through my networking script and I'll call you on the analysis."

"Great." He spins around to Louis, "Let's go. I have an idea on what we should do next."

Louis' phone beeps to indicate she has a text message. She pulls out her phone from her bag, thinking it might be a message from Aria, already breaking open the case with her techno-magic. She looks at the screen. "Oh my God!"

CHAPTER 25

Hicks looks over as he starts the car. "What's wrong?"

"I just got a text message." Louis stares at the phone, not sure what to do at the moment. She stares at the message.

"Yes, I heard the beep. What did the message say?"

She hesitates, is this the kind of thing she should share with her partner? Her mind works through the possibilities, razzing her, supporting her, either way she's got to tell him. The message is just too wildly unbelievable. "The text message came with a picture."

Hicks looks at her, eyes raised, "What's the picture?"

"Apparently, her name is 'Bethany'"

"Who's that?" Hicks looks at her curiously.

"I don't know, but she has a pierced nipple."

This comment gets Hick's immediate attention. "Oh?"

"Yeah, the message says 'Nice meeting you Will, call me later. –Bethany'"

"Oh no."

"Oh yes." Louis stares down at her phone's screen.

"Is she..." Hicks leaves a space in the end of the sentence, obviously hoping not to have to finish it.

"Yes, she's naked." Louis shows the picture to Hicks. The self-portrait seems to be taken in a tiny bathroom. Bethany's pierced nipple glitters with steel and jewels. A butterfly tattoo flutters over her right breast. She's anything but modest.

"Wow."

"Yeah, exactly." Louis is too stunned for any more detail.

Hicks drives to the insurance adjuster's office in silence until they are stopped at a red light, "So, what's her number?"

"Are you serious?" Louis' shakes her head. She knows exactly how this happened, the only thing to explain it really. He's drunk. He doesn't get fall-down drunk very often, but this time he has to be in rare form. He doesn't have his own cell phone number memorized very well, but he has her number. When 'Bethany' asked for his number he must have rattled of Louis' number. She's sure he wasn't looking for a naked picture of 'Bethany', or was he? It's the first time that Will cheating on her has really crossed her mind. A thought that seemed to bubble up on a daily basis with her first husband, the bastard. But she loves Will, and he loves her. Their marriage has been rock solid for so many years. That dinner, what was he trying to tell her? Was it that he's found someone else? Would that someone else be Bethany? She knows she should call him, clear up the confusion, but she's in the middle of a case. She needs to put these crazy thoughts aside for now, call him later.

Hicks puts the car in park. "We're here." He grabs two of the painting tubes from the back seat. "Ah, let's go."

Louis is still looking at naked Bethany. She exhales the air she's been holding and stuffs the phone in her pocket.

The bell rings as the detectives walk into the gleaming front lobby of the insurance adjuster. A little rat-like dog with bared teeth bounds up to them wagging a twiggy tale. The dog is surprisingly friendly, despite the bared teeth. Louis reaches down, holds out her hand and gives the little dog a pet.

James Henry shuffles his squat body into the lobby. The bright halogen lights bounce off his bald head. "Dobby?" He asks looking down at Louis.

Louis is confused for a split second until she notices that he isn't actually looking at her, but the dog. The dog peeks out from under Louis' legs and turns his head to point an ear toward Mr. Henry.

"Dobby, go lay down." He says forcefully pointing to the corner. The dog's tail straightens and stops wagging. Dobby walks to the little red doggie bed.

"Detectives. I'm so glad you came." The little man walks to the door in the lobby, "Come with me."

Dobby jumps up from his doggie bed, ears perked up.

"Not you Dobby. Go lay down." Mr. Henry says, scolding the dog.

Louis looks at the dog and smiles.

There are two desks in the room beyond the door. They couldn't be more different. One desk is clean. A small laptop sits on the shining dark wood. An elegant pen lies neatly on top of a spiral bound notebook. The rest of the desk shines under the lights. The other desk cannot be seen under the precarious stacks of paper. The space for the laptop is the only part of the desk that isn't two to three feet high. The black upholstered chair is covered in small white hairs.

Mr. Henry notices Louis staring at the messy desk. "My partner. He says he can find what he's looking for, but he never seems to be able to find it in a timely manner." He looks at Hicks, "What is in the tubes?"

Hicks says, "We were hoping you could tell us. We found them in Mrs. Mahoney's safe in the basement."

"Oh." Mr. Henry snatches the tubes from his hand.

Hicks says, "Make sure you wear gloves when examining the paintings, we may still need to process them for evidence."

He clucks his tongue. "I always wear gloves when handling precious artwork."

Louis is reminded of his attitude problem yesterday. "You said you have more information on the fake paintings?"

"Yes, yes. I took the liberty last night of taking a small paint sample from the 'Abstract #7' by Malcolm in the dining room."

"You took evidence from a crime scene?" Louis sneers.

"Well, ah, I… it was before you arrived." He trips over his tongue and expels out an excuse.

"You didn't know it was a crime scene until we arrived?" Hicks raises his eyebrows.

"Well, I, ah…"

"The dead body wasn't a clue?" Hicks asks.

Louis lets him off the hook, "And what did you find with your ill got evidence?"

"Ah, so I did some tests." Mr. Henry sits down at the perfectly clean desk. He types in his password, slowly, one key at a time, using only his two index fingers. Once the login is finally complete the three of them watch the screen flicker a few times making a chiming noise. Mr. Henry clicks on the only little icon on his screen, it being as clean as his actual desk. A web page comes up and the detectives have to watch as the login process is repeated. Only now he's fiddling with his phone.

"We have two factor authentication." He says.

Louis stamps and shuffles her feet. She reaches for her phone in her pocket, but is struck by the mental image of the very naked Bethany. She huffs and stuffs the phone back in her pocket.

Once Mr. Henry is finally done pecking in the password he clicks on the little blue button on the screen. Almost instantaneously a large red box appears stating 'Access Denied'. "Hmm." He ponders looking at his phone.

"Mr. Henry, why don't you just tell us what the report says?" Louis snaps.

"Oh, well the report is better… but… I guess." Mr. Henry turns his chair back around to face the detectives.

"The analysis of the paint indicates that this is not a genuine Malcolm painting."

"And how do you know for sure?" Hicks stares down at the little man.

"Malcolm only uses paint from a specific supplier. I used infrared spectrometry to analyze the organic compounds of the painting from the… crime scene and they didn't match the one's from Malcolm's supplier. There was linseed oil in the sample, and Malcolm's paint had none."

"Couldn't he have used a different paint for that painting?" Louis shakes her head thinking his evidence is hardly conclusive.

"Well… no actually." Mr. Henry straightens up and smiles. "I actually collected a sample of this painting two years ago when Mrs. Mahoney bought the piece. She wanted me to authenticate it again before we set the insurance price."

"Authenticate it again?" Hicks asks skeptically.

"Yes again. The piece was authenticated at the time of purchase, but Mrs. Mahoney likes to be thorough," He clears his throat, "especially when it comes to insuring the paintings. So many of the authenticators rely on their gut feeling because it's far too expensive to run tests on each piece."

"I see. So you can verify that the paintings are fake? In court?" Hicks asks, but as he asks he leans back toward the messy desks of papers. "Uh oh," he says.

Louis hears a quiet whooshing sound.

Mr. Henry rushes toward the toppling pile of papers but is just short of saving the stack from falling on the upholstered chair. "Damn," he mutters.

Louis hears a cat's muffled meow. An immense orange tabby cat peers out from the destruction of papers. The cat stretches and violently shakes away the papers resting on top. A few more papers fall to the ground.

Mr. Henry grabs the cat before it can do any more damage to the piles. "Off to the bathroom with you Crookshanks." He puts the cat under his arm and wrestles with it to the back of the room.

Hicks looks down at the disaster he created and grins at Louis, who is shaking her head.

As Mr. Henry comes back from the bathroom Hicks asks, "Dobby? Crookshanks?"

"My partner has a penchant for that kid's book, 'Harry Potter'," Mr. Henry says with disdain. He attempts to wipe the hairs from the cat off of his tweed jacket. "Anyway. Yes, I can testify in court that the paintings are fake."

"Have you seen the organic composition from other fake paintings, besides the ones at Mahoney's house?" Louis inquires.

"I have. Well, not this exact composition mind you, but very similar. And the piece was one of Mrs. Mahoney's paintings, but two years ago. In fact, hmm …." Mr. Henry crosses the room to a wall of filing cabinets. Without hesitation he pulls out a large set of keys, flips to the right key and opens one of the filing cabinet doors. He pulls a three-inch thick file from the drawer and slams the drawer shut. He walks back over to his desk, "I can't be completely sure, but I do believe the forger's style was very similar to that used in the Malcolm forged paintings." He flips through the thick pile of papers and pulls out an eight by ten glossy enlargement.

Louis peeks over Mr. Henry's shoulder. He lifts up the picture to examine the finer details and hits the painful side of Louis' chest accidentally. She lets out a short high-pitched scream.

Mr. Henry jerks away, "What? What did I do?"

"She's got shingles," Hicks explains.

"Oh, a most painful disease. I've had it myself," He frowns.

162

Louis isn't interested in a pity party. She takes a few deep breaths. "Just, give us the information and we'll be on our way." She says through gritted teeth, her eyes tearing up.

"Right. So the painting she had me authenticate in that case, *Winter's Eve*, by Winter Wellington, had far too many brush strokes. I noticed it right away." Mr. Henry holds up a copy of the painting. In it, a naked woman reclines on a rocking chair reading an enormous book. In the background there are of bookshelves packed full of gold inlaid books.

"Winter Wellington? Is that a woman or a man?" Hicks laughs.

Mr. Henry rolls his eyes, "A man." He looks at Louis, "Anyway, once I was suspicious I ran a test against the paint. The chemistry came out all wrong. I told her she was deceived."

Louis shuffles her feet, trying to push down the radiating pain, "Did she say where she got the painting?"

"I do have the bill of sale in the file. It doesn't say much, but I do remember she was quite angry. She asked me if I was sure, and I said I was. I distinctly remember her saying she was going to 'kill that woman'."

"Woman?" Louis looks confused.

"Yes, woman. She said, 'I'm going to kill that woman.'"

"Did she say anything else?"

"No, but she stormed out of here in a hurry."

Louis says, "One more thing, Mr. Henry."

"Yes."

Louis holds up her tablet in front of him, "Have you seen this woman?"

Mr. Henry squints and leans in close to a still made from the video Louis and Aria had watched earlier. "Can't say that I have. She does appear to be switching paintings though. Isn't that odd."

"Yes, thank you." Louis tucks the tablet back into her bag. "Can you make copies of that report, and the one of the Malcolm paintings?"

"Yes, of course." Mr. Henry storms off to the copier.

Hicks leans over to whisper to Louis, "I could have told her those boobs were fake."

***

The door shuts behind the two detectives. Hicks smiles, "We need to go to Chez Marin."

"The restaurant? You just ate three slices of pizza."

"Ha, ha," Hicks laughs sarcastically, "We need to go there and see if the staff knew Mr. and Mrs. Kitt. Quinn said the neighbors didn't seem to know them at all. People like that, they may not know their neighbors, but they'll know all the people at their favorite restaurant. And those people will know them, especially the bartenders."

"Good point, but that can wait. We need to look into those fake paintings and the Mahoney's hinky finances."

"You just want to go drool at your favorite muscular accountant."

Louis smiles, "No, I think the one victim that's alive is our biggest clue. You know what I say when the wife dies…"

"Yeah, it's always the husband."

"It's always the husband."

"I think it's him too, but I don't think we have near enough to nail him."

"No, which is why we need to talk to the accountant."

"I think we need to go to Chez Marin first. I know a bookie that hangs out there."

"Oh, so you plan on getting some betting in as well?" Louis steps out into the bright, hot day. She's counting the hours until the setting sun brings in a cool breeze.

"No, but I have a little hunch how we might connect the Mahoney's and the Kitts."

"Through a bookie?" Louis asks over the top of the car just before getting in.

"Yes, I've seen Charles Mahoney at the OTB a dozen times. He likes to bet the trifecta."

"That's where you have to predict the first, second and third horse right?"

"Right. And if they don't come in that order you get nothing. If they do, the odds are usually you'll win a pile of dough."

"So your theory is that Charles Mahoney and Neil Kitt may have bet together?"

"Well, they either bet together or saw each other at that restaurant. It's not very big, and if Charles was a regular of the bookie, and Neil and Sara were regulars of the restaurant..."

CHAPTER 26

Kristine pulls over to the side of the dirt road she's been traveling on for at least the last ten minutes, but perhaps it was more. Bob Dylan belts out *Knockin' on Heaven's Door*. She reaches over to change the station. Heaven isn't a topic she wants to think about right now and she's not a big Dylan fan. His nasal voice makes him sound like he's holding his nose because he's wandered into a kitchen cooking with expired meat. She hits the button to change the station, but the thinly veiled song describing a blowjob comes on. Unfortunately, just a hint of the catchy tune gets the chorus stuck in her head. She turns off the radio.

Wendell belts out his directions, "Bare left on Steele Road."

Kristine stares up at the screen. She's sure that Wendell said that already. "There's no road, unless you mean that driveway? What are you talking about?" This has happened before. She looks around, hesitant to take the road that looks like a driveway. She continues on down the road. She's fairly sure the road is also named Steele.

She shakes her head. She's not sure when she became so reliant on Wendell, but she's sure they are headed for a break-up soon.

Wendell told her a while ago that she was less than a half hour from Geneva, but the GPS still says she's a half hour from Geneva. A GPS must calculate time like computers do. She's spent many a late evening watching the progress bar on a particularly large document being downloaded creep across the screen, always estimating that she just has to wait a short time for the completion. In reality, the time is always off by double, or triple.

166

Computers live in their own time world, she thinks, one that is not governed by reality.

She moves the map around on the tiny screen, desperately trying to find the little checkered flag pointing her way to the tiny town. She can't find the flag, but the route seems to stop just a few miles up the road. Why then, would Wendell say she had a half hour still left to go? She looks around for her real map she's had packed in the car since long before Wendell arrived. She scours the car checking the glove box first and discovering a melted chocolate-covered energy bar; the kind with the women doing yoga on the front of the wrapper. The kind that make you feel good about yourself while absorbing all those empty calories. These fantasies of melted chocolate energy bars must be a symptom of her growing hunger. Did she even have lunch? She has to learn to take better care of herself, especially now that she has to take care of Bryan. But she can't think about that now, she must figure out how to get to Geneva, talk to Dennis Baxter's mother, and uncover some evidence that will keep this familial rapist and murderer behind bars.

The map is not found within the glove box, nor the side pockets or the pocket behind the seat. When she looks under the seat finding nothing but old junk mail, receipts and empty paper coffee cups she loses all hope. Out of the corner of her eye she sees a thick clump of paper. It's the right color and has a shiny cover, just like she remembers. "Ah ha." She smiles in satisfaction. Things are finally going her way. She unplugs Wendell from the dash. The little machine beeps and starts a little count down timer until she picks an option for keeping the GPS on even when unplugged. She takes Wendell and the real map out to the hood of her car. She unfolds the map to the index and searches for Geneva in the list of thousands of little cities and townships in her map of Western New York. She finds the coordinates and carefully unfolds the map, like she's done so many times before, at least before Wendell came along.

She compares the map on Wendell with the map in front of her. The old map gives her more context than the tiny screen on Wendell. She follows the highway she recognizes with her finger and finds the dirt road she turned on. "Old Richardson Road" on the paper map is "County Route 42" on Wendell. She sees now why Wendell is confused. The little dirt road she's been driving on is marked as private half way to Geneva. She'll have to turn around and go back to the highway, following a much smarter route. Time wasted, a frustration for Kristine at the best of times, and these are far from her best of times.

A pain of regret flows over her heart. She misses her sister's smile, her laugh. Kristine thought she would have all the time in the world to learn to be a good mom from her sister's example. Now she has to do it all on her own.

Just as she attempts to fold the map back into a shape that might resemble the one she started with, she hears a strange noise from the woods. She can't place the noise. Is it an animal huffing? Maybe a quiet whisper? She becomes very still, looking around to find the source. She hears it again, the crack of a stick? She isn't sure it's something she wants to stick around for. She folds the map not caring anymore if it is even close to the form she started with. She walks toward the door of the car.

"Hold it right there!" A gruff man's voice says from the edge of the woods.

Kristine stands still. She glances down at the phone on the seat.

"Who are ya?" He asks, but without allowing for an answer asks another question in a whisper, "Do you know them Richardson's?" His voice sounds like he's been smoking a pack a day for a half century.

Kristine thinks through her answer, and takes a deep breath. She starts to turn around to answer the man's question but he shouts at her, "Don't you turn aroun'. I gotta gun."

"Okay." She raises her hands in the air. "My name is Kristine Rocha. I'm looking for a route to Geneva."

"Well, this ain't the way. You don't belong here."

"Okay, just let me be on my way then."

"Bah. Geneva. What you want with that piss ant place anyway?"

"I need to speak with someone there, I'm a lawyer." She winces, knowing this isn't a brilliant thing to say in this particular situation.

"A lawya'?" His voice shakes, practically spitting out the question. "Lawya's ain't never done me no good. Took away half my land. Back taxes they say. Conspiracy, that's what I say. They're all in cahoots." He hocks a loogie from deep down in his chest, coughs and spits it out.

"I'm – ah – I'm not that kind of lawyer." She knows she's digging a hole, but maybe, she thinks, she'll be able to talk her way out of this mess.

"Not that kinda lawya'?" He scoffs. "Then what kinda pansy ass lawya' are ya?"

"I'm the kind that puts rapists and murderers behind bars." She starts to lower her hands slowly.

"Keep those hands up." He shouts. "You lawya's are all the same. You come looking for people, is that why you're here? You think you going to find something, take the away rest of my land? Who sent you?"

"No one sent me. I'm just trying to find the way to Geneva."

"This isn't the way. You can't get through up there, bridge has been out for years."

"I didn't know that, my GPS -"

"Who's that?"

"My GPS."

"Your what? You have someone else with you? Make him come out."

"No, it's a machine."

"You work for machines?" Again the man's voice becomes harsher. He coughs hard, finally dislodging another bit of phlegm and spitting it out.

"No, I don't work for machines. I use the machine to find my way."

"Find your way where?"

"Geneva, I need to get there, it's urgent."

"This isn't the way to Geneva, bridge has been out for years."

"Yes, you said that."

"Who are you?"

"My name is Kristine Rocha." This time around, she's going to leave out the lawya' part. This conversation is like a puzzle, she wonders if there is a magic phrase she can use to wrangle her way out of it.

"You know the Richardson's?"

"No. I -"

The man's voice cut's her short, "Then why are you here? You lookin' for something?"

"Yes, Geneva." Kristine's arms feel weak. She cannot remember the last time she's held them up for this long and if this circular conversation continues on, she's going to have to find some way to put them down. She starts to lower them, so slowly she thinks he might not notice. If she could just talk him into allowing her to get her phone.

CHAPTER 27

The sign on the Chez Marin says 'Closed', but Hicks proceeds through the unlocked door as if he owns the place. The restaurant occupies a single, narrow space in a strip mall. The atmosphere is generated from the heavy front drapes, and the tightly packed tables. Completely opposite from the immense place Louis went to last night, this place would only hold ten intimate couples. Busy and slow nights probably had the same number of occupants. Two men sit at the bar. Both men are dressed in starched fashion dress shirts. The men are hunched over in conversation, as though someone in the empty restaurant might overhear their private thoughts. Tiny glasses hold sips of deep red wine.

One man finally notices the bell on the front door ring, "We're closed." He says waving his arm without turning around.

"Jacque." Hicks calls out.

A scraggy man with a two-day old beard turns towards the door; a smile lights up his face, showing off his perfectly white teeth. "Bert, what brings you this way?"

"Oh, you know, just wanting to drop in for an aperitif after lunch."

"Well, you're too late. You need to have a pre-dinner cocktail," he raises his glass.

"Actually, I'm here on the job. This is my partner, Detective Louis Baker." He says stepping to the side, squeezing between two tables to let her by.

"Welcome to Chez Marin mademoiselle." He slaps on a faux accent and picks her hand up to kiss it.

Louis lets him kiss her hand, but stiffens up. She knows that she'd be a disaster in Europe.

"We want to talk to you about a couple of customers," Hicks explains.

He broadens his smile at Louis, but then breaks his gaze and frowns at Hicks. "I see. You don't come in here for weeks, now you want me to talk about my regulars?"

"Yeah, well. I haven't had the right kind of date for a few weeks. I know you don't approve unless they are leggy." Hicks elbows Jacque.

The man snickers, "Yes, you do need to bring in a few more of the leggy ones. Who is it you want to speak of?"

"Neil and Sara Kitt. They were here on Wednesday, I believe."

"Ah yes, she loves the Chicken Marengo. She's ordered that for years, but can never finish it. Mr. Kitt shares it with her or she has to take the swan home. He doesn't share it with her very often. She says she eats it Thursday's while pouring over her favorite books." Jacque raises an eyebrow, indicating he knows what kind of books Mrs. Kitt enjoys.

"Have you ever seen them in here with anyone else?" Louis asks.

"No." Jacque shakes his head. "They come here alone. They brought their daughter once, a long time ago. She graduated last year, from college I believe." He waves his arm across his restaurant, "Not too much room for extra people here, I'm afraid. I recommend reservations, but I always leave two tables open for my regulars. Not this asshole though." He points to Hicks.

Hicks laughs, "I can call ahead."

"I'll make sure Sam knows to make you wait for a month."

The other man holds up his tiny wine glass, smiling.

"What else can you tell us about them?" Hicks inquires.

"Mr. Kitt lost his job last year. He's a printer. He found another job, but he's very hush-hush about it. He never talks about work." Jacque looks to the side and takes a step back.

"And what else?" Louis presses on, noticing he has more to say, but is not so sure.

"And, I do not like to spread rumors about my regulars."

Hicks lowers his voice, "We're here to investigate their murders, Jacque."

"Murders? They're dead?" Jacque raises his hand to his face.

"Yes, so whatever it is you are holding back, please, out with it." Louis says insistently.

Jacque shakes his head, "One does not speak ill of the dead."

"Let's come at this from a different angle. I know Ricco is a regular here. Did Mr. Kitt ever meet with him?"

"No, no. Not with the bookie. The bookie only eats here. He has a healthy appetite. He knows not to do his business here. Anyway, a business like that is for Ricco to make money, not for any of his clients to make money. You know about the ways of gambling, Bert."

"Yes. Yes, I do." Hicks laughs.

Jacque sighs, "Ah, Mr. Kitt. I noticed a few months ago..." He frowns and rubs his slick black hair into place, "I noticed a few months ago that he had new credit cards. New ones every time he came in. So, when Madam Kitt was powdering her nose I asked him if he was okay with money. I knew it was none of my business, but you know, if one of my regulars is having money problems... well, I will give them a discount. I've seen it before, applying for all those cards, running up huge bills. But he said he got a job, a good paying job. One downtown. I asked him if he was still in printing. He laughed, said yes, 'in a way'. But that was it; Mrs. Kitt came back to the table. I don't like to talk money in front of the Madam."

An unnatural stillness fills the tiny restaurant.

Louis pulls out her tablet, "Have you perhaps seen this woman in your restaurant?"

Jacque studies the video still, "No. I don't think so, but you can't really see it very well."

Louis sighs, "What about receipts, do you have the credit card receipts from Mr. Kitt's last purchases?"

"Sam would have them; we must keep them for ages. Ridiculous, it takes up half of the back office." Jacque shakes his head.

"Great, we could use them now."

Jacque turns around. "Sam, take this detective and find some receipts from Mr. Kitt."

Sam nods his head and waves Louis to the back room. "Can I offer you a cup of coffee? It will take some time to dig through the receipts." Sam speaks, quietly but with a deep, soothing voice.

"Ah, sure." Louis replies, sitting at the red vinyl buffet restaurant style chair. She sits back and exhales.

The tiny office has two desks, both of them messy. The eight four foot high filing cabinets take up two walls. Sitting on a little kitchen cart is a fancy, but tiny espresso machine. Sam gets to work making the espresso. His hands glide over the controls like a wizard preparing a potion.

The loud noises fill Louis mind. She cannot think, and prefers not to. She stares out in a daze until Sam stands in front of her with a tiny cup of coffee. "Ah, thanks." She says more ineloquently than she would like.

"Cream? Or Sugar?" He asks.

"Sugar." She replies.

He hands her a few packets and a tiny spoon. He opens a filing cabinet, pulls out a rubber-banded wad of receipts and starts going through them methodically. "Your mind is troubled."

"Ah, yes, this case." She takes a burning sip from the cup.

"No, not a case, a husband." He doesn't look up at her.

"What?" She puts the cup on the desk next to her before she burns her fingers.

"You wear a wedding ring; the troubles are not your case, but your husband."

She tries to think of how her stress level could possibly be giving away her husband.

"Your wife then?" He asks finally looking at her.

"No, my husband, but how could you possibly know that?" She asks shaking her head.

"Thirty years behind a bar." He sorts through the receipts. "Ah, here's one." He hands the small, shiny slip to Louis.

"Can you find more?"

"Of course. But you should tell me about your troubles."

"Why?" Louis crinkles her nose.

"Because it will make the time go faster, and you want to get it off your chest."

"I don't actually." Louis picks her coffee back up.

"Suit yourself." Sam carefully puts the pile of receipts he's looked through back into the filing cabinet. He leafs through the files and pulls out another one. "Perhaps I should tell you a story?"

"It's your dime." Louis sips the perfectly brewed cup.

He starts into the tale without looking up, "I started behind the bar when I was old enough to look twenty-one at nineteen. My father ran this little hole in the wall restaurant on Pine.

He knew that he could lose his license, but he wanted me to learn the trade. He said, 'I have four regulars. They come in every night. Two scotch, neat, a whiskey on the rocks and a dirty martini.' He proceeded to tell me what scotch. Then he showed me how much ice to put in the whiskey and finally how to make an olive juice martini.

"I thought I was ready. He did show me a few other things and said I should get by fine. The night proceeded. The regulars came, and I served them their drinks."

He hands Louis another piece of paper. She sees that the name on the receipts is the same "Neil A. Kitt" but the last few digits not marked out on the card are different.

"At the end of the night my father checks the till. 'What is this?' He asked me. I stood there confused, I did some calculations in my head for how much I had made and looked at the total he rang up. They were quite in line. 'What do you mean?' I asked him. 'This is only half of what Tony makes. What did you say to the customers?' He asked me. 'Nothing.' I said. 'You said nothing to the customer?' He threw his arms in the air. 'If you want to be a bartender, you have to learn to talk to your customers.' I nodded my head.

"The next day I talked to the customers. I told them about my day, my girlfriend, and my tiny apartment. Still, my numbers were down. 'What did you say to the customers?' My father asked. 'Just stuff.' I said. 'Just stuff? These people are your customers, you don't just talk about stuff.' He shouted at me.

"I went to a bar near my tiny apartment the next day. I walked in and the bar tender greeted me with a big smile. I sat down on one of the hard stools. He leaned over and told me that he knew I was too young, but that he saw a heavy burden on my shoulders. He'd serve me a ginger ale, he said. He asked me why my family was giving me trouble.

"I was shocked. How could he know so much? I asked him. He told me that he just had a way of figuring things out, looking, listening to the things that are not said. He said that every person has a wavelength where all of their secrets are revealed. He said that you have to tune into those wavelengths.

"I asked him if I could learn these things. 'Sure,' he said. I worked as his busboy for two years, then his assistant for ten years. I'm now his bartender." Sam smirks and hands Louis two more pieces of paper.

She sees that none of the numbers match on these receipts either. "That should be enough. Thank you, Sam."

"You're welcome. I hope to see you in some time. I hope your wavelength reveals your inner secret to much more happiness next time."

She smiles and winks, "Me too." She leaves Sam to tidy up the receipts in the office. Hicks and Jacque are huddled over a plate of cheese. "Let's went," She says making her way to the door.

The door opens to the pressing heat and her phone indicates another text message. She stiffens up, grits her teeth. Her heart beats faster.

"Just check it." Hicks says.

"Maybe you should." She looks up at Hicks for guidance, but remembers the last, illicit text, "No wait, never mind." *How could Will give away his secret desires so easily?* She shakes her head and pulls the phone out from her pocket. She reads through the text, "Ah ha!"

"What?" Hicks opens the driver's door.

"Mr. Mahoney took a woman to his cabin in Naples." Louis says smugly.

"Whoa. The day after his wife died? That's kind of crass, even for a jerk like him."

"I know. Do you think we have enough on him now? Because I'd just love to catch him red-handed."

"Red-handed? He's not married anymore, and adultery isn't actually illegal."

"Right, whatever."

"How did you know he is at this cabin anyway?"

"David Huang."

"Who?" Hicks looks over at Louis, "Wait, that blogger? Are you seriously working with the press now?"

"I gave him a little quote this morning before you arrived. I told him I was sorry I didn't get it to him last night, but I gave him a little tip to follow our main suspect."

Hicks whistles, "Ballsy."

"I know. I don't know what I was thinking, but Mr. Mahoney is so guilty, and I know we don't have a shred of real proof. I thought, what could it hurt if we knew where he was?"

"We still don't have any real proof. We need one more stop, and then we can head to Naples."

"Where?"

"The OTB, I've seen him gamble there a few times, and he's not a sore loser, he's a violent tempered maniac."

"What if he's gone by the time we get to Naples?" Louis says breathlessly.

"Do you really think he's not going to take his time?" Hicks winks.

CHAPTER 28

Kristine's arms are aching. She can feel the blood draining from her fingertips. She's tried a dozen different verbal tactics, but nothing seems to be working. In fact, he remembered she was a lawya' at some point and the round of paranoia resurfaced like a breaching whale.

She decides to have another go at calming him down. "Look, mister, I just want to get back in my car and forget this place ever existed."

"Did you say mister?" The voice, growls. "I ain't no mister. I've got two ten pound boobs to prove that. Damn kids sucked all the life right outta me and left me with these huge boobs. Ungrateful brats. What good are those kids anyway? Always getting' into trouble. Damn son always accused of stuff he ain't done." Her voice, now that Kristine knows it's a 'her', trails off, muttering.

During the last long rant her phone rang and she stared at it like a man lost in the desert staring at a barrel of water. Now she has nothing to distract herself from the pain in her arms. If this raving lunatic woman is true to her word she's only got moments to live. What a life, she's spent too much time at work. It's only a job. If only she spent this weekend with her nephew, not here. She shouldn't be here on top of some random hill. She shouldn't be ranted at by a paranoid woman.

Kristine tries to break the rant again, if only for the possibility to lower her hands. "I'm very sorry. I couldn't really tell who you were since I can't see you. Now that I know you are a woman, maybe you can understand my situation."

"What situation?"

"I need to get home to my nephew. My sister just died," Kristine chokes on the words, "his mother. I need to take care of him." Kristine is at the verge of tears.

"What does that have to do with me?" The gruff woman's voice growls.

"Well, I just want to lower my hands, get into the car and drive away."

"No way. You'll be back up here in an hour. Looking for me, trying to take away my land. Stuff I do up here, none of your business. Definitely not the government's business, I tell you that right now."

"No, I won't come back." She says emphatically, shaking her head violently.

"You'll send someone then. Some of your lawya' friends. You thieves stick together, right?"

"No, my friend sells shoes to rich people." She knows better than to claim Louis as a friend at this point.

"I don't believe you. Lawya's always lie."

Kristine exhales, her arms piercing in pain, "Look, what do you want out of this situation?"

"What do you mean?"

"I mean are you planning to kill me? Hurt me?"

"I don't kill people. I ain't like that. And my family ain't like that either." She sneers.

"Fine, then I have to put my hands down. I cannot hold them up any longer."

There's a long silence. Kristine lowers her arms inch by inch until they are by her side. The pain of the blood rushing back to her hands is almost worse than holding them up. The silence continues and she starts to think maybe the crazy woman has left. She dares not to turn around though.

More silence continues until her phone rings again. The sound drills into Kristine's brain. Each ring, each little giggle from Bryan brings tears streaming down her face. Her mother. It has to be her mother calling. She must be especially worried that Kristine isn't answering. It will likely take hours to calm her down from two missed calls. Then her mind starts to wander into the worrying traps. What if something else has happened to her mother? To Bryan? What is she doing here in this God-forsaken place? She's in the middle of concentrating on the worrying, on the sound of the phone ringing and Bryan giggling when she hears the snap of a twig much closer than before.

CHAPTER 29

The OTB, only a few blocks from Chez Martin is packed with customers. It's the height of the racing season and every seat is full with even more people standing around staring at the endless sea of televisions. A gorgeous horse trots across the screen with a tiny blue and yellow checkered rider. Seeing Stars, presumably the horses name, scrolls along the bottom of the screen with descriptions of his odds, past wins, jockey, weight, and parentage.

Hicks walks among the throngs of people straight toward a man hunched over a substantial basket of fries. The large salt and pepper haired man appears not to have skipped any opportunity for indulging in his fries. His bulbous nose and pocked marked face display his vast experience with alcohol. The drink in front of him is a Bloody Mary, likely the only serving of vegetables he gets in a day.

"Ricco." Hicks pats the man's back.

He looks up from his fries curiously, but only grumbles, "Ah, Hicks." He lifts his Bloody Mary and gulps down an inch of the drink.

Another horse slowly trots on the screen in front of Ricco. He wipes his hands with a tiny paper napkin, lifts his mechanical pencil and scribbles a few notes in small spiral bound book lying in front of him. He lets out a grunt.

"Hate to disturb you during your prime business hours, Ricco, but we have a bit of a situation." Hicks leans in.

Ricco looks straight at Hicks, and raises a thick furry eyebrow. He doesn't say anything. Louis had been warned in the car about Ricco's 'business hours'. Apparently he doesn't like to be disturbed and has been known to have people thrown out of the OTB on occasion, specifically if they keep him from doing his work. His work primarily consists of keeping the books for very wealthy people and making money off of far poorer and less intelligent who bet their money away.

Ricco breaks his stare from Hicks, "Who's this?"

"This is my partner, Detective Louis Baker. We're here investigating a murder."

Ricco looks around the room, from left to right. "Seems all these low-lifes are still kicking to me." His heavy eyes reveal his annoyance and exhaustion.

"Right, a few people died this weekend, including Charles Mahoney's wife."

"Yeah, I read that in the crime blog."

Hicks looks over at Louis and rolls his eyes. She shrugs sheepishly.

Ricco grabs a handful of fries and stuffs them in his mouth, "What's that gotta do with me?" He asks, with his mouth so full that pieces of fries fall back into the basket.

"I heard Mr. Mahoney was one of your customers."

He doesn't look at Hicks but continues to chew. He watches another horse cross the screen and he wipes his hands. He picks up his pencil and writes another note. Louis looks to see the page is full of incomprehensible scribbles and numbers.

A bald man crowds a little closer to Louis. His aviator sunglasses are propped up against his forehead. His eyes shift around. His hands twitch, beating out a rhythm on his black slacks. His eyes meet Louis' and his hands beat in a faster rhythm on his pants. "Ah, when are you guys going to be done? I need to speak to Ricco." He glances at the large red digital clock.

Louis grabs her badge from her belt and flashes it to the anxious man, "Ricco is a little busy right now. Is there anything I can help you with?"

"Ah, no." The man backs away.

A few other men seeing the badge pack up their things and move away from Ricco.

"Seriously? During business hours?" Ricco growls. "Do not come in here and scare away my customers during business hours."

Louis growls in return, "Ricco, I'll happily stand here all afternoon and night. I can come back tomorrow, probably the next day too. I'll flash my badge as often as necessary in order to get the information I need."

Hicks laughs, "I wouldn't try to out-stubborn Detective Baker, Ricco. She has you beat by a mile."

"Fine, what is it that you want to know that will make you scurry out of here?"

Hicks smiles, "Is Charles Mahoney one of your customers?"

"Yes. Now go away." Ricco looks up at the television.

"Not so fast. How much is he in for?" Hicks asks.

Ricco keeps his eyes on the television, "Nothing, he's clear. Paid up in full, with interest, a week ago."

"How much was he down?"

"Two hundred forty three thousand, seven hundred twenty-two, and eight cents." Ricco takes another gulp from his Bloody Mary.

Just like a bookie to know what you owe them right down to the eight cents, Louis thinks. But now Louis knows where the two hundred fifty thousand dollars went.

Hicks steals a fry, "What was he betting?"

Ricco spots the stolen fry and sneers, "The trifecta. Last year he hit the trifecta in the Preakness, he lorded it over me for months, until he was down two hundred large. He wasn't too high and mighty after that. He came close a few times this year, but close doesn't count in the trifecta. He tried to double up, but I said 'Forget it, bring me the money or you're going to walk with a limp.'"

"You threatened him?" Louis asks.

"As with all my clients, I merely pointed out the cause and effect relationship with his betting habits." He says while squeezing the pulp out of the fry he's holding. "In my business you have to sometimes bring reality back to your clients."

"Did Mr. Mahoney get behind often?" Louis asks.

"Yes, but he's always been good for it. Is there anything else Detectives? I have a business to run." Ricco gulps down the last of his Bloody Mary then glares over at the bar.

Hicks pulls out pictures from his breast pocket. "Have you ever seen any of these people before?"

Ricco wipes his greasy hands again. He takes the short stack of pictures from Hicks then scrolls through them one at a time. He stops on the picture of Sara Kitt, but continues on again without further hesitation. "Nope."

"What about this woman?" Louis asks, holding up the tablet with the still from the video.

"Nah." Ricco shakes his head.

"Ricco, you're a terrible liar." Hicks laughs. "I'm fairly certain you've seen this woman before." Hicks holds up the picture of Sara Kitt.

"I don't know what you're talking about Detective Hicks." Ricco says smugly.

"Do you want us to haul you down to the station?" Louis asks.

Ricco rolls his eyes, "She goes to Chez Marin with her husband. That other guy." He sorts through the pictures and pulls out Neil Kitt's photo. "On Wednesdays."

"Right, and have you ever seen them in here or with Mr. Mahoney?"

"Nope, never." The cocktail waitress arrives with a Bloody Mary refill. Mr. Ricco takes a big gulp from the Bloody Mary. He wipes his chubby, whiskered face with a thin paper napkin.

"And you are sure you've never seen this woman?" Louis holds up the video still again.

"If I did, I wouldn't know. That picture is so blurry anyway. Is there anything else Detectives?"

"No, thank you," Hicks projects his voice across the room, "You've been extremely helpful with the Rochester Police Department, Mr. Ricco." Hicks grins and laughs.

CHAPTER 30

Kristine searches for the ringing phone. The ringing tone, like an old-fashioned phone, seems at once close and far away. She cannot find it. Every step she takes the echoing ring makes it harder to find the phone, like a phantom ring. Her house is a mess, of course, only making it even more difficult to find. She searches the cushions of the couch, sticking herself with a small bamboo knitting needle, "Damn it." A pain shoots from her fingertips, up her arm, up her neck to the back of her head.

The pain is fruitful however. She finds the phone, under the couch.

Kristine looks at the caller-id and rolls her eyes, "Hello?"

"What took you so long to answer? Why are you breathing so hard? Are you having sex? Do you even have a boyfriend?" Her mother would do well as a criminal trial lawyer. Her rapid-fire questions would surely confuse the defendant or witness in cross-examination.

"I was -"

She cuts Kristine off, "It doesn't matter. I'm going to be a grandmother!" The excitement comes out like a chorus of a pop song.

"What?" Kristine's mind reels. Her sister had only been married a few months. However, her off and on again relationship with Ethan Giammari lasted for nearly a decade. Her aunts, uncles and cousins had learned not to ask about Ethan's absence at family gatherings. Her mother, of course, hadn't.

Kristine fought with herself nearly everyday leading up to the big wedding. She wanted to tell her sister not to marry him, to find someone whom she really loved. But

187

every time she had the opportunity to talk to Kelly either her mother would somehow break-up the conversation before she could broach the subject, or her sister would just be entirely too happy. Kristine didn't want to be responsible for her sister's unhappiness. Maybe, she thought, they had worked through all the problems. Maybe they would be a happy couple. Kelly certainly seemed to be a radiant bride.

"It's not official, mind you. But a mother knows."

Kristine feels a rush of relief. The pregnancy is just another one of her mother's wild speculations.

"I hope it's a girl. Wouldn't a pink nursery be so beautiful?" Her mother trills at the word 'beautiful'.

"Sure, Mom. What makes you so sure that Kelly is pregnant?"

"She's been a little 'ill' if you know what I mean. She came over for dinner the other night and I swear she couldn't look me in the eye. Oh a baby! How wonderful." Her voice elevates to a high pitch.

"Well, try not to pick out baby names and sign up for preschools until you're sure, Mom." Kristine's sarcastic edge leaves a silence on the line.

"I don't know why you have to be so much like your father. He's always been the downer. I guess now that you're in your thirties it's time for you to be the downer."

The insult stings as though her mother reached through the phone and slapped her. She's unable to recover before her mother drops another conversation cruise missile.

"He's getting re-married by the way, your father. I don't know if the invitation made it to you yet, but Kelly got hers this morning in the mail."

And all is revealed. Her mother is making this baby business up to distract her from the reality of her father's marriage. He's moved on, and she hasn't. She likely won't ever move on, as long as her alimony checks continue to arrive on time. Why would she risk that money on another bastard husband? The first few years after her father left it was a steady diet of man-hatred.

No wonder Kristine couldn't stand having a man around for more than a few months. Eventually one of the topics of her mother's man-hating conversations would pop its ugly head into her relationship. Joey's refusal to make dinner, Sam's inability to clean up after himself leaving dishes lying around the house, or Scooter's habit of paying more attention to his computer, they were all insurmountable boyfriend qualities. Then she met Curtis, their relationship was picture perfect. She searched endlessly for bad habits, and found none, until she found out he was married. That, and the market in Northern Virginia for Lawyers pushed her to find a new home in Rochester, just a month after graduation. She hasn't really dated since leaving Virginia. Why bother? They all have horrible habits and secrets.

Kelly, however, is able to get past their mother's man-hating conditioning. She and Ethan are a happy couple. Perhaps they did decide to start a family.

Kristine comes back from her daydream. Her mother drones on about the upcoming wedding, or what she's learned of it since calling every single one of her even remote acquaintances in Fairfax. Her father, apparently, has finally convinced one of a string of receptionists that he's hired by their date-ability since leaving her mother more than twenty years ago. This one, she says, is a bit older than the other fresh-from-college bunch.

"You actually met her. That's what Jackie said."

"Where?"

"Law school. She graduated with you. Jackie said you were bound to have classes with her."

"If she went to law school, what is she doing being dad's receptionist?"

"How should I know?"

"Wait, what's her name?"

"Melinda Turlly, her father is Fredrick Turlly. He's on the town council."

Kristine repeats the name a few times in her mind. Georgetown was no small school, but she thought she knew everyone in the program. "Are you sure she graduated the same year I did?"

"Well, that's what Jackie said. She knows Melinda from your father's parties. Apparently Melinda has been hanging all over your father like a leech."

Then, like a flash, the image of Melinda appeared in her mind. Average height, average hair, average clothing. She gained a few pounds over the last two and a half years of too much studying, not enough sleep and exercise. Everything about her was average, except her serial monogamy habit. She clung on to men like they were the lifeboat in the sea of evil men. She never left a man's side at a party. She never studied in women-only study groups. She never ate dinner alone, and never had any women friends as far as Kristine knew. "Yeah, I think I remember her."

"Oh, well. I have few more calls to make."

"You're not telling everyone that Kelly is pregnant, right?"

"I would never do that." Her mother protests with a huff. "I let most people I talk to draw their own conclusions, like I did."

Kristine says her polite good-byes then plops down on her old green couch. Her mind wanders, thinking about how it might be fun to be an aunt to a little niece or nephew. She could take them to the park, or out to the zoo. She could use a good excuse to go to the little zoo in Seneca Park.

Her phone rings again. She picks it up just after the first ring.

"Did you talk to mom?" Kelly asks, annoyed.

"Yes, she -"

Kelly interrupts with a growl, "Damn it."

"What's wrong?"

"She told Aunt Sally that I'm pregnant."

"Oh no." Kristine stifles a laugh.

"Oh yes."

"So?" Kristine doesn't want to ask the question, but her sister isn't exactly forth coming.

"So." Kelly breaths a heavy sigh.

"Are you going to make me ask?" Kristine huffs impatiently.

"Sure, why not." Kristine can almost hear the smirk from across the phone lines.

"Well, are you pregnant?"

There's another long sigh from the phone. Kristine is sure she hears teeth grinding.

"Yes. I am. I'm about two months along and Ethan and I agreed to keep it to ourselves for another month. It was our little secret, Kris."

"Kristine." She corrects.

"Whatever, your little identity crisis is hardly my prime concern right now."

"So what are you going to do?"

"I'm going to have to make a lot of phone calls. I've been trying to get hold of mom, but she doesn't have call waiting and the phone's been busy for the last three hours."

"I imagine so, she's got so much news. Her favorite daughter is creating her first grandchild and her beastly ex-husband is getting married to the receptionist at last." Kristine laughs.

"She told you that, huh? Melinda isn't the receptionist. She's a lawyer in the law firm on her way to being partner."

"Partner? She graduated with me, how can she be so close to being partner?" Kristine's face reddens.

"Well, almost ten years of sleeping your way to the top and anything is possible, right?"

"Ugh." Kristine's heart is pumping uncomfortably. *Could it be jealousy?* She wants to forget all this business about her father and his career soaring new fiancé. "So, tell me about my future nephew."

"Oh, you're already picking sides? What makes you so sure it's going to be a boy?"

"Because mom wants it to be a girl. You know how she is about pink."

"Ugh, don't remind me." Kelly makes a sound that Kristine recognizes as Kelly's silent little laugh. "I don't think I'll even ask the radiologist to tell me the sex of the baby."

"That would just kill mom." Kristine looks up at the ceiling smiling.

Kelly cackles, "I know, won't it be great?"

CHAPTER 31

Louis squints into the horizon. The blazing sun shines brightly in front of long row of ominous black clouds.

Hicks looks in the same direction, "Looks like there's a storm brewing. We should check the radio for weather reports. Clouds like that could be hail, or a strong thunderstorm."

"Yeah, or my phone could tell us."

"Are you sure you want to head off to the cabin now?"

"Yes, why?"

"You said you wanted to talk to the accountant."

"We don't have time for that. We need to go out to Naples and catch that human centipede in the act." Louis sneers.

"Right." Hicks says, dubiously. He starts the car. "So Charles Mahoney is square with his bookie, Mr. Ricco."

"Yeah, so it wasn't money problems that lead him to kill his wife."

"Strike one for motive there."

"But what if Mrs. Mahoney caught him cheating? What if he's covering it up? She took that video, maybe that's his secret lover stealing the paintings and selling them to cover his gambling debts?"

"You're hell-bent on that train of thought aren't you, Baker?" Hicks laughs.

"Yes, well, his wife died yesterday and he's off doing God knows what with God knows who at some cabin in the woods."

"Yeah, but is this about Charles Mahoney, or is it about -"

Louis' phone rings, interrupting Hicks right before Louis knew he was going to say 'Will'. She stares at Hicks, her blood boiling. She clenches her fist. She's ready to punch her hand into the dashboard. Her hands shake as she reaches for her phone, but brushes accidentally against her painful right shoulder. A spark of pain courses through her. She pounds her fist on top of the car.

She manages to pull the phone out of her pocket. The caller-id scrolling across the phone puzzles her. She answers curiously, "Mrs. Rocha?"

"Why isn't she picking up her phone? What could she possibly be so mad at me about? I'm doing all the work here. I've got all the paperwork for the funeral. I've called so many people. I couldn't possibly cry any harder than I have over the last 24 hours," She sobs. "Why would she give me the silent treatment? I mean, what? What have I done to deserve this?"

"Whoa, whoa." Louis says, "Slow down. What's going on?"

"Kristine isn't answering her phone. She has to be ignoring me. Honestly I have no idea why she would do this to me." Mrs. Rocha blows her nose, "She's the only... family... I have left in this... whole world." Her voice comes out as a sobbing stutter.

"I'm sure she's not ignoring you. Maybe she's in a place with bad cell phone reception?" Louis looks at Hicks.

"She hasn't picked up for more than... two hours!"

"She said she was going to follow up on a lead for her case. She said it was out of town. You know the country around here."

"No I don't. I don't leave town, not since the accident."

"Right. Well, the backcountry around here can be very... remote. There are a lot of places with no cell phone reception."

"Well, she should call in. I need her opinion on the services, and I want to talk to my grandson."

"Oh, well Bryan is with Aria. You can call her -"

"With whom? A stranger? Kristine left the only grandchild I will ever have with a complete stranger?"

"Well, she's not exactly a stranger. I've known her for -"

"Frankly, I don't care how long you've known her, Louis. I don't trust her. What kind of qualifications does she have?"

"Qualifications?"

"Yes, is she certified in CPR? Does she have a certification for early childhood development?"

"Well, yes the entire squad had to take the CPR course for -"

"She's a cop? Are you kidding me? Kristine left my precious grandchild with a cop?"

"She's not exactly a cop."

"She works for the esteemed Rochester Police Department?" Her sarcasm cuts through the sentence like a knife.

"Yes, she does work for our squad in computer forensics."

"So she's completely unqualified to take care of a ten year old?"

"Actually, she's very competent. She's been taking care of her nieces and nephews since she was a teenager. She's taking very good care of Bryan. If you want to speak to Bryan and find out for yourself how he's doing I can give you the number."

"Yes, thank you." Mrs. Rocha huffs.

Louis proceeds to give Mrs. Rocha the number. "I'll see what I can do about locating Kristine for you, Mrs. Rocha."

"Yes, well tell her I need to speak to her immediately."

"I'll pass that message along."

Louis hangs up the phone. She exhales deeply.

"Whew, she sounds like a force to be reckoned with. I now know where Miss Rocha gets her lovely demeanor."

"You have no idea. When I first met Kristine she was a wreck. We had this little 'who's family is more messed up' contest. She won by a landslide, and my dad threw me through the front door once. Her mother called almost everyday, Kristine would shake our entire room with fear and anger. Mind you, it was a little room, but it was sturdily built in the 1850's."

"That's messed up. Now I know why you and I haven't had that 'who's family is more messed up' contest. My mom's eccentric and my dad was a jerk, but no one ever threw me through a door."

"Yeah, I can't say I didn't deserve it a little. I got on my parents' nerves a lot. My teenage years were not my shining moment."

Hicks laughs, "So what now?"

Louis thinks. "Naples is what... an hour away?"

"Yeah, probably. What about ADA Rocha?"

"She's not answering her phone from her mother. She's probably in the middle of an interview with a witness. She probably doesn't want to answer the phone, especially not from her mother."

"Good point." Hicks smiles, "I wouldn't want to answer the phone to get reamed like that either."

"She also probably didn't want to tell her mother that she left Bryan with Aria. I'll call her now. If she doesn't answer I'll call her again when we get to Naples. She said she wasn't going to be longer than a couple hours anyway. She's probably wrapping up the interview right now. Maybe she'll return the call to her mother?"

Louis pulls out her phone. She dials the number for Kristine letting the voice mail pick up after five rings.

"You've reached Assistant District Attorney Kristine Rocha. I'm not available right now, please leave me a brief message with your full name and phone number. Please repeat your phone number very slowly and I will return your call as soon as I can."

"Hey Kristine. It's Louis. Your mom is pretty frantic to get hold of you. Please call her as soon as you can. I sorta spilled the beans about Bryan being with Aria. She seemed pretty ticked. Hicks and I are headed down to Naples to follow a lead. I should be back in town in a few hours. Maybe we can have a late dinner? I had such a great time with Bryan this afternoon. He's a super smart kid. Anyway, call me."

***

"Where exactly is this cabin?" Hicks asks.

"David said it's up Parish Hill Road, inside the park."

"I bet we'll be able to spot that Bentley. There can't be too many of those up in these parts."

"I wouldn't imagine." Louis looks up to the darkening sky, "I hope we beat this storm." A loud rumble rolls through the car.

"You had to jinx it didn't you?"

"Sorry, but you know I don't believe in all that superstitious stuff." Louis laughs.

"Yeah, but I do. So keep your walking under ladders and breaking mirrors to yourself, okay? I'll be throwing some salt over my shoulder."

"Sure, no problem. I'll make sure to keep the umbrellas closed indoors around you as well."

"Thank you. Is that so much to ask?" Hicks grins. "Here it is, Parish Hill Road." He steers the car onto the road. A light rain falls on the car. Hicks turns on the windshield wipers and headlights.

Louis squints into the growing darkness. Signposts dot the roadway. 'The Hide-away', 'Stolen Moments', 'Jones-ing', to name a few.

Headlights come toward them quickly around a corner. The car veers into their lane, "Holy shit!" Hicks exclaims and steers the car within inches of the ditch. "God, how fast was she driving?"

"What makes you think it was a *she*?" Louis tilts her head.

"I'll rephrase the question. How fast do you think that male or female complete maniac was driving?"

"At least eighty, but sixty is dangerous on these roads, in this condition."

Louis then spots a black painted sign with gold embossed lettering, 'Preakness Trifecta' and laughs. "There it is. He must have bought it last year."

"Nice. Ricco said he gloated. I think naming his cabin in the woods after his big win counts." Hicks smiles. He pulls onto the road.

A short way down the driveway the sprawling cabin appears in their view. While it does look like a cabin, the scale of the house makes it appear more like a mansion. Louis sees that, like the Mahoney's house, the cabin also has large artwork visible from the driveway.

"Where's the Bentley?" Hicks cranes his neck around the property.

"Maybe he took another car?" Louis speculates.

"Oh, there's a garage, over there, just behind the… it's not a cabin." Hicks points.

"You're right, definitely not what I would imagine a 'cabin' would look like at all." Louis laughs. "Let's knock on the door, see if we can get the weasel to explain these strange transactions. Maybe find out who he's sleeping with, and how long that's been going on."

"Let's not discuss his love life, unless there's some sorta connection with the case." Hicks puts the car in park. He looks over to his partner. "Personally, my money is on Holly to be the mistress."

"Yeah, something seemed off with his personal assistant. I mean, who can hold the puke bucket that long for your boss?"

"Let's not talk about puking." Hicks frowns.

The detectives walk up the short staircase. Hicks takes his turn at knocking on the door. "Mr. Mahoney?"

There's no answer at the door. A deep rumble comes from miles away. The rain makes tinkling sounds on the cabin's tin roof. Hicks leans in, pressing his right ear to the door, cupping his hand to his left ear. "I don't hear anything…"

"How could you over the thunder and rain?"

"Shh… wait. I hear something." Hicks backs up a step. He pounds on the door much harder. "Mr. Mahoney, it's the Rochester police, we need to talk to you." He shouts. He leans back to listen to the door. "Did you hear that?"

"What?" Louis asks. She pushes her head to the door to listen. She doesn't hear anything.

"I heard glass smashing."

"You just want to get in there without a warrant."

"I definitely heard something."

Louis walks over a few feet to the considerably large picture window. The window is unhindered by any curtains. On your own land, with neighbors so far away, you don't need curtains. You can bound about buck naked if that's your purgative. It's a beautifully decorated house without all of the overly modern furniture in the main house they had visited yesterday. The art is different too. Instead of the stark abstract pieces there are landscapes, some very large, some small. She doesn't see anyone in the living room, although the lights are on. She sees two sets of shoes scattered on the floor. One pair are men's dress shoes, obviously Mr. Mahoney's. The other pair are strappy high heel sandals she's sure she's seen before, but can't quite place.

"Do you see anything?"

"Shoes."

"What is it with women and shoes?" Hicks shakes his head. "Come over here. I swear I hear something."

199

Louis walks back over to the door. She concentrates on the sounds from behind the door. She tries to block out the sound from the gathering thunderstorm. She hears an indistinct thud, then a far away cry of "Help!"

The detectives lock eyes. "Did you hear that?" Hicks asks.

"Yeah, that sounded like someone's cry for help."

Hicks breaks into action. He reels up and smashes his shoulder into the door.

"Are you serious? This thing is a couple hundred pounds at least."

"Do you have a better idea?" Hicks rubs his arm.

Louis pushes Hicks out of the way. She turns the handle to the door and the door swings open.

"Oh." Hicks smiles sheepishly.

"Mr. Mahoney? Holly? Is anyone in here?" Louis can hear the echo of her voice in the large cabin's space.

"In here!" Groans a voice from somewhere deep inside the house.

"Where are you?" Louis calls into the house.

"Back here!" The voice shouts a little louder.

Louis proceeds slowly into the house. Hicks keeps a short distance. Both detectives have one hand on their side arms.

Louis tip-toes through the house. She takes the hallway, just past the brightly lit oak and brass kitchen. A gurgling sound, emanating from one of the rooms, echoes down the hallway. She pulls out her gun.

She opens the first door, peering around it slowly. The room is not lit. She turns on the light and sees a large sleigh bed covered with an intricate quilt, ablaze with fall colors. She concentrates for a moment on the gurgling sound. She's sure it isn't emanating from this room, but that's all she's sure of.

Hicks taps her on the shoulder and the sudden, piercing pain flows through her body like hot lightning. She leaps up, but keeps from screaming by biting the inside of her lip so hard she can feel the warm blood and taste of metallic. She holds her breath, for fear of letting it out with a scream.

She turns to Hicks. He's making a gruesome, but apologetic face. She follows his pointing to a partially open door near the end of the hallway.

Hicks steps in front of Louis. She's still trying to control her breathing, and her need to scream.

There is a loud creak in the floor. Louis' phone vibrates in her pocket. As the detective's move closer, Louis can hear moaning and a gurgling sound.

Hicks pushes the already open door wider. He looks into the room, "Call the paramedic."

"What is it?" Louis peeks her head around the imposing Hicks. The bed, a white quilt, is stained dark red with blood.

Hicks rushes across the room, ducking behind the bed. "Mr. Mahoney's no longer our number one suspect."

Louis follows him and watches as Hicks applies pressure to Charles Mahoney's chest. She pulls out the phone, steps slightly out of the room, dialing 9-1-1.

Charles' chest gurgles. "She came back." His voice is raspy.

"Who came back?" Hicks asks, stress in his voice.

"She did. We were…" He gasps for breath, "and then she left."

"Who left?" Hicks asks again, insistently.

Louis walks back into the room, "Paramedics are on their way."

Hicks looks up at Louis, his hands are a deep shade of red, "Good."

"Her heels," Charles' glazed eyes look up at Louis. "I heard them… in the hallway."

"What's he talking about, I'm not wearing heels."

Hicks shakes his head, "He keeps saying 'she left', 'she came back'"

"Did he say who?"

"No, maybe he doesn't really know her?" Hicks speculates.

"Maybe it was the woman who left her heels at the front door?" Louis asks.

CHAPTER 32

Kristine blinks a few times, unable to focus on anything. An overpowering smell of cat urine and musk fill her nostrils. She tries to reach her hand up to her nose to pinch it, but cannot move her arms more than a few inches. She feels her skin crawling, but chocks it up to paranoia. A blaring TV from across the room provides the only light.

"Shirtless, sexy men are filling up the silver screen this summer…" The television blasts.

She blinks a few times more. Through her blurry vision the room looks like a surrealist painting. It's a very dark, surrealist painting. She realizes she's actually seeing the room sideways. She tries to move her arms again, but realizes they are tied behind her back. She squeezes her right hand. A bolt of pain crawls up her arm to her neck. After recovering from the pain, her arm feels like she's being stuck with tiny pinpricks. She tries to right herself by pulling up her knees, then using her face to prop herself up. She makes a loud grunting sound, but she's sure if there is anyone in the room they wouldn't have been able to hear it over the booming television.

"I don't know about you, Mark, but I'm going online to buy those movie tickets right now…"

Kristine's eyes try to focus, but the room is still a blurry mess. She wants to take a small break. She closes her eyes and tilts her head back against the wall. The moment her head touches the wall she feels a sharp stabbing pain. She lets out a little yelp, still certain that no one would be able to hear her over the television.

The room floods with light, and then plunges into a greater darkness. She looks around and realizes that she's sitting on a kitchen floor. There are bits of crumbs littering the linoleum. A tiny army of ants is marching along the floor. She swallows down the encroaching sickness. She can just make out the sound of water dripping right above her.

There's another flash of light, another plunge of darkness following the flash.

"Later on Entertainment Tonight, who's been married for twenty years and didn't know -"

The television is abruptly silenced like the plug has been pulled. The room is now so dark that Kristine can't even see the details she had a few moments ago. The fear and pain mix in her brain to create monsters she hasn't had the time to think about in years. Her mind feels the army of ants crawling up her body.

"God damn it." A husky voice calls from another room. There's rustling of papers and the sound of furniture scraping along the wood floor.

She starts to remember where she was, and what she was doing last. She was in the car, lost. She got out to consult her map, since Wendell was no help at all. Then, there was a man, a harsh voice from the woods. But it wasn't a man at all. It was a woman. Did she get a look at the woman? No, she was just a voice. She was a paranoid woman who didn't trust people, especially lawyers. What is it that she said, "you come to take my land, like those other lawya's."

The monster in Kristine's mind takes the form of a large old woman. A woman that is hell-bent on getting rid of her. Will she die of abuse? Starvation? How long can she last here on the kitchen floor without food or water? Is she bleeding from a head wound? How long has she been here? What will Bryan do without his mother, or even his Godmother? What twisted things will her mother teach poor Bryan?

There's more rustling sounds, then a dim flickering light appears. Kristine can make out the outline of a table

204

in front of her. The legs she can see clearly but the top of the table is covered with oddly shaped objects, including what must be a doll with wild hair.

If it is dark outside, how long has she been here? How long will it be before someone finds her? How long until someone comes looking for her? Why didn't she tell Louis where she was going? Is Bryan still okay? Why didn't she just let someone else follow this wild goose chase?

The flickering light grows larger on the ceiling as the candle and whoever is holding the candle comes closer. Kristine's mind again fills with a nightmare vision of the monster holding her captive. How did she get here from the road? The woman that carried her here must be of a considerable size.

Something furry brushes her arm. She pulls away and lets out a short scream.

"Who's that?" The voice calls out.

Kristine shivers. She tries to scoot away from the furry beast. Then she hears the cat's light purr and breathes a sigh of relief.

"Who's that?" The voice calls out again.

"Your captive." Kristine barely recognizes her own rough, dry voice. She suddenly feels extremely parched.

"My what?" The voice now has a face, and a body, lit by a small candle. The sight of the petite woman fascinates Kristine. She is old, but not as old as Kristine had thought. She's wearing a sweatshirt with a white cat peeking out of a teacup. How did this little woman drag her to this place? She knows now that she can't be too far from the car.

"Your captive. You brought me here and tied me up." Kristine feels bold now that she can see this diminutive woman. This frail woman doesn't come close to resembling the gigantic monster in Kristine's imagination.

"Right. Well you shouldn't be snooping around my property." The woman snarls.

"I wasn't snooping around your property. I was reading a map and trying to get the hell out of here."

The lights flicker back on. The television booms to life with the Jeopardy theme song. Kristine's blurry vision becomes sharper. The woman's twiggy body stands above her. The woman's beady eyes stare at her. She wonders if it is even possible that this tiny woman dragged her from the car by herself. Maybe she had help in the form of a much larger man?

The woman comes closer, still staring at Kristine. She grabs the cat from the top of the kitchen counter, and then slowly shuffles back into the other room.

Kristine shouts after she's left the room, "What are you planning to do with me?"

There's no response, presumably because the woman cannot hear her over Jeopardy. "This henchman from 'Goldfinger' wears a steel rimmed bowler hat."

Kristine smiles, "Odd Job" she murmurs.

"Who is Odd Job?" The contestant repeats, but in the form of a question.

"Correct. Pick again." Alex Trebek answers.

"Can I have 'Bond Henchmen' for four hundred Alex?" The contestant asks.

Kristine can feel the rope burn, but manages to work some of the rope free. She formulates a quick plan in her head. She pulls her feet around and under herself, pushing up on her hands. She searches the countertop. It's covered in piles of dirty dishes. The smell of rotting food almost knocks her back. She cannot find what she's looking for on the counter. She doesn't want to fish around blind through the dirty dishes either. She turns around, pulling open a drawer. She turns back and see's some junk in the drawer, but no knife and no scissors. She pulls open another drawer. There is a random assortment of silverware in large quantities, but only butter knives in the drawer. She pulls open another drawer and hits the jackpot. She turns around and slowly walks her hand through the drawer, feeling the dry wooden handle of the chef knife on top of the pile, trying not to cut herself.

Kristine shuts the doors she's opened. She drops the knife, then slowly wiggles her way back down to the floor.

CHAPTER 33

Louis meets the two paramedics at the cabin's door. "What took so long?" She asks.

The seventies throw-back looking paramedic, complete with a Burt Reynolds furry mustache says, "Nice to see you too." The mustache reminds her of the description that her father used to have for the paramedics that arrived on scene when he was a beat cop. "Ten gauge syringe toting cowboys," he used to call them.

Burt Reynolds speaks up as they hurry down the hallway, "Some freaked out woman had the road blocked. We had to call the police to come get her."

The paramedics walk into the bedroom, shoving Hicks aside, and swiftly get to work. Louis watches the blur of the two men, their equipment out, and pressure applied.

"Shallow breath sounds. I hear gurgling." The taller one says.

"Could be a collapsed lung." Burt Reynolds speculates.

Hicks shakes his head and grumbles, "I wish he would say who he was talking about."

"Maybe he doesn't even know her? Maybe she's an escort?" Louis walks out of the bedroom.

Hicks follows her down the hallway. "All he said was that she came back. He heard her heels. So where did she go? Why did she go? Why did she come back?"

"I don't know. But let's start with what we do have."

"What's that exactly?"

"We have the shoes from the living room."

"Are we going to go around looking for Cinderella? See if the shoe fits on someone in the kingdom?"

"Don't get snappy with me. If we do find a suspect we can compare the toe prints."

"Seriously?"

"Yeah, we caught that idiot last summer robbing banks in his bare feet. And whoever owns those shoes is a prime suspect. They're pretty expensive shoes as far as I can tell. Cece might be able to help us narrow a search of where they were purchased, if they were purchased in the area."

Hicks looks down at his bloody hands, "I need to get cleaned up."

"We can go as soon as I bag those shoes." Louis walks out of the cabin toward the car to grab an evidence bag. The rain is pelting down on her head hard. Large drops of rain pound on her shoulder and the pain seems to double for each little tap.

When she gets back to the cabin her tears mix with the rain, but she's sure Hicks can see the pained expression on her face.

"You look like hell." He confirms her thought.

"Thanks."

"Isn't it about time for you to take those pain killers yet?"

Louis looks at her cell phone for the time, six p.m. She notices she has several new text messages, three from Aria, one from Bethany and a two voicemails. She dials the number for Aria, "Hey Aria…"

"Hey, you didn't return my call from earlier, so I sent you a bunch of texts."

"I haven't read them yet. We found Charles Mahoney shot at his cabin."

"Oh no."

"Yeah. You want to give me a re-cap of the messages?"

"Well, I was able to decrypt the hard drive from Victoria's laptop."

"What did you find?"

"Identities, credit cards, and her diary."

"Identities?"

"Yeah, hundreds of them. I'm pretty sure they're stolen. It's going to take me a long while to track down the real people, probably even longer to find the fake ones."

"More fakes on this case. Fake paintings and fake identities."

"Yes. Also, I need to leave to go to family dinner tonight. As it is I'm going to be a little late."

"Oh sure. No problem, thanks for working the weekend."

"Yeah, well, have you heard anything from Kristine?"

"No. You haven't? She should have been back at least an hour ago."

"No, I haven't heard a word. Her mother called though."

"Yeah, sorry, she really wanted to talk to Bryan, so I told her where he was."

"No problem. We didn't talk long, she really did want to talk to Bryan."

"How's he doing?"

"Pretty awesome. He's a great kid. He got tired of watching me work, so he started watching a movie. I think it'll be done soon. I've seen this one with my nephew."

"I'm worried about Kristine, she should have called by now. Let me call her. I'm sure it's nothing, just her getting caught up in a case. I'll call you right back." Louis hangs up the phone and dials the number for Kristine. The phone rings a few times, then Kristine's message picks up. She waits for the beep to leave a message, but instead of a beep the voice mail message says, "Code 714: This voice mail box is now full."

Louis rolls her eyes. No doubt Mrs. Rocha filled the voicemail with her rants. Louis looks around the room. The strappy sandals remind her of Cece. It'll be at least another hour before she can get back to Rochester. Maybe she could call Cece? She'll probably be mad about interrupting her date, but what are friends for if not helping out in case of need? She did get jealous when Kristine didn't call her for help with her cat. She dials the number.

A quiet song starts playing from the living room. Louis frowns while listening to the ring in her ear. She starts trying to find the tinny song playing somewhere in the living room.

Cece's voicemail picks up, "You know the drill."

Louis hangs up and searches for the song again, but it's no longer playing. She dials Cece's number again to leave a message this time. She listens to the phone ringing in her ear, and hears the song playing in the living room again. "Oh no."

Hicks looks at her, "What?"

"Do you hear that?"

"Yeah, it sounds like trumpets."

"Yes, it's the trumpets from 'Boogie Shoes'."

"What's that?"

"Cece's ringtone."

"Oh no."

"Yeah, find it. Never mind, you're still covered in blood. Stand back." Louis growls in frustration, "This isn't going to be good."

Hicks scoffs, "When Cece's involved, it's never good."

There's a knock on the door. Hicks walks over, opens the door with a wad of tissue from his pocket. Two uniform policemen are staring at Hicks' bloody hands.

"Mr. Mahoney?" The officer looks at Hicks puzzled. His shiny gold badge says 'Sylwester.'

"No, I'm Detective Robert Hicks from the Rochester Police Department."

"Oh. Where's Mr. Mahoney?" Sylwester asks looking past the detectives and around the room.

"He's in the bedroom back there, about to be taken to the hospital." Louis pipes up while nonchalantly looking for Cece's phone.

"And you are?" The other officer asks Louis.

"His partner, Detective Louis Baker." Her eyes focus on a black shiny object sitting between the couch and the magazine rack. Louis shutters to think how Cece is involved in all of this. She doesn't even own a gun, and wouldn't know the first thing about using one.

"We're here because Mr. Mahoney was reported shot." Sylwester continues to stare at Hick's bloody arms.

Louis looks up from staring at the phone. "Yes, he was shot. We called it in."

"Did he say anything?" Sylwester continues to stare at Hicks.

"Not much that made any sense." Hicks stares back at the young officer.

Louis notices, to her great relief that Hicks fails to mention that Mr. Mahoney said that it was a woman, and certainly fails to mention Cece.

"I see. Because we have his Bentley down at the station. License plate reads 'M-A-H-O-N-E-Y'."

"Oh?" Louis shifts her eyes between the two officers. The second officer has a scar above his left eyebrow. His name badge is highly tarnished, although he doesn't look much older than Sylwester.

"Yes. There was a woman driving the car." Sylwester pulls out his notebook from his breast pocket.

Louis lets out a big sigh.

"Her name is Cecelia J. Grant..." He continues until he hears the paramedics enter the kitchen.

The paramedics walk by the four officers wheeling Mr. Mahoney out the door. Burt Reynolds looks back at Louis, "We'll be taking him all the way to Rochester Memorial. He's fairly stable, and we don't have good facilities down here for gun shots."

Louis breaks her look from the Naples uniform police officers to give Burt Reynolds a little smile, "Thank you."

Sylwester continues, "You said your name was Louis Baker?"

"Yes, I'm Louis Baker."

"She said that she didn't know anything about anyone getting shot. She said to talk to Detective Louis Baker of the Rochester Police Department. I explained to her that she was in someone else's car and that someone else had been shot."

"Right." Louis starts to tap her foot impatiently. Hicks shoots her a look that reads: *We are both in hot water now.*

Sylwester twitches his face, "So, why don't we start from the beginning?"

Louis takes a deep breath, hearing the rain beat harder on the roof of the cabin.

***

"...So right now I need to find my friend Kristine." Louis finishes. She's breathing hard, as the story came out in a few long breaths.

"I see." Sylwester stuffs his hand in his pocket.

"Do you mind?" Louis asks.

"Do I mind what?" Sylwester looks at her, confused.

"I need to go."

"We still have a lot of talking to do."

"Right, but not right now. I've got two friends. One of them is in your custody and the other is missing. I need to find -"

Hicks interjects, "How about I stay with the two of you. I'll check in on Cece and figure out what I can do, most likely call her a lawyer. Louis, you go find Kristine."

Sylwester stares at Hicks, "Well hold on now -"

Hicks interrupts again, "She'll return just as soon as she finds Kristine Rocha, the assistant district attorney." His booming voice echoes in the large space.

"Oh." Sywester says quietly.

"Yes," Louis grabs his attention, "I think she may be in danger. She was following a lead on a case that's falling apart, the Hewitt case, you know it?"

The nearly silent officer with the scar pipes up, "We are familiar with that case. Detective Baker, please come back to pick up Detective Hicks after you find ADA Rocha."

"Thank you." She swiftly walks to the door.

Hicks starts in, "I need a clean shirt and you need to call in the crime scene technicians. Do you have good ones down here?"

Louis misses the response as the door shuts.

She jumps into the car, pulls out her phone, and then presses speed dial for Aria. She picks up on the first ring, "Aria, can you help me find Kristine?"

"She's still not answering her phone?"

"No. I'm really worried at this point. Her voicemail is full too."

"Okay, hold on."

Louis listens to sound of rapid-fire key pressing then hears Bryan's tiny voice, "Whatcha doing?"

"Ah, I'm looking for a cell phone. Remember, how we did with some of those number's earlier?"

There's a faint reply, "Yeah, but you didn't find any of those."

"Right, let's hope we find this one." There's more tapping.

"Louis?" Aria asks.

"Did you find her?" Louis pulls the car's seat up about a foot. She adjusts the mirrors, ready to roll.

"Yes, remember, the cell phone tower thing is only accurate to about ten city blocks."

"You don't have to give me that disclaimer every single time. Where is she?"

"There are only two towers her cell phone is pinging off of… It looks like she's not moving either, or one of the towers would be out of reach by now."

"Where Aria?" Louis asks impatiently.

"About ten miles South of Geneva? I think she's on Steele Road…" Aria hesitates, "But I'm only guessing."

"Fine. How many houses are in the area?"

"Ah, okay, so if you map out… Wait a second." There's more typing sounds. Louis starts the car and puts it in drive. She puts the gumball on top of the car. Her hand comes back soaking wet. She sets the windshield wipers on high velocity. She calculates the distance to Geneva in her head. She yanks the car in reverse. Mud goes flying in every direction when she puts it in drive.

"Okay, I'm about twenty minutes away. I'll call you in fifteen minutes for an update. Will you be able to tell me about the houses in the area?"

"Yeah, I almost got it now. But when you call back I'll have more info. I better call my mom."

"Sorry Aria. Tell your mom I'll make those special peanut butter cookies she likes so much." No one needs to know she makes them from a tube from the fancy grocery store.

"She'll be happy to hear that."

***

The windshield wipers are barely able to keep up. Lightning bolts flash in the distance. She peeks on a hill and sees a car, Kristine's blue Corolla, in the middle of Steele Road.

Louis whips out her phone, a little too quickly, brushing against her painful shoulder. "I found her car." She says, gritting her teeth.

"Ah. That was quick." Aria sounds startled.

Louis walks up to the car, the pain piling on top of her shoulder. "Yeah, she's not here though," she shouts, barely managing to get through the loud sheets of rain.

"Okay, I have your location. There are three houses close to there. At 455 Steele are Mr. and Mrs. Emery, then at 490 Steele is Mrs. Garrigan and ... oh. Wait, what case did you say she was working on?"

Louis blinks away the rain from her eyes, "The Hewitt case, why?"

CHAPTER 34

Kristine feels the last of the rope pulling free from behind her back. Her arms have stood the test of multiple endurance trials today. She'll have to put 'being held up at gun point' and 'sawing a rope, behind her back with a large, dull kitchen knife' into her regular exercise routine.

The final Jeopardy theme starts playing in the background. *Who is Alexander the Great? It's an easy one today.* She rubs her wrists to get feeling back into her hands. She stands up in the kitchen with the knife in front of her. She hears the rain beating down on the roof, but only just barely over the blasting television.

She looks around in the dim light and spots the front door. It's just past the detritus of the room, and more importantly, the television. She hopes Alex Trebek will hold out the suspense long enough for her to make it to the door. She gets down on her hands and knees and crawls through the ramshackle house. The door is within a few feet of the television. Her heart races in her chest so hard she can feel the thumping on her rib cage. Should she stand up and run for it? Or should she slowly crawl and try not to get noticed? She looks down at the dull knife. The woman said she had a gun, so she's bringing a dull kitchen knife to a gunfight.

She decides to rely on the slow, hopefully unnoticeable crawl. She's within eight feet of the door, but spots a picture on the wall that stops her. *I know that picture.* She ducks behind the television to get a closer look. The picture is unmistakable. The high school superstar, the child molester, and the child murderer, Dennis Baxter, stares back at her with a chipped-tooth smile. The picture was all over the news after he was named the prime suspect and DNA match to the murderer.

What Kristine can't comprehend is why this woman would have his picture, hanging so prominently on the wall, unless... She bolts up from her position on the floor. She spins around wielding the knife. The shrew shrieks in surprise. Kristine moves closer, not spotting any gun. She steps in front of the television and screams. "Turn it off!"

The cat jumps out of the woman's lap. She fumbles around, knocking her glass off the small nightstand. The smell of cheap whiskey permeates the air. Finally, the rolling credits from Jeopardy stop. The room is dark and silent. The only sounds come from the pelting rain.

"Who are you?" Kristine emphasizes each word with her knife.

"Nobody." The woman snarls.

"Who are you?" Kristine repeats.

"Eudora Baxter."

"I thought so. What was your plan tonight?"

"I don't know." She growls. "I was waiting for my son."

"Your son is in prison. He murdered his step-daughter."

"That's what you and the press say. But I say he didn't touch any of those little girls! He would never hurt anyone!" She stabs her finger in the air.

Kristine's mouth opens. Her heart skips a beat. "Did you say *girls*? There were others?"

"That Sherry, she started all this mess. He didn't go near that girl or that little red-head, what was her name?"

"I have no idea, but I intend to find out." The puzzle pieces fall into place now. Baxter molested other little girls of his girlfriends and other wives. They didn't have any proof and didn't want to come forward to put their families through the stress. Why would they need to when there was iron clad DNA proof pointing to the culprit?

She'll find them all. She'll search every previous address he ever occupied. She'll subpoena every mother.

Kristine backs up slowly toward the door, still waving her dull knife. "I'm leaving now, but I'll be back. Just like you said, I'll be back and I'll bring the cavalry with me."

"You gonna take my land, my son away from me, you bitch!" The woman gets up from her chair, shaking her fists.

Kristine spins around, running toward the door. In two steps she's turning the knob. The door flies open and there stands her friend, Louis Baker. Through the rain she can see her car off in the distance lit up by the small flashing light on top of Louis' cruiser.

"It's about time you showed up." Kristine says.

CHAPTER 35

Kristine stands in front of Louis holding a kitchen knife.

"What's going on?" Louis shouts through the rain.

Kristine steps out of the house. She makes a beeline toward the car. Louis hustles to catch up.

"Eudora Baxter took me hostage." Kristine screams.

"Hostage? I thought you were out here investigating the Hewitt murder?" Louis shouts and points toward the cruiser.

Kristine grabs her things from her car, locks the door, and races toward the cruiser.

The doors slam. "I was following a lead from Sherry Bowden. She said to talk to Dennis' mother to find out what happened. I found a call from Sherry's daughter just after the DNA was found for Dennis. The DNA that turned out to be botched."

"Wait, how did she take you hostage?" Louis slicks back her wet hair.

"Can you turn the heat up? I'm freezing." Kristine shivers.

"Yeah." Louis switches the defroster on the car to mix with the floor heat. She switches the heat knob from somewhere in the middle to full heat. "So tell me, what happened."

"I was following a lead, but damn Wendell told me to turn left, or maybe right for some road that didn't exist."

Louis rolls her eyes. "Wendell? The GPS? When are you going to get a new one?"

"Very soon. I'm throwing that one in the trash."

"So, you were lost?"

"Yes, then I got out of the car to look at a map."

"You still have a map?"

"Yes, and I was looking at the map when this crazy woman starts ranting at me. She said she had a gun. From her deep voice I thought she was humongous." Kristine flails her arms around to emphasize the size.

"What did she say?"

"She thought that I was going to take away her land. She said that this isn't the way to Geneva. She said the bridge was out. And then I made a critical mistake telling her that I was a lawyer."

"Hold that thought. I need to call Aria."

"Is that how you found me?"

"Yes. I don't know what I'd do without her."
Kristine smiles.

"Aria? Yeah, I got her." Louis looks over at Kristine, now noticing blood running down the back of her head. "Yeah, she doesn't look to good... I'm going to take her to Memorial, you want to meet us there with Bryan?"

Kristine feels the back of her head with her fingers. She trades off staring at her bloody fingers and looking at Louis.

"No... I think she'll be okay, but we better get her checked out... Yeah, talk to you later. And, thank you!"

"Okay, now tell me how you got that bump on your head." Louis says calmly, the car approaching ninety-five on the freeway.

"I don't know. I was talking to her, telling her about Bryan, then I don't remember... I woke up, hands behind my back, on the floor in her kitchen. It took me twenty minutes to cut through the rope with this dull knife." Kristine holds up the knife.

"You can put that away now, Rambo. When was the last time you slept?"

"I don't know. Tuesday night, I think? There was that jury selection on Thursday afternoon. Wednesday I was up all night doing the research. I thought if I prepared enough, asked the right questions... Then, yesterday..."

"You need some sleep. We aren't the spring chickens we used to be."

"Remember that time you were on the beat all night downtown? It was a slow night."

"Yeah, and I saw you, with your books."

"Remember what you said?"

"I said, 'You look like you're going to win the case of a decade.'"

"I did too. That was my first big case. I had more than enough witnesses, and physical evidence to put the 'Burb Husband Bandit' away for five whole years!"

"I know you did. You always do your homework."

Kristine's phone rings.

"Oh, by the way you need to call your mother." Louis shrugs sheepishly.

Kristine rolls her eyes. She answers the phone, "Mom?"

Louis can year some shouting from the other end of the phone, over the blasting heater, the thump of the rain and the mechanical whirring of the wiper blades.

"Yes… Well… Yes…" There's a long silence then she blurts out quickly, "I need to go see a doctor about my head, but I'm okay… No, Mom… Yes, Mom… but… No… but… Yes… I mean, no…" Kristine breaths a deep sigh.

Louis looks over to see her silently nodding her head, as if this is the only way Kristine can get through to her mother, somewhat telepathically.

"Mom, okay, that's enough. I'm a grown woman." Louis can hear more shouting. Kristine takes a long breath. She then begins to start shouting over her mother, "Mom, I'm doing the best I can. My friends, Louis, Cece and Aria are helping me through this. I'm going to solve this case. I'm going to be back to Fairfax for Kelly's funeral. You don't need me to pick out flowers. You already know that she loved Calla Lilies. You wanted to call me to check up on me. I'm sorry I'm disappointing you, but you're just going to have to live with the disappointment."

Louis would give anything to see the look on Mrs. Rocha's face at this very moment. She's watched Kristine build up to the point of bursting many times, but her frustration usually subsides over time. Louis knows that we never stop being our mother's daughter, even after years of being out in the world.

***

Bryan's face is pressed up against the window in the emergency room. Aria stands behind him, poking away at her phone. Louis helps Kristine out of the car. She's been crying the last few miles to the hospital. She confessed all of her worries in the car. She worried over Bryan. Where was he going to go to school? Would he find friends in Rochester? Would he want to stay here? She worried over her mother, alone in Fairfax. How was she going to manage without her sister's constant attention? Finally, she worried over her own life. Would she ever meet a man? Get married? Have a child?

Louis couldn't help but smile at the last comment. "You have a child now. One that's already potty trained even."

Kristine emits a stifled laugh. "You've got a point."

The sliding doors open. Bryan rushes to hug his aunt. "Where were you?"

"I was…" Kristine smiles down at him. "I was unexpectedly detained. But I'm here now."

"Okay. Aria says that you need to see a doctor. Did you fall?"

"Not exactly, but I hit my head on something and Louis likes to be extra safe."

"I went to the doctor when I hit my head on the monkey bars at school one time. I had to have three stitches." Bryan points to the top of his scalp. "It really hurt. I hope you don't have to have any stitches."

"Me too."

"But if you do, we can go get ice cream. Mom took me for peanut butter and chocolate chip ice cream when I got my stitches."

"Sounds like a plan. Let's go talk to the doctor."

Louis reaches out to touch her shoulder, "Wait, Kristine. I'm sorry to leave you, but I need to get back to the crime scene in Naples."

"No problem, Bryan and I will take a cab home." She looks down at Bryan, "Have you ever been in a cab before?"

His eyes open wide, "No. Grandma H. says they're gross."

"Well, I guess you'll get to see for yourself."

CHAPTER 36

Louis walks into the tiny Naples Sherriff's office. A little bell like one in a coffee shop rings. She shakes her umbrella out and puts it in a stand by the door. "Quite the downpour. Is it expected to lighten up?"

"What do I look like, Louis? The weather woman from channel ten?" Cece's biting tone and glaring eyes come from the wrong side of a tiny jail cell. The brightly colored floral wrap dress from this morning is wet and torn in a few places. Louis looks down to see she's wearing plastic soled canvas slip on shoes. She holds back a little laugh, knowing that Cece must be burning up inside wearing such cheap shoes.

"Where's Hicks?" Louis asks.

"Seriously? You go and rescue Kristine, leaving me here in jail, and all you want to know is where Bert is?" Cece spews out a short scream, much like a teenager given two weeks detention for disrupting class.

"Yes, and I suggest you sit tight until your lawyer gets here."

"Is Kristine coming?" Cece asks, timidly.

"No, she's in the hospital." Louis hears laugher from another room. "You did call someone else, right?"

"No, but Hicks did. He says he has a friend." She groans.

"Good. He's got lots of friends. I'm sure one of them is an excellent lawyer."

"Louis, you got to get me out of here. This guy smells." Cece stands to one side, revealing a scrubby man lying on the small bench in the cell.

"Let me go see what's up. I'm going to want to talk to you, but I'm a cop and I want you to be protected from saying anything…" Louis stops herself. She breaks eye contact with Cece.

"You mean stupid." Cece frowns.

"Well… yes. Sit tight, I'll be right back." Louis walks toward the sound of the continued laughter. She opens the door to the tiny break room. Hicks is sitting at the little table with a uniform police officer. His badge reads 'Yates'. His head is tilted back and he's wiping tears from his eyes. Styrofoam boxes fill the small table. She can see a fishtail sticking out of one container.

"Baker! Sit down, have a bite to eat." Hicks' boisterous voice booms through the small room.

"Don't mind if I do." Louis searches the room for another chair. Yates stands up, hands her his chair then pulls up a crate to sit on. He's tall, but the crate is so short Louis can only see his head above the table.

Louis opens the container. A large fried fish sits atop a bed of homemade fries. She takes the little plastic fork and flakes off the fish between the skin and the bone, just like her father taught her.

Yates takes another bite from his fried fish, "So this bike cop dumps ink all over himself?" He shakes his head laughing.

"That's not the best part." Hicks clears his throat. "So he molests the hell out of the machine, leaving a trail of inky evidence. He finally finds this tiny slip of paper, no bigger than the nail on his pinky finger, which of course is now covered in ink." Hicks chuckles. "So our lieutenant comes in the next morning, wanting to know who in the hell defiled the copier. She has us all lined up with our hands out."

"No." The laughing cop shakes his head in disbelief.

"Oh yes. Only problem with her little interrogation is that our 'bike squad' cop is home, washing his only proper uniform for homicide. So I make like I'm guilty, right? I'm hiding my hands behind my back. She gets all suspicious, orders me to reveal my hands."

"Did you?" The cop on the crate asks.

"Of course I did. She stared me down. It was all I could do to keep from laughing my ass off."

"Nice. Hicks, I can't believe we didn't meet before now. You are one hell of a storyteller. It gets pretty boring around here. About twice a week we have to pick up ol' Larry from the..." He looks up, searching for something. "...bar. Shoot. I can't remember the name of the bar. It used to be ol' Larry's place called 'Naples Bar'. Nice and simple. But it's changed hands so many damn times." The cop shakes his head. "What was I saying? Oh yeah. We have to pick up ol' Larry and put him in the tank to sleep it off. That's the highlight of the day most days. Occasionally we get a speeder. And last year they found that big stash of pot in the attic of that pretty house down on main..." He looks back up at the ceiling, "But, since you all came to town we have an attempted murder and a hysterical woman crashing her stolen car in the ditch. Plus ol' Larry." He laughs hard.

"Hey, Baker, did you obtain the location of our esteemed Assistant District Attorney Kristine Rocha safe and sound?" Hicks beams.

Louis swallows her bite of fish. "I found her. But I wouldn't say safe and sound. She had just managed to escape being kidnapped by Eudora Baxter."

"Kidnapped?" Hicks asks.

"Yeah, apparently she got lost when chasing a lead. She pulled over, just so happens, in front of the Baxter residence near Geneva. It turns out that isn't too much of a coincidence after all. Kristine had quite a bump on her head, so I took her to the hospital."

"Wow. She's alright though?"

"Yeah, I think she'll be fine." Louis shovels another big bite of fish in her mouth. "Why is it taking so long for your lawyer friend to show up, Hicks?"

"Ah, he said he was bailing one of his clients out of jail, but he'd be here as soon as he could."

"You couldn't get someone who was available?" Louis raises an eyebrow.

"Busy night, I guess. It is Saturday." Hicks shrugs.

There's a little bell sound. Yates pokes his head out the door, "Let me check this out." He comes back a moment later with a scraggly looking man in a rumpled suit. His brown plaid shirt is half untucked. His suit jacket has a rip in the pocket.

"James, how the hell are you?" Hicks stands up, then wipes his hands on a napkin. He reaches across Louis to shake the man's hand.

James hunches his body over, "Sorry, Detective Hicks. I got here as soon as I could."

Hicks looks the man over, "You look terrible. I mean, worse than usual."

"Yeah, I... haven't slept in a couple days." He straightens the front of his greasy hair with his fingers.

Hicks looks at him sideways, "You're not on the stuff again, right?"

"Nope, four hundred seventeen days sober, man." James pulls out a red coin with a pyramid in the center.

"Great." Hicks makes a short sigh. "So, James, this is my partner, Detective Louis Baker." He turns to Louis, "Baker, this is James Shoemaker, a defense lawyer I know from drug enforcement. He has got a lot of scumbags off, but for all the right reasons. He's just about the best defense attorney I know."

Louis shakes her head, "She isn't mixed up with drugs, Hicks."

"I know, but whatever is going on, James will get her out of it."

James smiles confidently at the complement. "Thanks, Hicks. What kind of trouble is the woman in?" He sets his tattered briefcase on the table. He pulls out a small notebook, its edges look like it was used for a puppy's teething toy. He pulls out a stubby, chewed pencil from his breast pocket.

Yates speaks up, "Well, we found her in a ditch on Parish Hill Road. Turns out the car was taken, allegedly stolen, from Mr. Mahoney."

Hicks picks up the story, "Right, and following a lead on the death of Mr. Mahoney's wife, Baker and I were up at Mr. Mahoney's recreational property. We found him shot in his bedroom. He was mumbling something about a woman returning, although he didn't name the woman. It's not looking good for your client, councilor. But since she's a friend of ours, we need her to be protected. And more importantly for our investigation, tell us everything she knows."

"Hmm..." James scribbles a few notes. "I see, and you don't suspect she actually did the shooting?"

"I can't see it." Louis shakes her head. "I've been surprised many times in my career. The evil things people are capable of doing to each other, is beyond my comprehension. I've known Cece for years; I can't see her doing this." *Maybe to her ex-husband, but not this guy.*

***

There's a quick knock on the break room door.

Louis peeks her head out. "Is she ready?"

"Yes, she's got an interesting story to tell, for sure." James wrings his hands, "But before she tells you the story she would like you to drop the charges on stealing the car."

"I think we can arrange that."

"Great." James beams a smile, but his eyes are weary.

Hicks and Louis walk out of the break room. Louis looks into James' sad eyes, "But she better tell the whole story, not leaving out anything."

"Yes. I believe she'll be quite cooperative. Right this way." James opens the door to a small room.

Cece sits hunched in a folding chair. She's fiddling with the cheap canvas shoes, half sliding them off. She looks up, "Louis. I swear. I didn't know anything about a shooting. I just -"

"It's okay, Cece. But we need to know what happened. Everything that happened. From the beginning."

"Right. Okay." Cece straightens her dress and stops fiddling with her shoes.

Hicks pulls up a folding chair for Louis. They both sit down in the room. James remains standing.

"Okay. Where do you want me to start?" She switches from looking at Louis, to Hicks, to James.

Louis sets a hand on her leg, "Start from where he picked you up at work."

"Okay. Well," She looks up at her lawyer.

His soothing voice comes out in a half whisper, "It's fine. You'll be okay as long as you tell them the truth."

Cece takes a deep breath, "So, he walked into the shoe department. I was clearing out my register. It's weird though, I'm pretty sure he didn't remember my name."

"What makes you think that?" Hicks furls his brow.

"Well, I caught him looking down at my name tag. And then he called me by name, kinda weirdly. He said something like. 'So, Cece are you ready for a big adventure, Cece?' " She flicks her hair out of her face, "So, we walk down to his car, he parked in the handicap spot out in the front. He's lucky he didn't get his car towed. I told him that." She laughs. "I got comfortable in the car. They were leather seats. They felt like new shoes. Then asked him where we were going. He said it was a big surprise. I said I liked surprises. We didn't talk much on the way. We listened to music, classical I think? Every once in a while I asked him where we were going, like it was a game. When I asked 'Naples?' he said I was close. So we passed Naples, then we went up this long winding road. He was driving pretty fast and there are a lot of really tight corners. I was a little scared and told him to slow down. He told me to relax and sit back in the seat to enjoy the ride. When we got to that... I don't even know what you call it, a cabin? Anyway, when we got there I got out of the car. I felt a little woozy from the heat and the drive. I wanted a cup of coffee. He said he didn't have any. He said he had wine. I asked for a glass of water. He seemed disappointed."

Cece takes a deep breath, "Is this what you wanted to know? I mean, like details?"

Louis smiles, "Yeah, keep going."

"Okay, so I had some water. We started talking and then...we were making out on the couch. After a bit he asked me if I want that wine now. I said, yeah, sure. So he left to get wine and I was just looking around the room, poking into things and I saw a picture of this beautiful woman. She looked a lot like you, Louis."

Louis nods, "That would be Julie Mahoney."

"Yeah, well I asked him who it was and he said it didn't matter. And I thought of that conversation you had with Will this morning and decided to be a pain. So I said, 'Of course it matters you have a beautiful woman in a picture on the table. Who is she?' And he said, 'My late wife.' I was in shock, of course. Then I asked him when she died. He said, 'Yesterday.' And I said, 'But you made this date with me two days ago.' Then he said, 'We have always had an arrangement.' I was all upset and we went back and forth a few times. He asked me to drop it and handed me the wine. I'll tell you right now, something about the wine didn't taste right, but I drank it anyway. I started feeling a little woozy, like I was in the car. I felt like the room was spinning, but then we started... making out some more. Then, I don't know what happened, but it felt like someone was watching us. I swear I saw a little Asian guy in the window, just before it started to rain. I screamed. Then Charles was trying to figure out why I was screaming, but by the time he turned around the Asian guy was gone."

Hicks looks at Louis. Louis raises her eyebrows as if to say, Oops.

Hicks looks back at Cece, "Did you see anyone else?"

"No. I don't think so. But there were two cars in the driveway when I left."

"Two cars?" Louis scrunches her face, "Wait, we're getting ahead of ourselves. So you screamed, then what?"

"Like I said, Charles was trying to figure out why I screamed. We talked for a bit. I said I felt funny. He started being really charming. He was feeling me up. He lifted me, but stumbled a little. It's not like I'm heavy." Cece rolls her eyes. "It was like he was drunk just on one glass of wine. I think I was too. That never happens to me. Two glasses, maybe, but not one." She leans her head back and looks at the ceiling. "I can't remember but he must have carried me all the way to the bedroom. My head was spinning. Then he was all over me on top of the bed. I started thinking about if it was the bed he shared with his wife. I got all creeped out. I pushed him away, but my arms were... I don't know, weak."

"Did you tell him no?" Louis' eyes widen.

"Yeah, I was really freaking out. He was like, 'It's okay, just relax.' But I was like, 'No. Take me home. I don't feel good.' Then, he said, 'Stupid bitch.' I remember that really vividly. I tried to get up, but he wouldn't let me. My head was spinning." Cece puts her hands up to her forehead.

Hicks shakes his head, "What happened then?"

"I don't remember everything. I got out from under him, somehow. I screamed. An Asian guy just appeared out of nowhere. He dragged me out of the house and sat me on the wooden bench. The rain was starting to come down pretty hard. I got up, opened the door and reached in for Charles' keys by the door. I ran to the car in my bare feet, got in and started it and drove down the driveway. I almost hit the beat-up car, but even if I did, I wasn't going to stay."

"How many cars were there?" Hicks asks.

"Two"

"Two cars?" Louis clarifies.

"Yes... one of them was all beat-up, the other one was... white?"

Louis looks at Hicks and back to Cece, "Just white?"

"It was *really* white."

"Did you see anyone inside the car?" Hicks asks.

"No, it was dark and raining at that point. I didn't see anyone, and I don't think I could have. Besides, I was still woozy."

Louis takes a deep breath. "I think Charles will have a hard time pressing charges about the stolen car. If you said 'No' and asked to be taken home."

"Is it bad?" Cece grimaces.

"I think you'll be okay, we just need to find this Asian guy..." Louis looks over at Hicks, "I'm sure he'll verify your story. We need to find that white car. You don't have a gun registered do you?"

" I hate guns. I can't believe you carry one all the time." Cece rolls her eyes.

"Okay, you need to stay here. The Naples police won't be able to release you until your story checks out."

Cece huffs. "Can I at least get my shoes back?"

"I'm afraid they are being logged into evidence."

"Those are Jimmy Choo's. They better be in the condition I left them."

Louis smiles, "I'm sure they'll be fine."

The detectives shuffle out of the tiny room. Louis looks over to Hicks, "So what now?"

"You look terrible. I'm going to take you home."

Louis feels a tingle of pain in her shoulder. She checks her pockets. "I can't remember where I left my pills."

"Yeah, I think you left them back your desk. When are you supposed to take them?"

Louis checks her watch, "About three hours ago."

"It'll take another hour to get back to Rochester, so we better get going." Hicks points to the door.

"We have leads to follow here." Louis protests.

"I believe your husband told you this morning that you need to let people do their jobs."

Louis mumbles, "I don't want to talk about Will."

Hicks opens the door, but Yates rushes to stop them, "Detectives? What's the story? Where are you going?"

"I need to get Detective Baker back to Rochester. The techs are scouring the scene at the Mahoney's cabin. Ms. Grant gave us a few leads, and a good reason she stole the car."

Yates leans forward, "A good reason?"

"She was being sexually assaulted by Mr. Mahoney." Hicks says.

"So she stole his car?" Yates asks, giving them both a look that says 'that won't fly in any court'.

"She asked to be taken home." Hicks says, "He refused. Called her a 'stupid bitch'. I don't think Mr. Mahoney will be pressing charges. And there's a witness."

"A witness? Where?"

"I have a feeling it's someone we know." Hicks looks over at Louis, "He's from Rochester, I'll track him down tonight. Most likely from his Twitter feed."

"I see. Does Ms. Grant know who shot Mr. Mahoney?"

"No, but I suspect that person was driving a white car."

"We didn't find any white cars at the scene." Yates says, "Lots of people drive white cars."

"Yes, I know. Look, just be on the lookout for suspicious white cars." Hicks says sarcastically, "I need to get back. Have your guys call me if they find anything. In the mean time our dear friend, Cece, is in your hands."

"We'll take good care of her."

Hicks leans into the uniform cop for what looks like a conspiratorial whisper, "Whatever you do, don't give in to her pleas for her shoes back."

***

Louis can hear the chainsaw snores from the front door. The living room is muggy hot. She opens a window in the front of the house then wanders to the kitchen in the back of the house to facilitate a cross breeze. Almost instantly the house takes on the feel of standing in South Dakota. Her fever started rushing back on the way back from Naples. Hicks turned up the A/C so high Louis was violently shaking. She had adjusted the seatbelt to try and cover herself a little more, but felt the spark of pain shoot through her body. She's happy to be home, even with Will's loud snores. He probably did get drunk, just like Kristine said.

She's exhausted. She's sure that she'll be able to sleep, even with his thundering snores. She walks into the bedroom and is hit with a rush of cold air. The central A/C in the house has been out of service for weeks, but somehow Will managed to get the window unit in the bedroom working in one way or another, even in his drunken condition. But she hasn't been home for two days. Perhaps he got it working on Friday?

His snores are loud and clear. She rubs his back, trying to calm him. His snore is interrupted and comes out like one long echoing choking sound coming through a clogged drainpipe. She can smell the strong musty alcohol permeating the corners of the room. It could be scotch, or maybe bourbon.

He opens his eyes. He blinks at her. She knows he's not really awake. "Will?"

"Hmm?" His eyes are open, he's responding, but she knows he's not really there.

"Did you have a good time tonight?"

Will closes his eyes. Within a minute his snoring increases its pace and volume.

"I hope you did. Because we need to talk." Louis tucks his blanket up around his cold shoulder. "I want to know what's going on with you, Will. I want you to tell me

why you're being so secretive. What are you holding back?"
She reaches over to turn down the A/C's fan to low.
"Sleep tight, we'll talk in the morning."

Will coughs. He slowly opens his eyes. "Mm hmm."
He mumbles. Gradually his snoring starts up again.

Rochester Herald Staff writer David Huang reports:

June 14th 11:04pm: On a tip from Rochester police, David Huang followed prime murder suspect, Charles Mahoney, 29, of Rochester to Naples. The suspect had a woman, Cecelia Grant, 38 of Rochester at his cabin just one day after his wife, Julie Mahoney, 25, passed away in their home. Julie Mahoney's death has been reported by the medical examiner's office as 'suspicious'.

Upon hearing screaming at the recreational property, reporter David Huang entered the residence of Charles Mahoney in Naples to rescue Cecelia Grant. Whereupon it is alleged she stole Charles Mahoney's late model Bentley Continental GT, crashing it into a small tree near the south end of Parish Hill Road.

Police interviewed the reporter David Huang looking to confirm Cecelia Grant's statement in the matter.

Police are now looking for a white car, possibly a late model Mercedes, last seen speeding away from the recreational property.

Sunday

Chapter 37

Kristine's eyes blink into the bright sun seeping into her bedroom from the slits in the blinds. She moves her head and feels the pain from the bump and stitches she got the previous evening's adventures. She wiggles her fingers and feels the phone she's been holding all night. The conversations she had with all of those disgruntled women permeated every corner of her dreams, but perhaps it was the pain medication. She sits up. She tries to shake off the fuzzy bits of her mind.

From the corner of her eye she can see Houdini is glaring at her. He's hidden half behind a fold in the quilt. "Sorry sweetie." She pets his furry body. "I think we'll make it a lounge around the house day today. What do you think?" He meows at her. "Yeah, I know. Promises. Promises." She smiles.

She thinks of Bryan. She wonders if she kept him up late with her phone calls. She had better be quiet and let him sleep. She thinks about her refrigerator. Does she even have anything to make him breakfast? Maybe she can slip out, get a quick cup of coffee and a couple croissants while he's still sleeping? Is he old enough to leave alone for a few minutes? She better not risk it, what if he woke up and wondered where she went?

She sorts out the notes lying on the nightstand, reminding herself of the painful conversations well into the night. She tucks her feet into her warm slippers. She puts on the thick pink robe her mother bought her last year. It's a size too big, but comfortable to lounge around in the house, especially on the rare occasions when she has guests. But Bryan isn't a guest. He's her new family. She smiles. She wants to rush down the steep stairs and hug him with all her strength.

She paces at the top of the stairs. The floor creaks loudly in the same warn spot. Her mind keeps recycling her thoughts, from her agonizing conversations last night, to the vision of the frail, but fierce Eudora Baxter holding her hostage. Kristine's imagination swirls with thoughts of Mrs. Baxter with a gun she never saw.

She wants to put the thoughts aside and focus on Bryan. She checks her watch: eight a.m. She remembers her sister telling her that when Bryan started kindergarten he was sleeping almost eleven hours a day, but since then he sleeps about nine to ten hours. They got home at eleven p.m. It took him a while to get into his pajamas and settled from all the crazy excitement, but he had to at least slept eight hours. Perhaps he's been awake, waiting for her to come down?

She decides to leave the case in bed, or at least by the nightstand. She slowly descends the ancient, creaking stairs. She sees the couch with a big lump in the middle under her green acrylic blanket and a pink throw, also purchased by her mother. She wonders how he can be so tightly balled up under two blankets when it's already pushing the lower eighties in her little house. She walks over to turn on the window air-conditioner. If they're going to laze around the house all day, it might as well be comfortable, electricity bill be damned.

She shuffles through the refrigerator. There's a small carton of milk. She opens it up, and then sniffs inside. Her nose crinkles at the sour smell. She drains the rest down the sink in chunky clumps. Kristine opens the little wooden bread box, hoping that magically there would be mold-free bread hidden in there she forgot about.

Unfortunately, she's got no such luck. The breadbox, given to her by her sweet Uncle Reggie, has only a box of crackers. She reaches into the nearly empty box. She mindlessly munches on the handful of buttery crackers left.

Sounds of ringing and Bryan's little boy laughs make her smile. Her mother is calling again. She grabs the phone from the oversized pocket of her robe. "Hey mom."

"Kristine. How did all your *important* calls go last night?" After getting her mother calmed down from the hours she went missing and left her favorite grandchild with a stranger, Kristine tried desperately to end the call by saying she needed to make a few important calls for work. This, of course, threw her mother into another, uncontrollable cycle of anger. It was only after another half hour of consoling, and a hint that she had to pee, that she was allowed to hang up. Her mother absolutely hated to talk to people while they used *the facilities.*

"I only have a couple more women to track down. Thanks for asking." While the calls were agonizing, they were at least productive.

"Good. I made a few calls myself this morning. We have Reverend Brown; he did that service for the Mitchell's. Do you remember?"

Kristine thinks, "I don't think so. Was I there? Or was that Kelly?"

Her mother continues unabated, "The Giammari's are going to play guitar in remembrance of their son. Apparently they all did that together, the four of them. I can't believe Ethan never mentioned it."

Maybe he did and you just never listened.

"They want to know when you'll be getting in on Monday, so they can spend some time with Bryan."

Kristine hesitates, she hadn't thought of it. "Ah, I'm not sure. I've got a court hearing at ten-thirty. Then Mr. Pucket wants to meet me at noon."

Her mother is incredulous, "You haven't purchased tickets?"

"Ah, no. Sorry, I've been a little busy. I'll -"

Her mother interrupts, "Well, you get that done right now. Send me the reservation information as soon you can. I want to give the Giammari's a solid time of your arrival. I don't want to give them any reason to take Bryan away."

"Why would they do that, Mom?"

"Well, you never know. Ethan's sister, Megan, is a mother. They could try and take custody."

The thought had never crossed her mind. Why would Megan want to take Bryan away?

Her mother continued on, "I'm sure you're fine, dear. She has a family of her own. I just wouldn't want to give the Giammari's any excuse to take Bryan away from you."

"Yes, well."

"So you'll send me the reservation information?"

"Yeah. I'll get right on that."

"Great. Can I talk to Bryan?"

"Well, he's sleeping right now."

"Oh." Her mother groans. There's a brief sound on the other end of the line of shuffling of papers. "Well, can you wake him? I want to talk to him about the service. I thought maybe he could read a poem."

"A poem?"

"Yes, I thought that he could read Shakespeare's *Fear no more the heat o' the sun*. It's really touching. I think it might be a memory he could keep for the rest of his life."

Kristine's voice lowers to a whisper. "A memory of his dead parents' funeral? Are you sure?"

"Yes." Her mother says with resounding conviction. "I think it would be good for him. And he'll need to practice the poem today."

"Right." She says, not even bothering to hold back the sarcasm. "I'll wake him." Kristine walks over to the couch.

The moment her hand touches the blanket she knows something isn't right. "Oh no." A chill runs through her spine.

CHAPTER 38

Louis wakes to the loud banging of pans from the kitchen downstairs. The room is briskly cool. She can still smell the lingering scent of scotch in the air. Her eyes blink into the bright sun seeping through the sides of the dark shades she bought while working the night shift.

Will's lack of ever getting a hang over after a heavy night of drinking is a cruel unfairness. Everyone has asked about his secret to a life free of hangovers, but he has always shrugged and smiled, "Just lucky I guess." The bedroom fills with an echoing sound of a large metal lid hitting the hard tile floor. Louis rolls her eyes. It must be time to get out of bed. He didn't even bring her coffee and the paper, as he usually does on Sunday mornings.

She pushes the covers off her body. She is knocked back with a pain so great she though she may be struck by lightning. She reaches over to the nightstand for her medication. She takes it, dryly swallowing the large harshly chemical pill. Her face contorts. She leans back into the fluffy pillows. She's grimacing through the pain.

She listens to glasses clanking together, refreshing in her mind the previous evening's messes. She cannot understand why Cece would get herself into a situation like that. Driven out to a remote place and being taken advantage of by Charles Mahoney. But she can see the charm in him. She wonders how many other women he's isolated and manipulated to do what he wants. He's a man with great wealth. Every real case she's needed to investigate boils down to either jealousy or money, or ultimately jealousy of money. Charles Mahoney has a gambling problem. What if he had someone steal those paintings and sell them? What if she caught them? Then he would have a reason to kill her. So he has the motive. She was home that night, but unexpectedly, an opportunity. The means is missing from that triangle. Plus, there was Tim and Victoria, and the Kitts, how did they die with the same symptoms? If Charles Mahoney killed his wife, why kill those other people? What connection do they have? Furthermore, who shot Charles Mahoney, and why?

She looks up at the slow moving ceiling fan, concentrating on one fan blade spinning in a circle when Will busts into the room. She looks up, grimacing from the continued pain.

"Oh, you're up." He grumbles. He quickly turns his back to her. He flings open his dresser's top drawer and rummages through it.

"I think your banging around downstairs woke me right up." She mutters through her gritted teeth.

He looks over to her, sneering. "I was washing the dishes."

"I heard that."

"They've been sitting in the sink the last three days. Do you want to go smell the rotten food in the kitchen?"

She looks up in time to see his eyes narrow, "Wait, you're pissed at me?"

He whips his head back to his task, "What are you talking about?" He mumbles.

"You're pissed at me. I can see it in your eyes."

"I'm not even looking at you."

"You were. And the fact that you won't look at me now says a lot."

He turns to look at her, "Well, Detective Baker, what do you suppose I have to be mad about, exactly?"

"I don't know, exactly. I'm sure you're mad I went out yesterday after you told me to stay put. I'm sure you're mad I haven't been home for a few days. But I don't know, exactly, why you're pissed at me. There's something else bugging you, something that's been nagging at you for a while. I want to know what that is, and why you needed to chat it up with Bethany yesterday."

"Bethany?" His confusion looks genuine to Louis.

"Yes, Bethany. That perky, pierced woman." She stabs at the air.

"I don't know what you're talking about." He shakes his head.

Louis reaches over to the nightstand. She clicks around on her phone. She thrusts up the screen to Will, while still lying on the bed. "Does this ring a bell?"

He squints at the tiny screen, "Oh, Beth."

"Beth is it?" She rips the phone away.

"But how -" His confusion is palpable.

"Well, I believe in your drunken state you probably gave her my number instead of your own."

"Oh." He says, his eyebrows rising.

"So, tell me why you felt the need to tell Beth about your fantasies. Tell me why she felt the need to send you naked pictures from the washroom?"

He stands there, is mouth agape.

"Never mind, don't tell me that. I don't want to really know right now. Right now, I want to know why you won't tell me what you're so mad at me about." She feels a little stronger. She struggles to sit upright on the bed, mashing her teeth through the pain.

He rubs the thinning dark hair at the top of his forehead with two fingers. He exhales, guiltily. As he sits on the end of the bed, well away from Louis, he exhales again. "I don't know where our relationship is going."

Louis shakes her head, "What?"

"You have your career. I have mine." He hesitates, looks into her eyes, "You don't get paid that much. Right now we are relying on my paycheck to keep things afloat."

"Wait, are you saying we having money problems?"

"No, just -" Her cell phone interrupts him with a beep for text message, "Just let me finish." He says in a rush.

She doesn't look at the phone. Although she's terribly tempted, she doesn't break eye contact with her husband.

"Last week I met with the Director of Operations at the Bank." He looks down at his hands, "I'm going to be promoted."

She smiles. She can't help it. He must be worried about their pay differential. But she's never really worried about the difference between what she makes and what he makes, or what she does and what he does.

"You're not listening."

"I'm listening. I'm confused, but I'm listening." She's still smiling.

"There's a catch. The promotion comes with -" Her cell phone beeps again. He rolls his eyes and growls in frustration.

His frustration giving her just enough time to try glance at the phone and figure out who's texting her. She knows it's got to be Hicks.

He catches her glancing at the phone. "The promotion comes with a move."

There it is: a live bomb in the room. Her breath is taken away for a moment. "What? A move to where?" Her whole body shakes. The pain swells up from her shoulder and radiates through her entire body in one flash.

"A move to Washington, D.C."

"D.C.? Are you serious? I can't move to D.C." She pounds her fist into the bedding.

"Yes. Yes, you can." He says forcefully.

"No. No, I can't."

"Louis -"

"No, my life is here. My career is here. My friends are here."

His face becomes stoic. "I noticed you didn't put me in that list? Where do I fit in?"

Louis stares at him, unsure of what to say to defuse the bomb.

"Well, your husband isn't going to be here, come fall."

245

"How can you be saying this?" She searches the room, hoping to find some explanation for the crazy things she's hearing.

"I've wanted this promotion for five years. The branch here in Rochester is small town. I would head a team of twenty people working specifically on branch operation information security. This could be huge for my career."

She shakes her head, "You sound like a brochure. Why couldn't you do that here?"

"The Director of Operations -"

Her phone starts ringing. "I'm going to take this, but we aren't done. Not by a long shot." Her phone rings again. "You can't just give up on our twelve years of marriage for a job opportunity."

They exchange dirty looks, the phone ringing insistently in the background.

"Hello?" Louis says, impatiently.

"Louis? It's Kristine." She sobs. "I can't find Bryan."

"What? What do you mean you can't find Bryan?"

"Ah, I came down from my room. There was a lump covered by some blankets on the couch. I thought he was sleeping so I left him alone. When I finally tried to wake him up, he wasn't there. The lump was just a pillow."

"Where could he have gone?"

"I don't know. I thought maybe he went outside, or... I don't know. I've been outside, shouting for him. He hasn't -" She sobs again, "Louis, what am I going to do?"

"Stay right there. I'll put a BOLO alert out. What was he wearing?"

"I don't know..."

Louis looks at Will, he's already staring her down. His nostrils are flared. She can see his chest rising like someone was filling a giant balloon in his chest. She breaks her stare from Will.

"I don't know." Kristine whines, "His bag is gone. What if someone took him?"

"In my experience, at that age, he probably left on his own."

"You have experience with this?"

"Of course, disappearing children fall under our department. If he did wander off, the best thing for you to do is stay put. I'll call the squad and we'll have a dozen cops looking for Bryan in less than twenty minutes."

"Okay, call me when you know something?"

"Yes, of course."

Louis assures Kristine that everything is going to work out fine. She looks up at Will, "I have to go."

"Yes, I know. You always have to go." Will rolls his eyes.

"I can't believe you are plotting me as the villain. You've known about this for weeks, I know you have. Why couldn't you have brought it up any one of the other last fourteen days?"

"Why do you think I scheduled that dinner?"

"I don't want to talk about this right now. I need to find Bryan."

***

"Okay, we are looking for a white male child, ten years old. His name is Bryan William Giammari and he's approximately four feet three inches tall, weighing sixty-seven pounds." Hicks' thundering voice pronounces each important syllable with unmistakable clarity.

A little voice peeps up from the back of the room, "I have a picture of him from yesterday."

"Aria?" Louis walks over to her.

Aria clicks a few times on her tablet. Bryan's smiling face, his blue plaid shirt and his knobby knees surround the uniforms from each of the ten televisions in the squad room. Aria's tiny voice squeaks out sharply, "I just sent an email replying to the BOLO with the picture. You should all have it in your squad cars by the time you get downstairs."

"Thank you." Louis smiles, but her smile dissipates quickly when she spots Lieutenant Olsen storming into the room.

"What's going on here?" She surveys the room.

"Lieutenant Olsen, we are looking for a missing child." Louis points to Bryan on one of the many televisions.

She looks around the room, "I didn't authorize this search. It's Sunday. I don't have the budget for so much overtime." She looks around the room, "Why exactly is Ms. Park here?"

"She was with the child here most of yesterday. I thought she would make a good witness."

"What child? Why was he here?" The Lieutenant points to the floor.

"His name is Bryan Giammari. Aria watched him while ADA Rocha was busy tracking down a lead in the Baxter case."

"Detective Baker, you better start making sense."

"Yes, ma'am. If you care to step in the hallway with me, I'll bring you up to speed on the situation." Louis opens the door for the angry woman to step through.

They exchange heated words. Unfortunately, glass windows surround the squad room, so Louis is sure she has become a muted TV show for the entire department. She refuses to turn and see if the attention is on her, at least not until Lieutenant Olsen stomps away.

Louis gets Aria's attention by tapping on the glass and waving her over. "That's a nice picture of Bryan."

"I took it yesterday to show him how the camera works." Aria smiles. "Good thing."

"Thanks for coming in."

"I got here as soon as I could. But it seems like Lieutenant Olsen doesn't want me to be here." She sounds like a scolded child.

"Don't worry about her. I want to know everything you guys talked about yesterday. Did he give any hints of running away?"

"He asked me a lot of questions."

"Like what?"

"He wanted to know how the buses worked here in Rochester. He said he rode the metro, that's the commuter train, in Alexandria. So, I showed him the website. Like how you can map any two points and the bus will tell you what routes to take, and which parts you have to walk."

"Oh dear."

"What? You don't think I should have told him?" Aria makes a pained expression.

"No, it's fine. We just need to take that into account. Did he say where he wanted to go? Did he give you an example?"

"As a matter of fact he said he wanted to know where his aunt lived and he wanted to map from there to where she worked. I was thinking he was going to try to get her to ride the bus for environmental reasons, you know how kids are these days."

"Oh that's good. Hold on." Louis bursts open the door to the squad room. "Hicks, take a couple of uniforms over to Kristine's office."

Hicks smiles, "What makes you think he's there?"

Louis phone rings. "Kristine?"

"My keys are missing."

"Did you leave them in the car out in Geneva?"

"No, I used them to get into the house last night. Now they're not here." Her voice is full of panic.

"Do you need them to get into your office?"

Kristine speaks hesitantly, "Yes..."

"I think I know where he is. Sit tight."

She hangs up the phone, "Hicks, never mind about the uniforms. Let's went."

***

The tarnished brass knob turns freely in Louis' hand. She turns around to look at Hicks, "It's unlocked."

He shrugs, "Well, lawyers do have long hours. Could be that someone is in there working."

"Let's hope it's Bryan." She shuffles through the long hallway. She's been to Kristine's office a thousand times. Sometimes to drop off notes on a case, sometimes to follow up on a trial she's interested in.

Louis snakes through the hallways straight to Kristine's office door. She opens the door, also unlocked. The room is a small disaster area. There's a pile of books on the floor, and the drawers to the filing cabinets are all opened.

Hicks looks behind the pile of books. "Nothing."

"Damn, it looks like he was here." Louis sighs. "I'll call Kristine."

Louis watches Hicks leave no stone unturned, looking behind Kristine's assistant's desk.

"Kristine? We're at your office... I know, I know... Well it looks like he was here. There's a pile of books on the floor... oh he did that yesterday?... Your drawers are all open, do you know what he might have been looking for?... Damn, really... That's, well, okay... yeah, we'll keep looking. You stay there... don't cry, it'll be fine... I'll call you back in a bit." Louis sighs and hangs up the phone. "She's a wreck."

Hicks continues poking around the assistant's desk, "What was the kid looking for?"

"Kristine found divorce papers filed by Kelly at the house on Friday. Bryan must have seen her file the paperwork into the filing cabinet when they were here yesterday." She points down at the pile of books, "He also made the book fort yesterday."

"That explains the books and the filing cabinet. But what about the assistant's desk?"

Louis looks over at the desk, "She didn't mention anything about that. Weird that he would pull out the drawers. And why would he empty them?" Louis asks, noticing the two empty file drawers. "Seems strange."

"Where do you want to try now?" Hicks doesn't look up at Louis, but continues to poke through the desk.

"I need to think. The uniforms already have the bus depot covered, and the airport."

"The airport? How would he get anywhere at the airport?"

Louis shrugs, "A kid has done it before. An eleven year old snuck onto a flight from London to Rome without a ticket or even a passport."

"Okay, but that's a big airport. I'm pretty sure that isn't going to happen here."

"No, but he could try."

"True." Hicks smiles.

"Wait, he was here a long time."

"Yeah, so?"

"He had to have gone to the restroom in the time he was here."

Hicks raises an eyebrow. "Let's check it out, but then be ready to think of somewhere else."

Louis steps into the hallway. She can't remember the last time she used the restroom in the building, or where the nearest one is located. She looks left. "I'll go this way, you go that way."

"Okay." Hicks marches off to the right.

A few yards down the hallway Louis hears voices.

CHAPTER 39

Kristine runs to the sound of knocking on the door. Her mind's eye sees Bryan standing at the front door and her enveloping him with a huge hug. She opens the door and slumps in disappointment.

"ADA Rocha?" The skinny, redheaded, freckly-nosed, uniform cop smiles.

"Do you have any information about Bryan?"

"Ah, no, ma'am. Detective Baker asked me to come here with Ms. Park." He moves to the side and points toward the car.

In a split second a tan streak whips by her legs. The uniform cop bends down and scoops Houdini up with one quick movement. "And where do you think you're going?" He stares the cat down. He turns the cat back around and tucks him like a football under his left arm. He sticks his right hand out to shake, "My name is Patrick Quinn. I'm sorry we had to meet under these circumstances."

"Thanks for catching him. I need one less thing to worry about today."

"I'll be happy to keep a good watch on him. May I come in?"

Kristine stands aside, "Yes, of course."

Quinn keeps hold of the cat and walks into the house.

"Why did Louis send you both here?"

He's still holding the hapless cat. "She said that Aria would be best to calm you down."

"What?" Kristine shakes her head violently. "Has there been a call? Is Bryan being held for ransom?"

Aria steps into the house, "What he means to say is that we came here to help you. Louis wishes she could be here, but she's got a good lead on where Bryan might be."

Quinn carries the cat toward the tiny kitchen table.

"Thanks, Aria." Kristine's eyes tear up. She lingers, looking past Aria. She spots a boy bouncing just down the street. She starts running his way. Her heart sinks another level when she realizes it isn't little Bryan striding up the sidewalk toward her, but another, much taller boy. "I can't take this."

Aria drops her computer bag in the small hallway. "Come inside, I'll make tea."

"It's already so hot." The tears stream down her face, "How can you think of tea?"

"I'll make iced tea then." Aria smiles.

Kristine steps inside the house and shuts the door, but not before taking another peek toward the street. "Is this really happening?"

"Yes, but we're going to find him. He'll be just fine." She says softly.

Quinn pipes up, "Chances are really good if we find him in the first five hours."

Kristine looks at him in horror. "And if we don't?"

"Well in that case -"

Aria interrupts clearing her throat and staring down Quinn, "It's not important right now."

Kristine keeps her eyes on Quinn. "Quinn, I think you can put the cat down now."

"Right." He places the cat on the floor. Houdini whips his tail a few times in anger, and then runs up the steep steps to the attic bedroom.

Kristine's phone rings. She looks at the caller-id and screams in frustration.

"What is it?" Aria asks.

"My boss, D.A. Pucket. I can't talk to him right now, I've got to leave the lines open."

Quinn fumbles getting his phone out of the holster. "Here, take my phone. Call him back."

"Thanks." Kristine grabs the phone before he drops it on the floor. She hands her phone to Aria. She runs to the garage.

"Mr. Pucket?"

"Who's this?"

"It's Kristine. I needed -"

"Kristine. I have a meeting with the mayor in less than an hour. I read through your email, but I hardly think this is sufficient evidence to convict."

"No, probably not, but it may be enough evidence to continue on with trial. I have at least four women out of twelve ready to testify tomorrow."

"Four?"

"Yes, four of them caught him in the act. The other eight were suspicious. Katy Bowden is sixteen. She's the one that called the office wanting to report on Dennis Baxter's behavior when she was just nine."

"What if the judge doesn't allow the new evidence?"

"Then we are sunk. Sir, this is the best evidence we have. I'm sorry it's not more, but I need to get back to what I'm doing."

"Are you following up on more leads for the hearing tomorrow?"

"No, my nephew has gone missing. There's an Amber Alert. Sir, I really must go." Right now.

Kristine abruptly hangs up. Not something she would normally do to her boss, but today isn't a normal day.

Aria and Quinn are exchanging hushed words when she returns.

Quinn looks down at his feet and mutters, "I'm sorry. I didn't mean to scare you."

"I just – I don't deal with missing children cases. I don't deal with that many children cases at all." She frowns.

Aria lays a hand on Kristine's shoulder. "Bryan's search is in good hands. Earlier this year she found a thirteen year old runaway; the girl was found in a

254

hamburger joint twenty miles out of town. She was shaken up, but safe and sound. The guy who abducted her was caught for speeding. The officer didn't see the Amber Alert until after the stop, but he saw the girl and put two and two together five minutes too late. The guy freaked and dropped the girl off at the hamburger place. Louis was there within a few minutes, got the girl and the guy who took her. Louis is good, really good." She looks down at the table, "One thing at a time. We'll let the other twenty people looking for Bryan do their jobs."

Kristine's cell phone rings a tone she is very familiar with. Aria hands her the phone, looking at her hopefully, but Kristine stops her, "It's just my mother."

She answers the phone without giving her mother a chance to speak, "Mom, I need to keep the lines clear. I can't talk right now, I don't know anything." She hangs up the phone.

Within seconds the phone rings again. Kristine growls in frustration. "Mom, I can't talk right -"

"What if Bryan called here and I was calling to tell you that he's fine?"

Her frustration rises to the top, "Well did he?"

"No but -"

Kristine mashes the button down to hang up on her mother. She screams in frustration when the phone rings again, but stops when the ring is different from her mother's special tone.

Aria looks at Kristine expectantly.

Kristine looks at the caller-id. But her eyes are too blurry to make out the text.

CHAPTER 40

The voices from down the hallway turn to a piercing, echoing scream. Louis picks up the pace, running toward the sustained high pitch scream. She bursts into the small kitchen.

Louis runs over to see Bryan sitting on the floor screaming. "Bryan?"

Bryan stops screaming and looks at Louis.

She reaches down to pick him up, but he pulls away. "Bryan, it's me, Louis."

He looks at her again. He wipes tears from his eyes. "Louis?"

"Yes, it's me." She reaches down again to pick him up, this time he comes easily. "Are you okay?" She holds him tight, but on the left side of her body, away from the pain.

"Yeah… I got scared." He sniffles.

She hugs him closer, "You scared your aunt."

Hicks comes into the small room. "Bryan, thank God. I heard the screaming and came running."

"It was a spider." Bryan says.

"Where?" Louis asks.

"Over there." Bryan points to the floor.

"Find it and kill it, will you Hicks?" Louis asks.

"Yeah." Hicks says.

"I need to call Kristine." Louis pulls out her phone.

The wavering voice on the other end of the line asks tentatively, "Hello?"

"Kristine? We have Bryan. He's okay."

"Oh my God." Kristine sobs. "Thank you." Louis listens as Kristine tells the other people in the room that

Bryan is okay. She comes back on the line, "Where did you find him?"

"At your office. He found the papers."

Kristine lets out another sob. "He's too damn smart. What am I going to do? Let me talk to him."

"Here you go." Louis hands the phone to Bryan.

"Aunt Kris? ... I know... I'm sorry... don't cry... I'm sorry... okay." Bryan starts to cry. "Here, she wants to talk to you."

Louis can hear sobbing on the other end of the line, "Kristine? We'll be there as soon as we can."

"Thank you. Thank you so much. I don't know how you do this."

"I'm really glad we found him so quickly." Louis smiles and hangs up the phone. "Hicks, get on the phone to Alec in central. Tell him to call off the Amber Alert and call in all the uniforms before the lieutenant blows a gasket."

"Got it." Hicks walks out of the kitchen.

She sets him on the counter to get a good look at him. "So, young man."

He looks into her eyes, ashamed. "I didn't – I mean, I – just wanted – I mean -"

"You wanted to find out what was in that folder." Louis points to the purple folder opened on the tiled floor.

"Yes." He wipes his nose with the back of his arm.

"Why didn't you just ask your aunt?" She rubs his shoulder.

"I did. She didn't want to talk about it." He fiddles with his fingers.

Louis gives him another big hug. "Sometimes adults don't want to discuss things right away. You need to be patient with us. You have to be especially patient with your aunt. She's got a lot going on, and she's going to need your help."

"My help with what?" Bryan frowns.

"Your help with raising you up to be a good, law abiding boy."

"Law abiding?"

"Yes, you aren't supposed to go traipsing around town without your guardian knowing where you're going."

"Oh. Are you going to arrest me?" His lower lip whimpers.

"Not this time. I'll let you off on a warning. But remember, don't do it again. Always tell your aunt where you are going and when you're going to be home."

"Right." He nods heavily.

Louis helps him down from the countertop. "Let's went."

"That's not right." Bryan shakes his head.

"What isn't?"

"You should say 'Let's go.' Not 'Let's went.'"

"Ha. That's what my dad always says. 'Let's went.' He got it from a TV show when he was growing up."

"Oh. 'Let's went.'" He mimics.

They walk into the hallway.

Hicks sticks out his hand for Bryan to grab, "How did you get all the way here by yourself?"

"Oh, I walked to Mt. Hope Road and waited for the 24 bus. I waited for the courthouse stop and then pulled that yellow cord thingy. Then I walked here from that stop."

"Wow, that's pretty brave."

"Then I used Aunt Kris' keys. You can tell which key is the right key by matching the number on the door with the one on the key. Then I punched in the key code on the alarm using Aunt Kris' poem."

"She taught you a poem?"

"Yeah, it's how she remembers the code. She said she worries that she'll forget the code with all the stuff she has to think about."

Louis exchanges looks with Hicks, winking, "And he's only been in town a day and a half."

***

Louis smiles, the only good part of looking for missing children is taking them home to their families. The car is barely parked and Kristine runs to open the back seat's door.

She's crying hard when she pulls him out and then holds him tight. "Don't ever do that again." She sobs.

"I won't, Aunt Kris. I'm sorry." He cries back.

"Why did you go off like that?" She carries the oversized little boy toward the house. A few steps away she turns around, "Louis, I don't know how I'll ever repay you."

Louis smiles. "I'm sure we'll think of something. We're a little over due for diva night out already."

"I'll figure something out when I'm back from Virginia." She walks back toward the house.

Aria and Quinn are heading out the door and Kristine stands aside for them. The blazing sun bears down on the four of them outside on the front lawn.

"Thanks for coming out, Aria. I knew you'd be able to keep her calm." Louis smiles.

"Yes, she was a wreck. I don't know what I'm going to do when I have kids. Maybe lock them in the house forever."

Louis takes one of the large cases from Aria. "It won't do any good. They'll find a way to escape. Better to teach them to be independent and responsible."

Aria wipes her brow, "Good to know. I'll think about that in like a million years when I find a husband and decide to have kids."

Louis sees Hicks lean over to whisper in Quinn's ear. Quinn smiles coyly.

"Now what?" Hicks asks.

"Oh, in all the excitement over the last evening and morning I forgot to tell you more I learned from Victoria's computer."

"What else did you find?" Louis fans her face with her hand. "Man it's hot out here."

"Pushing the nineties by now I think." Hicks adds.

"She had forty different folders with different identities inside them. They had social security numbers, credit cards, and full credit history reports, including little essays with personal stories."

"Maybe she was a private investigator? They would have personal information like that."

"I don't think so. I did a brief background check on Victoria Wallace. Here's what she looks like." Aria holds up her phone. An older black woman stares back at Louis.

"Maybe they just have the same name?" Louis speculates.

"And the same social security number? Tim is also not his real name either."

"So they were running some sort of identity scam?" Hicks asks, catching on.

"They must have been."

"What about the Kitts?" Louis asks.

"That's they're real name. I don't know how they were involved."

Louis snaps her fingers, "Remember what Neil Kitt did for a living?"

Hicks rolls his eyes back, "He was a printer. He must have provided the social security cards and identity cards. That's why he had all those credit cards."

"Right." Louis shakes her head. "So what about Julie Mahoney? I can't see how she fits into this puzzle."

"I don't know. She had money, lots of it. Maybe she was just an innocent victim?" He scratches his head, "Or maybe she was funding some sort of scam with the Kitts and Tim and Victoria?"

Louis snaps her fingers, "We still haven't talked to Carlos!"

"The handsome accountant?" Hicks smiles, "You're right, we haven't talked to him yet."

CHAPTER 41

The detectives enter an older non-descript office building, taking the familiar, slow, wood paneled elevator to the fifth floor. The marble engraved directory in front of them when the elevator doors open contains dozens of listings. The forensic accountant, Carlos Alvarez, is at the top of the list.

Over the last two years Carlos' office receptionists have never once been the same, even on the same day. The receptionist on this particular occasion is a tall thin black man, smartly dressed in a skintight suit. His Italian plaid shirt and striped tie mismatch in Louis' mind, but are actually quite fashionable, at least according to Cece. Louis can't figure out what he's even doing here, dressed this way on a Sunday.

Louis walks up to the desk. Her short frame is nearly eye-to-eye with the man seated at the desk. "Good afternoon. We need to speak to Mr. Alvarez."

"Mr. Alvarez is in, do you have an appointment?" His voice is so soft you can barely hear it, like a puffy white cloud given a voice.

On a Sunday? "No, we don't. But he should be expecting us."

"I see. Your name, please?"

"I'm Detective Louis Baker and this is Detective Robert Hicks." She points to her partner standing next to her.

"Very well. Please have a seat."

Louis walks over to the angular white leather couch and sits down. Hicks sits down as well, but within moments starts to slide forward on the seat involuntarily.

"Mr. Alvarez? I have Detectives Louise Baker and Robert Hicks here to see you."

Louis scrunches her face.

"Don't sweat it." Hicks whispers, "I'm sure pretty boy didn't mess up your name on purpose." He straightens up from sliding further down in the leather chair.

Louis leans over slightly to see Carlos bustling down the hallway. His muscular chest is barely contained in his button down blue shirt with small white pin stripes. His bright red tie swings from side to side across his gorgeous well-toned body. Louis unconsciously licks her lower lip.

"Speaking of pretty boy," Hicks mutters.

Louis shushes him.

"Detective Baker. I'm so glad you could stop by." Carlos reaches to pat her on the shoulder, but she quickly ducks out of the way.

"Sorry Carlos, I have a little… injury," she says pointing at her chest.

"Oh, of course." Carlos' stare lingers in Louis' eyes.

"Yes, nice to see you too, Carlos." Hicks says dryly.

Louis clears her throat, "So, Hicks says you found a few things in the Mahoney's accounts?"

"Yes, let's go back to my office and I'll show you the accounts."

The sound of a new text message echoes down the empty hallway. Louis pulls out her phone and reads off the message. She halts in the middle of the hallway.

"Louis?" Carlos asks.

She doesn't look up.

"Ah, Baker, are you okay?" Hicks turns his head at an angle.

She doesn't look up. She stares into the screen of the phone. She's trying to stare down the phone, begging it to be something else.

"Baker, seriously…" Hicks says slowly, then runs his fingers atop his bald head. "It's her isn't it?"

"Her who?" Carlos whispers quietly.

"She's ah…"

Louis doesn't look up, but snaps, "She's nobody."

"Ah, whoa," Carlos darts his eyes from Hicks to Louis. "If you want to leave… I can email you the report, and some of my findings. I have the report ready now. Although, you might still need me to walk you through the finer details."

Louis looks up, stuffs her phone in her pocket. "Forget it. I already have." She exhales unconvincingly.

"Ah, I guess." Carlos says. He walks purposefully around to his desk. He sits, arranging the three stacks of papers so that each stack is perfectly spaced. "So, I went back a year on each of the Mahoney's accounts, at least all of them we had a warrant for.

"I found that up until three months ago the wife made regular, even payments into Mr. Mahoney's personal funds. An allowance, if you will."

"Well, she did come from money right?" Hicks asks, looking over to Louis.

She's staring at the floor intently. Her grinding teeth and short huffs can be heard between the gaps in conversation.

"Right, her parents, Mr. and Mrs. Johnson, opened a trust that has been supplying her with a monthly income." Carlos addresses Hicks while staring at Louis.

"How much is the payment?" Hicks leans over to peer at the papers that Carlos is still straightening nervously.

"Twenty thousand dollars."

"A year?" Hicks asks.

"A month."

Hicks whistles admiringly, "Twenty large? How does someone spend twenty thousand dollars in a month?"

"Artwork apparently." Carlos hands Hicks a piece of paper. "She's bought several significant pieces in the last year. I circled each of the purchases and the cost of insurance. All of the artwork came from legitimate dealers. I checked them."

"So, what happened three months ago?" Louis finally joins the conversation.

"Well, three months ago the payments to the husband stopped."

"That must have pissed him off." Hicks laughs.

"I don't know, but he drained through his account pretty quickly. The money was all gone by the end of the month. His credit card maxed out at a hundred thousand. He opened a new credit card and maxed that one out at fifty thousand in a few weeks.

"Then, last week the wife paid off all the overdrafts, the credit cards and supplied the husband with three hundred and fifty thousand dollars on top of it all."

"Why?" Louis squints curiously and shakes her head.

"'Why' is not in my purview, that I would leave up to you, Detective." Carlos winks. "Two hundred and fifty thousand dollars was then transferred on the same day from Mr. Mahoney's private account to his business."

"If she spends so much on artwork, where did she get all the money to pay off his accounts?" Hicks asks.

"I assume she sold some of her artwork. There was a deposit of nearly a half million dollars a day before she paid off all the debt."

"I don't understand. He funded his business through his personal account? Is that legal?" Louis raises an eyebrow.

"Well, it's not illegal. It's not a public business, it's privately owned by Mr. Mahoney. The funding will likely be a headache for his tax account, but nothing more. The problem is…" Carlos hesitates.

"The problem is what?" Hicks probes.

"The problem is, from what I can tell, he's been diverting funds from the business account into a shell company. The payments to the shell company are highly irregular. Well, I'm fairly sure it's a shell company."

"You lost me." Hicks grins and lets out a little laugh.

"Shell companies are legitimate businesses that do not have assets or operations, or typically employees. Legitimately they can exist to shelter companies from liability, certain taxes, or they can hold patents or copyrights. The shell company's owner may then gain income from those intangible assets. However, shell companies are sometimes used to commit fraud or launder money.

"We don't have the proper warrant for investigating the shell company that Mr. Mahoney's funds have been diverting to. He isn't the named owner of the company, and I haven't been able to contact the actual named owner. This makes me highly suspicious."

"I've been highly suspicious from the start." Hicks laughs again. "When the wife dies, the husband is always the prime suspect. Strike one. That he was overdraft and suddenly his wife saves him? Strike two. Now we find out that he's laundering money. Three strikes, he's out."

Louis smiles at the baseball analogy. "I agree, it's not looking good for Mr. Mahoney. Shall I set up that meeting with Holly now?"

"You can't stop thinking of that cheating angle can you?" Hicks shakes his head.

"Its always cheating and jealousy, Hicks. But let's go talk to Mr. and Mrs. Johnson, first. If they are supplying that much money to their daughter, they've got to be keeping pretty close tabs on her."

"Good point. Rich parents always know what their kids are up to, even if they don't want to admit it." Hicks winks.

***

Louis presses the doorbell again. The three-part melody they heard last time repeats. The large oak door opens. The woman standing before her is sheet white, except for her puffy red eyes and black streaked mascara. "Mrs. Johnson?" she asks.

"Yes?" She says without fully making eye contact.

"I'm Detective Louis Baker and this is my partner, Detective Robert Hicks. I'm so sorry for your loss."

"The police were here yesterday, and the day before."

Louis is confused by the comment, but she's seen various shades of shock in her time. Everyone experiences lost differently, "Yes, ma'am. We just need to ask you a few more questions."

She doesn't say a word, but opens the door a little wider and stands aside for the detectives to come in. A balding man with a thick mustache comes rushing down a large spiral staircase. "Shirley? Who is it?"

She doesn't look up, "It's the police."

He rushes to her side. He puts his arm around her shoulders, as if he was holding her up. "Honey, why don't you go back to bed? I'll talk to them." He looks at the detectives, "Go on into the sitting room, I'll be right there." He points over with a tilt of his head.

Louis watches as he slowly walks her up the staircase. She takes a deep breath. She looks at Hicks, "She didn't look so good."

He looks around the room, "No, definitely not." He walks over and sits down on a shiny gold couch with gold fringe at the bottom. "Hmm… not as comfortable as you might think."

"Scoot over." She grumbles.

The bald man comes back down the stairs. "You're detectives?"

Louis and Hicks stand up. "I'm Detective Robert Hicks, this is Detective Louis Baker." Hicks reaches his hand out to shake the man's hand.

"Dean Johnson." He sits in a matching gold armchair. "We answered a lot of questions yesterday."

"Yes sir. We had some questions about your daughter's relationship with Charles Mahoney." Louis clarifies.

Mr. Johnson looks down at the floor. "Jules and Charles were married for five years. They met, dated, and got married. They were going through a rough patch, but what couple doesn't have problems?"

"Did Jules ever elaborate on what kind of issues she was having with Charles?"

"Normal issues." Mr. Johnson says sternly.

"Right, we were trying to get some information on the nature of the *financial* relationship." Hicks changes the subject, "Your daughter had a monthly trust set up by you?"

"The particulars of a trust are not public, but yes, we set up the trust. She receives a monthly *income*." Mr. Johnson corrects.

"Twenty thousand dollars?"

"That is the monthly amount." He raps his fingers on the hard, whitewashed wooden arm of the chair.

"When was the trust set up?" Louis asks.

"The day she was married." He twitches his mustache with his fingers.

"Since the day she was married?" Hicks frowns.

"Yes."

"You didn't think that Charles Mahoney could provide for your daughter?" Louis clarifies.

He scoffs, "Are you kidding? My daughter has expensive taste in art. And Charles Mahoney could hardly keep his business afloat. I told him six months ago to look into manufacturing that new drug, Shoftikin, but he said the equipment was going to cost too much." He shakes his head, "One must invest in the right technology to make money." His fist slams down on the chair.

Louis bites her lower lip, hesitating. "Do you know if your daughter was involved in drugs?"

"Drugs? No. She wasn't involved in drugs."

"Did she have any friends that were involved with drugs?"

"What are you trying to imply, Detective? If you know something, about family business, it would behoove you to keep family business private."

Louis is surprised by the response, "Sir, we don't know anything about family business, should we?"

"No." Mr. Johnson looks away.

"Sir, your daughter was most likely killed by someone she knew. Did she have any friends we should be looking into?"

"I think that's quite enough questioning for now." Mr. Johnson stands up. "I need to go check on my wife."

Louis walks toward the door, but spins around before opening it. "Mr. Johnson, Julie was your only child?"

He stares at her, not answering.

"Were there any other relatives that we should speak to? Anyone in particular she may have been close to?"

He turns away from her. "There's no one except my wife and I."

Louis nearly slams the door. "Another strike out."

"Why did you ask him about other relatives?"

"There were pictures on the wall of two girls in a few snapshots. In one of them they were wearing the same dress. I thought maybe one was a close cousin? She could have been stealing the paintings? Maybe this cousin was jealous of the monthly trust."

"You mean monthly *income* from the trust." Hicks says.

"Right."

Hicks smirks, "So, what are we waiting for? Let's go talk to Mr. Faithful, shall we?"

CHAPTER 42

"Not you two again." Charles groans from his hospital bed.

"You'll just have to deal with us until we find your wife's killer, Mr. Mahoney." Hicks plasters a smile on his face.

"Charles, please." He corrects.

"Charles." Hicks echoes back.

"We need to know everything that happened last night. Start from when you were driving to the cabin." Louis pulls out her electronic tablet. She pulls the little pen out to take careful notes.

Charles rolls his eyes. "OK, but when I'm done you guys are going to leave?"

"Sure, we'll be checking out your story. Just like we did with 'The Jamaican.'" Hicks says smugly.

Charles looks from Hicks to Louis then back to Hicks.

"What you didn't think we were going to spend the whole evening chasing after a fake drug dealer did you?" Hicks sneers and rattles the hospital bed's rails.

Louis plays the good cop and reaches out her arm to hold Hicks back, "Just tell us what happened yesterday."

"Well, I drove that ungrateful Bi-" Charles stops himself, "woman up to the cabin in the Bentley. She seemed a little scared of the cars handling, if you know what I mean." He smiles smugly, "I mean I drive that route so often…" He looks up at Louis. "Anyway. We had a few drinks. She got a little loose." He smiles. A silence hangs off of his sentence. Charles exchanges looks with both of the detectives again, seeming to waiting for a question. When none comes he continues, "So then she had this little freak out about seeing someone outside. I told her there wasn't anyone for miles. She got all frantic, so I took her to the bedroom. We were getting hot and heavy when she pushed me away. She said she wanted to go home. I said that I would take her when the drinks wore off. I didn't want to be drinking and driving, you know? But she left." He hesitates.

Louis makes a few notes on her tablet. Her hands are barely able to sustain contact from all the frustrated shaking she's doing. "And then?"

"And then, she came back. She shot me." He points to his chest.

"You saw her shoot you?"

"No. I heard her heels. She was wearing those fancy shoes. She sells fancy shoes, you know?"

"You didn't see her?"

"No. I *heard* her. I just told you that." He rolls his eyes.

"OK, let's talk about your bank account." Hicks leans in.

"What about my bank account?" Charles stares at him.

"You have a bit of a gambling problem, Chuck." Hicks points his finger at Charles.

He shakes his head, "I do not have a problem. My debts are paid."

"Your debts are paid because your wife paid them."

Charles huffs, "So what?"

"So, now that she's paid up all your debts you felt like bumping her off? Maybe deflect the suspicion by getting shot. I noticed it wasn't a mortal wound."

"You think I planned on getting shot? Do you know how much this hurts?"

"I'm familiar, yes." Louis thinks back to the pain she felt when a domestic got out of hand last year.

"So you know." He nods.

"I know that you arranged to see Cece before your wife was killed, and continued to keep that date." She stares him in the eyes, but looks over to see Hicks' stern 'We agreed not to bring that up in this interview' look.

"Yeah, Cece, that's her name." Charles taps the top of his head. "Not sure why I can't remember that."

Louis rolls her eyes. "You're missing the point. Your wife was still alive when you made that date."

"So?" Charles looks at the detectives, and the look of confusion on his face is unmistakably genuine.

"So, do you make it a habit of cheating on your wife?"

"Cheating?" Charles breaks out laughing.

"If you cheat regularly maybe one of your mistresses got jealous and-"

Charles laughs and winces a pained expression, "You gotta stop making me laugh so hard. It really hurts."

"Okay Chuckles," Hicks billows, "Why don't you bring us up to speed on the big joke?"

Charles looks at the detective sideways. "I wasn't cheating on my wife. We had an arrangement." He smiles and raises his eyebrows.

Louis takes her turn at the confusion, "What kind of an arrangement?"

"I guess it doesn't matter too much now, she's dead." He takes a deep breath. "I met her at a bar, a bar *full* of women. But I was striking out left and right. She walked up to me and handed me a pink martini. She proceeded to tell me all about the bar, 'Betty's'."

Hicks cracks a smile and laughs, "No wonder you were striking out. Are you dense or what?"

Louis looks at Hicks, "What am I missing?"

"Baker, it's a lesbian bar."

"Oh." Louis exchanges looks with Charles and Hicks. "Wait, your wife was a lesbian?"

"Yeah. Like I said, we had an arrangement. Her parents paid her way through art school, but they wanted her to get a real job, and a real husband." Charles smirks.

"So her parents were going to cut her off if she didn't get married?" Hicks asks.

"Yes, so she told me all of this over a few 'dates' before we got married. I met her parents. Her dad loved me, mostly because I was not a woman. They practically gave up hope when she was in college."

"I see." Louis' wheels turn in her mind. "Why didn't you tell us all this before?"

"Part of our arrangement was being discrete. I got a hefty allowance. In exchange I couldn't tell anyone that she was a lesbian. Thanks to her, my business stayed afloat when a lot of businesses fail."

Hicks says, "Why did she cut you off?"

"We had a little disagreement. I got drunk and threatened to tell her father what was really going on."

"But then she paid your bills?" Louis asks.

"Yeah, I promised not to tell her father, and said I wouldn't get into so much financial trouble. I promised to go to Gamblers Anonymous."

Louis scoffs, "But she died, surely you could have told us?"

"Old habits die hard, Detective. Holly didn't know, and I didn't want to tell her either."

"Are you having an affair, I mean, sleeping with Holly?"

Charles smirks, "Of course."

Louis shakes her head. "Is it possible that Holly was jealous of your wife?"

The question clearly takes him by surprise, "I don't think so. I mean, I told her that Jules and I were going through a rough patch. That was the story for everyone. That we were going through a rough patch. Jules told her parents that a bunch of times. We were going to file for a divorce, probably next year. Her lover was getting a little uncomfortable with our arrangement. It's not like Jules was going to wake up one day and say 'oh after five years of fake marriage I think I'm going to become straight.'"

"Her lover?" Louis eyes light up.

"Yeah. The woman detests me. She loves to talk, and what she loves to talk about most is how much she hates me."

"Wow, hostile environment, huh?" Hicks laughs.

"Yeah, but Jules was never like that overly fem-bot stereotype. Frankly, I don't know what she saw in Tina."

"Tina… ?" Louis leaves space in the question for a last name.

"Hmm. I think I heard her last name once." Charles squints his eyes, willing the memory to come back. "It was something really common. Like, Jones. No, not Jones. Oh, 'Smith,' Her name is Tina Smith. They met at an art auction. Jules told me that under her pistol attitude was a teddy bear. And she was really hot in bed, that part I didn't mind hearing *all* about."

Louis rolls her eyes. "Give us a brief description of 'Tina Smith'?"

"Ah, sure. Jules said she like to -"

Louis cuts him off, "A *physical* description."

"Oh yeah. She's about five and a half feet tall, maybe a little taller. She is always dressed to the nines, especially shoes. Jules always wanted her to take her shoes off at the door, but she always pranced around on the white carpet with her heels. She's got red hair. It's dyed though, so I don't know how red her hair really is. She wears it up in a curly poof kinda thing." Charles strains to hold his hands up to emphasize the poof. "I don't know what else?"

"Did she smoke?" Louis asks.

Charles shakes his head, "Oh no. Jules didn't like smoking. She made me quit a few years ago."

Louis swipes through a few pictures in her tablet. She holds up a picture to Charles, "Is this her?"

"Yeah, yeah, that's her." He says. He leans in closer to the tablet, "What is she doing?"

"Stealing your artwork." Louis says.

"Seriously?"

"Do you know if Mrs. Mahoney kept Tina's number in a contact book or... Why is it that we still can't find your phones?"

"I have no idea," Charles shrugs, "But Jules synced her phone with her computer. You can look at her contacts and appointments there."

"Alright, if you think of anything else you neglected to tell us, call us okay?" Hicks motions toward the door.

As the door swings shut he grumbles, "Did you really have to cut him off?"

***

"So, what are you thinking, Baker?" Hicks cranks up the A/C in the car.

"Smith." Louis looks over her notes from the case.

"They met at an art auction. I wonder which one. I wonder how we could find Tina Smith?"

"I'm going to guess right now that she's not in the phone book, or if she is, she's not the right Tina Smith." Louis says, devoid of the usual hopefulness.

"I'm sick of this cases wild goose chases."

"Yeah, why do I feel like we've got all of the important information about a day late?" Louis looks up from her notes. "Wait, maybe this is starting to make a little sense?"

"How so?" Hicks looks over her shoulder to the notebook.

"Tina hated Charles, and loved Julie Mahoney. Lovers do crazy things. Maybe she got tired of their fake relationship. Maybe Tina tried to cut Charles out of the equation and killed Julie instead? I mean, she did come home early."

Hicks looks at Louis, skeptically. "But what about the other victims?"

"Smith. That's the name on the house we went to. Both the Kitts and Tim had directions to that house."

275

"But that was Jane Smith, not Tina Smith." Hicks corrects.

"We already know there was identity fraud going on." Louis rolls her eyes, "So how do we go about finding Tina or Jane Smith?"

"She's not going to go back to that house. And we have a guard at the hospital door in case she comes back." The silence hangs in the air while the two detectives think. Louis is startled when Hicks' phone rings. "Don't be so jumpy." He pulls the phone out of his holster, "Detective Robert Hicks."

Louis listens to the muffled sounds of the other side of the phone call.

"Wait, wait. Let me put you on speaker so my partner can hear." Hicks clicks around looking for the right button.

"It's that one." Louis leans over and presses it. Accidentally touching her sensitive shoulder, she winces. "Damn."

"Detective Hicks?" The familiar voice Louis cannot place asks. "Is everything alright?"

"Yeah, just me fumbling with the phone. Go ahead and repeat what you told me a second ago, Peterson."

"Sure. So we have a preliminary toxicology report back on Victoria Wallace, Tim Sherman, Neil Kitt and Sara Kitt."

"And?" The detectives ask in unison.

"In all four cases we found high levels of para-Methoxymethamphetamine, otherwise known as PMMA"

Louis says, "Long word, is that significant?"

"Yes ma'am. PMMA has been known to cause severe hyperthermia."

Louis asks, "Hyperthermia? Isn't that when you are cold?"

"No, ma'am. That's *hypo*-thermia."

"Oh. So where does PMMA come from?" Hicks asks.

"It's similar to the street drug, ecstasy and has been known to be sold as ecstasy. We haven't seen any cases here, but there were high profile cases recently in Norway, Germany, and in Canada. About ten years ago there was a string of deaths in Florida."

Louis says, "Hold on, did you say Germany?"

Hicks looks at her. "What are you thinking Baker?"

"Julie Mahoney just came back from Germany on Friday."

"You think she brought the drugs with her?"

"No, because that doesn't explain the other deaths, but something bugs me about Germany. Charles said she came home early."

Peterson says, "One more thing, detectives."

"What is it Peterson?"

"We found PMMA in that house you raided on Friday."

Louis says, "So now we know where the drugs came from."

"Did we find any prints in the house?" Hicks asks.

"Not my department. I know the print shop is pretty backed up, though."

Hicks sighs, "Thanks, Peterson."

"You're welcome, detectives. Good luck."

Rochester Herald Staff writer David Huang reports:

June 16th 8:39pm: In a statement released an hour ago Rochester police have found evidence of paramethoxymethamphetamine (or PMMA) in five victims experiencing hyperthermia (or extreme fevers) this week.

PMMA has been known to be sold as ecstasy, but has far deadlier effects on the body. Police warn that PMMA is five times more toxic than ecstasy.

Rochester police also confirm PMMA was found at the house raided in Marketview Heights on Friday.

MONDAY

CHAPTER 43

Quinn rushes into the squad room waving a piece of paper. "I got it!"

Louis rolls her eyes, "What have you got, Quinn?"

"I've got the preliminary report back from the fingerprint analysis on that house in Marketview Heights. You were right Detective Baker, the fingerprint people wanted to get rid of me as soon as possible."

Hicks shakes his head, "Teaching someone else your nasty tricks, Baker?"

"What does it say?" Louis asks.

"They found fingerprints from Mr. Kitt on the door knob. And one print on the back side of the door that belongs to several people in the system."

"Whoa. Did you say one print that belonged to several people?" Louis asks.

"That's what the report says." Quinn frowns.

Louis shakes her head, "I told you this case is all about identity fraud."

"Certainly seems that way, Baker." Hicks stares at the phone, "Hand me that list. I'll search through the database and see if that print lines up with any of our suspects."

Louis snatches the report from Quinn's hands. "Not so fast." She clicks around a few screens, "Whoa."

"What is it?" Hicks gets a little to close to her shoulder. She shifts her body away, "Don't be like that. What is it?"

"Take a look at this picture, one of the four with the same fingerprint."

"She's, what, eight?"

"She's nine, but take a look at the name."

Hicks starts heading down the stairs to the car, "I know where we're going next."

***

The large oak door, with its lion's head knocker is adorned with a bow made from velvet black ribbon. Louis uses the knocker hesitantly.

"Now who's not paying attention?" Hicks smiles.

"What are you talking about?" Louis looks down at her clothes, thinking she may have spilled her coffee on herself without noticing.

"There's a door bell." Hicks points to the little button to the left of the enormous door. "You used it last time." He pushes it in. The chimes ring in a familiar three-part melody.

"Oh." Louis takes a deep breath. An overwhelming sweet perfume of the last honeysuckles of spring fills her sinuses.

The large knob turns and the woman they saw yesterday stands before them. She looks even more pale and fragile.

"I'm sorry, ma'am. We need to speak to you about your daughter."

"You were here yesterday." She says, groggily. "She's still dead, right?"

"Not that daughter, ma'am."

"I don't -" The pain on her face turns to shock. She takes two steps away from the door.

A man's voice calls from beyond the door, "Shirley? Who is it?"

Louis hears the knob on the door rattle. Shirley Johnson stares into her eyes, her pupils come out of focus.

Louis lunges past the door and catches the woman in her arms just moments before she hits the floor. The burning pain in Louis' shoulder nearly knocks her out as well. She takes deep breaths.

Louis' ears fill with whooshing sounds. Through the pounding in her ears she can hear rapid stomping on a set of stairs.

"What the hell?" Mr. Johnson asks, but to Louis' ears it sounds underwater.

She hears Hicks shouting, "Baker? Baker?"

She waves Hicks away from her face. She lifts Mrs. Johnson off of her shoulder and Mr. Johnson comes along side and supports her. The woman's head lulls all the way back without anything supporting it. She's out cold.

"What the hell happened?" Mr. Johnson asks.

"I'm not sure myself." Hicks looks at Louis.

***

"My wife took a pill." Mr. Johnson says twitching his mustache while walking down the spiral staircase. The man sits down at the golden antique sofa. "She hasn't been the same since we lost Jules. A parent shouldn't out live their children."

"Again, I'm very sorry for your loss, Mr. Johnson." Louis says.

"Now, can you tell me what the hell is going on?" Mr. Johnson looks at Louis, his eyes filled with a mix of frustration and rage.

"Sir, we found some information." Louis hesitates.

"Like I said last time, whatever you found out about Jules should be kept private. Whatever it is, I'm sure we can deal with it as a family, not have it out in the open." He waves his arms toward the front door.

He knows she was a lesbian, Louis thinks. She shakes her head, "We know Julie had a friend. But we found some information on your other daughter." Louis pulls out her tablet and hands it to Mr. Johnson. "Is this her?"

"This isn't… this is…" He shakes his head. "Wendy." His voice is barely audible.

"So, you haven't seen her hanging around?" Hicks clarifies.

He shakes his head. "Don't you think I would have known Wendy?" He says angrily. He goes back to staring at the photo. "I've been looking for her for seventeen years."

"It's not the best picture." Louis points out.

"It's a mug shot for Christ sake!" Mr. Johnson shouts, then sighs, "She's so beautiful, exactly how the age progression photo company said she would look."

Louis leans over to see the picture, thinking it may have accidentally moved to one of the other pictures, since the picture she remembers is a mug shot of a hooker picked up four years ago on the streets of Albany.

Mr. Johnson traces out the woman's face.

"She went missing when she was nine?" Hicks asks.

"Yes, two days after her birthday." Mr. Johnson doesn't look up.

"You were at the park?"

He sighs, "We were celebrating her birthday. There were… purple balloons, her favorite color. Shirley was setting up a game for the girls. Julie wanted to go to the bathroom, so I took her. When I came back, Wendy was gone. We never saw her again."

Louis thinks hard. Why did they find Wendy's print in the house where drugs were manufactured?

Mr. Johnson looks at Hicks, "Is she alive then? This picture looks old."

Hicks clears his throat, "Her fingerprints were left at a house in Marketview Heights."

Mr. Johnson's expression is pained, "In Marketview Heights? She's here? But… I thought she was…"

"You thought she was what?" Louis asks.

He lays the picture down on the antique ornate coffee table, "I thought she was in Germany."

"Germany?" Louis thinks back, *Julie was in Germany before she died.* "Is that why Julie went to Germany?"

"Yes, she…" He sighs again. His hands come up to his face to fiddle with his bushy mustache.

"Sir," Hicks attempts to get his attention, "Sir, we believe that your daughter had a relationship with a woman, Tina Smith."

Mr. Johnson's nostrils flair. His face turns red, "She was married, to Charles Mahoney. Tina was just a friend."

"We need to talk to Tina. Do you have any contact information for her?"

"No." His lips purse, he hesitates, but then sits up straight.

The detectives stare at Mr. Johnson silently. Louis leans forward, "We believe your daughter, Wendy, may have been involved in the murder of your daughter, Julie. She also may have attempted to murder your son in law, Charles."

He shakes his head, "You can't be serious. What proof do you have?"

"Wendy's prints were found in the house in Marketview Heights. There were traces of PMMA-"

He interrupts, "That doesn't mean anything." He rests his head in his weathered hand. "We looked for her for so long. The police said, to be gone that long, she was likely killed. We gave up hope. There was a ransom, you know. We paid it." Tears well up in his eyes. His face freezes, "You have to go."

"Sir?" Hicks looks at him.

Mr. Johnson stands up, "Out!"

***

Louis sits in the passenger's seat, fiddling with her phone. She receives another message from the very desperate Bethany:

```
Hey Will. I'm sorry I ddin't hear
from you yesterday. You must have
needed to sleep off all those scotchs
:) Lying here on my bed thinking about
your lusty handucff fantasy. Come tie
me up.
```

The picture is indeed of her lying on her bed. She looks like she's been primping and preening herself for an hour to get her hair just so and her makeup just right. No one gets out of bed and looks that gorgeous. Her mind wanders over the idea of playing along. How far would it go? How long would it take to set up a meeting with this needy woman? But then what would she do?

Hicks breaths over her shoulder, "Damn. Why can't I get sexy women to text me pictures like that?"

"I guess you just need to meet the right desperate woman, Hicks." Louis tucks the phone away.

He smiles, "I thought I had."

Louis looks at him sideways. She checks her watch.

He laughs, "I hope she gets here soon. Or I'm going to have to use those bushes over there in a bit."

"Seriously? Why didn't you go before we left?"

"He kicked us out of the house."

"Well then, stop drinking that coffee."

She reaches to grab the coffee from the holder in the center console, but Hicks stops her hand from reaching the cup. "You can't take a man's coffee away from him. That's undue cruelty."

"Look, over there." Louis points to a woman walking up the steps of the Johnson's house. "She's thin, and wearing heels."

284

Louis steps out of the car. The woman looks around. Louis follows her gaze across the street to a white car. She turns back to see the woman's smile sour quickly.

"Hicks!" Louis points to the white car.

Hicks runs toward the car.

The woman turns her back.

"Police, stop right there!" Louis shouts.

Mr. Johnson comes running from his house, "No! She's going to get Wendy!"

Louis picks up speed, "Tina Smith! Stop right there!"

The woman's heels knock against the concrete like an engine throwing a rod. Louis catches up to her in four long strides. The force of her tackle drops the woman to the ground.

Louis screams.

"Get off me!"

"Tina Smith, or whatever the hell your name is..." Louis groans, "You're under arrest for theft."

Hicks is out of breath when he catches back up to Louis.

"You look a little light handed for arresting our suspect, Detective Hicks." Louis says.

"Yeah." He breaths deeply. "She... got away."

"No kidding?"

"Got her plates though... I'm pretty sure it was Julie Mahoney's car, but with different plates."

"Good, get an APB out."

Louis lifts the small woman up to her feet. "Those fancy shoes hamper your agility. You need to think ahead for your next get away."

Mr. Johnson looks at the detectives. His fists form tight balls, "How could you do this? You're ruining everything."

"Mr. Johnson, we are going to find your daughter. Count on it." Louis shoves the woman into the car.

CHAPTER 44

Kristine looks over at Bryan. He's watching a cartoon. It's one she doesn't recognize with a talking grouchy bird and a blue dog. He laughs hysterically at a joke Kristine barely understands.

Her notes are spread out on the kitchen table. She piles the papers up. "Bryan? Let's do something together."

There's no response. She walks into the tiny living room. She tries to get his attention again, "Bryan?"

He swings around quickly, "Mom?" He realizes his mistake and frowns. He starts to cry.

Kristine sits next to him on the couch, "Honey, I'm so sorry." She grabs him for a big hug.

He blubbers, "You sound just like her."

"Of course I do, Bryan. We were sisters." She runs her fingers through his hair and kisses his forehead.

"I want to go home." Bryan cries.

"I know you do, honey." Kristine's heart sinks. It's the moment she's been waiting for. He doesn't want to be here. "But can we try out living here in Rochester for a while?"

He looks up at her and shakes his head. He sucks in a bit of snot.

She reaches over to pull out a tissue from the box and hand it to him. "If I move back to Fairfax it'll be a lot harder for me to find a job, Bryan."

"You can stay home," He whimpers, "and take care of me. Like mom."

"I can't honey. I have to earn money."

"But why?" He whines.

"So we can eat. So you can go to a good school."

"I don't wanna go to a good school. I just want you to be home."

"Bryan, that's not how life works."

"It's not fair!"

"I know..."

His crying is inconsolable. She rocks him, rubs his back and hugs him tightly. She starts to cry along.

His crying suddenly stops, but she continues. She feels like her emotions are a megaton freight train driving across country at high speed. Just because there's an obstruction on the tracks doesn't mean her freight train of emotions is going to stop on a dime. His big brown eyes look at her, but she continues to sob. He consoles her with a hug, and then he rubs her back.

"It's okay Aunt Kris." He says.

Her sobbing continues, but weakens. She reaches over for a tissue. She blows her nose, hard. "We're going to need a lot of time at the therapist."

"What's a therapist?" Bryan asks, sounding out the word awkwardly.

"Someone we can go to and talk about all the hurt we have."

He reaches for a tissue and rubs his eyes. "Is that like a marriage councilor?"

"Yes. A lot like a marriage councilor. How do you know about marriage councilors?"

"Mom and dad went there. Mom said they had to go there because of all the hurt that mom and dad had."

Kristine thinks about her sister. Why didn't Kelly tell her that she was going to a marriage councilor? Why didn't she say she was having troubles with Ethan? Was it because she didn't want to tell Kristine everything wasn't the pillar of perfection? She sighs; it was most likely because she didn't want to disappoint her older sister.

"How often did they go?" Kristine asks.

"Every Thursday night. I used to watch Cross &
Cross with mom on Thursday nights, but she said she had
to go with dad to marriage counseling instead."

*Thursday nights. They weren't out on a date, they were in
counseling.*

"Grandma H. doesn't like Cross & Cross. She made
me watch house decorating shows." He grumbles.

"Yeah she likes those." She's not a big fan either.

"They're boring."

"I know." Kristine wipes her eyes again. "Let's go for
a walk."

"It's hot outside."

"Yeah, but we need the walk."

Kristine hears the phone ring, her mother's special
ring. "Good afternoon, Mom."

"I thought you were going to be at the airport by
now? The Giammari's are anxious to see Bryan."

"My hearing went late, I was just going to call you. We
are booked on a later one this evening."

"Is that Grandma H.?" Bryan asks.

Kristine nods her head. "Here, why don't you talk to
Bryan?" She hands over the phone without waiting for an
answer.

Bryan smiles, "How's Pete? … My gecko… Are you
feeding him the fruit flies?... Oh good… Did you dust
them with the stuff from the blue shaker?... Yeah, you can't
forget that part. Mom says that baby geckos have to have
more vitamins…"

There's a long silence. Kristine smiles, it's nice to be
able to pass her mother off to someone else.

"Yeah, I practiced the poem… but I don't understand
any of the words. What does exorciser mean? Is that
someone who exercises?"

What kind of poem is she having him recite?

"Aunt Kris and I are going for a walk… Love you,
bye." Bryan hangs up a little too quickly for her mother to
have responded.

Kristine blows her nose into a tissue. She smiles at Bryan. "Maybe we can find a better poem to recite for the funerals tomorrow?"

"Okay, I don't like that one, I don't understand the words."

CHAPTER 45

Tina Smith's glassy gray eyes stare at the blank walls. She polishes her nails against her little blue dress, holding them up to examine the shine.

"We have a little movie to show you Tina." Louis says. "Do you like movies?"

Tina rolls her eyes. "Is it starring anyone I know?"

"Yes, I believe you know her quite well." Louis punches play on the tablet. "Do you recognize her?"

Tina leans in, "What is this?"

The movie of a woman in a flowery dress and heels is played out on Louis' tablet. Once the seven minutes has played through Louis clicks on another. The same woman is shown replacing another painting on the opposite wall.

"What do you think that one is worth, Hicks?" Louis asks.

Hicks scoffs. "Two hundred?"

"Are you serious? That painting is worth seventy thousand dollars!" Tina protests.

"The one you took down, or the one you're putting up?" Louis asks.

Tina purses her lips. She stares at the one-way mirror beyond Louis' gaze.

Louis says, "Turns out that neither painting is worth that much."

Tina scowls, but remains silent. She picks away at the blue nail polish on her finger.

"Do you want to know how I know that?" Louis asks, rhetorically. "I know because a certain insurance adjuster has the originals in his office. You see I looked at the dates on these videos. They were recorded months ago."

Tina wipes her hands on her dress, "So?"

"So, if she knew you were stealing her paintings, why didn't she say something? Why didn't she turn you into the police? That got me thinking. After what Charles Mahoney told me…"

Tina rolls her eyes again, "He said something intelligent? Let me mark that in my calendar."

"Yeah, he told me the Julie had a lover. He told me that you were her lover. Of course she wouldn't want to turn in her lover to the police." Louis says. "You were stealing her paintings, but she wanted to make sure you weren't really stealing her paintings. So she replaced them with fakes. Well, she replaced them with fakes before you replaced them with fakes."

"Fine, I switched some of her paintings with fakes. And, according to you I didn't even switch out the real paintings, so what are you going to charge me with? Stealing fake paintings?"

Louis bangs her fist on the table, making Tina jump. "No, Murder."

"Murder? I didn't kill anyone."

"Well, you look pretty good for it from here."

Tina shakes her head. "I didn't kill anyone. I'm telling you. I don't know who-"

"But I think you do." Louis cocks her head. "Who drove you to Mr. Johnson's house this afternoon?"

Tina looks at Hicks, then back to Louis.

Hicks says, "Where's that smart-alec comeback now, Tina?"

"I loved her." Tina says, whimpering.

"Who? Julie?"

"Yes, Julie. I loved her. She was going to get a divorce."

"Then she was going to marry you?" Louis asks.

"Yes, then she was going to marry me. She had some savings…"

Hicks thumps his fingers on the table. "Which she used to pay off Charles' debts?"

291

"That's not all of it." Tina's eyes start to moisten when she shakes her head. "She had the paintings…" Her lower lip quivers.

Louis says, "Which you were trying to steal. You see how I'm confused?"

Tina looks down at her lap and sighs.

Louis says softly, "Tell me who drove you to Mr. Johnson's house."

Tina bites her lower lip. She looks straight into Louis' eyes. A tear falls down her face. "Wendy Johnson."

Louis slides a cell phone across the table, the cell phone Tina had in her purse. "I need you to call her."

Tina shakes her head, "I can't."

"You can." Louis says, "I need you to call her and tell her that you got away. That Mr. Johnson knows where the painting she's been looking for is."

Tina looks at her, puzzled. "How do you know where it is? How did you know she's looking for a painting?"

"Because I've seen it." Louis smiles. "And if I were her, in the middle of this murderous scheme she's got going on, I would have left town by now. Why didn't she? Because she needed that painting."

Tina picks up the phone, "Where is the painting?"

***

Hicks sneezes loudly.

"Shh!" Louis scolds.

"Sorry, there's so much cat hair. Between Crookshanks and Quinn's uniform."

"It's Ms. Rocha's cat." Quinn says.

"I don't care. You two shut up!"

There's a short silence, then Quinn asks, "Why do you think Wendy's going to come here?"

"Shh! I see a light!" Louis pushes Quinn's head down.

After a long wait a cone of light trails along the back wall. Giant shadows of papers and filing cabinets look like a moving city skyline.

There's a computer screen glow. A click-clank of computer keys, then the dim light goes red with a short horn sound. "Damn it."

The clinking of keys dangling is the only sound in the dark room. There is a heavy clunk of the filing cabinet opening.

Louis stands up, slowly, quietly. Her gun is out, pointed toward the suspect. "Now!"

There's a quick flash of light.

"Wendy Johnson, you are under arrest."

***

Louis places a pad of paper and pen on the table in the interrogation room. "Wendy…"

"Don't call me that."

"We are charging you with breaking and entering, but we believe you murdered Tim Sherman and Victoria Wallace."

"That's not their names."

"Yes, well we need to find out their real names so we can inform their real families. I need you to write down what you know."

"Why's that? So their families can have some peace?"

"Exactly. You also murdered Neil and Sara Kitt. I know that's their real name. What exactly did they do?"

Wendy silently stares at the one-way mirror.

Louis moves to stand in front of her reflection, "And then there's your sister, Julie."

Her fierce stare into Louis' eyes tells a lot of what she needs to know. "She got a little too close to whatever you were up to. You manipulated her into falling in love with your girlfriend."

"Ha! In love. She didn't know what love was."

"Your sister or your girlfriend?"

"She hasn't been my sister for seventeen years. She's the one that should have been taken. Then I could have been coddled by my parents and given everything I ever wanted. I could have..." Wendy stops herself.

"You could have what?"

"Nothing. You have no evidence. I didn't murder anyone. I think Tina did it. Like you said, she's the one that Julie fell in love with."

"Yes, but you're the one we caught breaking into Mr. Henry's office."

"Tina made me do it."

"Well, I'm quite certain she's the one that told you Julie's paintings were in Mr. Henry's office. I'm also quite sure you're the one that wanted to track down one particular painting."

"It wasn't even there."

"No, you're right. It's not there. It's here, being thoroughly examined by Mr. Henry."

Wendy's eyes grow large.

"That's right, Wendy."

"Stop calling me that."

"Would you prefer if I call you by one of your aliases?" Louis flips through pictures on her tablet. "Jane Smith? Or maybe Susan Jones?"

"Shut up."

"Oh, look at this little innocent picture. You're what? Eight."

"Nine."

She flips back to the picture from four years ago. "Your father was crushed by the thought of you walking the streets in Albany. He couldn't even fathom you murdering your own sister."

"My father? The man who lives in that fancy house, giving all his precious money to his only daughter? He isn't my father. My real daddy was a painter."

"What did he paint?"

She hesitates, "It's not important."

"Your real father and real mother were sick with worry seventeen years ago. They got the call. They paid the ransom and never heard from your abductor again."

"No way, he was too cheap to pay the ransom."

"He paid the ransom."

"You don't know what you're talking about. Daddy said they didn't pay." She protests, looking to the one-way mirror for help.

"They paid the ransom, Wendy. Your abductor didn't want you to know that, but they paid. The police back then didn't want him to pay, but he paid it."

"Daddy said they didn't pay." Wendy's voice sounds like a small child. "You're lying."

"I'm sure we can find documents to prove it."

"You're lying!"

"I'm not lying, Wendy."

"Stop calling me that!"

"Wendy, whatever the man told you, he wanted you to think you were isolated from the world. He wanted you to think you couldn't run away, that you wouldn't be welcome back at your real home."

"Stop talking about daddy like that!"

"Wendy." Louis leans in, "Who ever this man was, he wasn't your daddy."

Wendy screams in frustration, "Get out! Get out!"

"Alright, I'm going to go talk to Tina, or whatever her name is. I'm sure she'll love hearing about how you tried to frame her."

Wendy lunges over the table.

Louis smiles. "Ah. I'll make sure to add 'assaulting an officer' to your charges."

***

Louis looks outside to the full moon. It's so large on the horizon that it fills the squad room's window. Crazy things, they say, tend to happen on the full moon. She begins to believe the myth. She shakes her head.

"Why did you say we didn't find her prints in Mr. Mahoney's cabin?" Hicks asks. "We haven't even got the report back yet."

"I just guessed." Louis shrugs.

Hicks shakes his head, "What I don't get is why kill Tim and Victoria? Or the Kitts? And why with this PMMA stuff?"

Louis stares at Hicks for a moment without saying anything.

"What?" He asks. "You got that look on your face again, Baker."

Louis thumps her fingers on the table. "Make a list of everything that the Kitts and Tim and Victoria purchased in the last two weeks."

"You got it." Hicks turns to plug away at the computer.

She pushes back her chair and looks across the room, "Hey Quinn."

"Detective?" Quinn calls back.

"Call Peterson in toxicology. Ask him about the PMMA in Germany. Ask him if they caught the guy."

"Yes ma'am." She watches Quinn write on his tablet.

"Hicks, did you call Kristine?"

"Yeah, ADA Rocha said she'd be here as soon as she possibly could. She was on her way to the airport with Bryan. She says she has fifteen minutes to spare." Hicks looks past her, "Speak of the devil. There she is now."

Kristine is holding Bryan's hand. He looks tired. They both look like they've been crying.

"Are you okay?"

"Yeah. We just need some sleep."

"I'm sorry to call you in, but no one else was available."

"Bryan, go with Detective Hicks."

"But -" Bryan whines.

"I promise I'll only be a minute or so."

His little chin wavers.

Hicks sits down at his desk. "Bryan, come over here. I have this really neat game on my computer."

Bryan slowly walks over to the detective.

Louis pats Kristine's shoulder and points her toward the interrogation rooms. "I found our killer her name is Wendy Johnson. Julie's lover, Tina Smith, her real name is Amy Lindow, is writing down her statement. It was a love triangle, and identity theft ring. I think I can get Wendy to confess and save the city a few hundred thousand dollars." Louis opens the door to the room, more of a closet, behind the interrogation room. "But I need your sign off on taking the death-"

"You found her! Why the hell is she in here?"

Louis is stunned, "Who?"

"Marcie. She hasn't been returning my calls."

"Marcie? Your paralegal?"

"Yes, Marcie." Kristine points to Wendy.

"You're kidding?"

"No. What does she have to do with this?"

"Her name is Wendy Johnson. She's our killer."

"What?"

"I have no idea what she was doing working as your paralegal, but she killed five people this weekend, including her sister."

"My God. That woman knows me. She knows my phone numbers. She knows where I live."

"Kristine, calm down." Louis rubs her shoulder again.

Kristine pushes her away, "Calm down? Are you kidding? You want me to strike a deal with this psychopath?"

Quinn walks into the room. "Oh sorry, ADA Rocha." He says, "Detective Baker? I have that information you wanted on the PMMA in Germany."

"Perfect, tell me." Louis says.

"They did catch the guy in Germany distributing the PMMA five years ago." Quinn raises his hand to his face, "His name is Peter Snow."

"Excellent, go find out everything about Peter Snow, and whether he had any connection to Mr. Johnson here in Rochester, or anywhere else."

Quinn smiles, "I'm on it."

Hicks walks into the room holding out a paper printout. "This is a weird list, Baker, but I see the pattern you were looking for."

"What pattern?" Kristine asks.

"Let me see that." Louis looks through the list. "Do you have a pen, Kristine?"

"Right here." Kristine hands her a heavy silver pen from her yellow summer jacket.

Louis smirks. She quickly circles seven items from the list and then hands the paper to Kristine. "Notice anything about those items?"

"They are all orders from chemical manufacturers." She points to a circled item half way down the page, "This one is from a pharmaceutical company, Charles Mahoney's company."

"Exactly."

"What was she making?" Kristine asks.

"PMMA, similar to making ecstasy, but deadly." Louis says. "Kristine, I think I've got enough on Wendy to take her down. Just take the death penalty off the table and we could save the city a ton of money. I think we could get a confession."

"I need to think about this. You better tell me more."

***

Louis "Hey Wendy, sorry this is taking so long."

Wendy's head pokes up from the table. Louis can tell she's been sleeping. "What? Oh."

"We're checking on your story. Can I get you a soda? Maybe a coffee?"

"No."

"How about a cigarette? You smoke, right?" Louis pulls out a pack of cigarettes from her pocket and throws them on the table.

"There's no smoking allowed in here." She growls.

"Oh, our lieutenant says we can make an exception."

"Why?"

"She's just generous." *Or she has no idea.*

"Fine." Wendy's hands shake opening the package. "You gotta light?"

Louis pulls out a lighter and a little tin can from her other pocket. She lights the cigarette hanging from Wendy's mouth. She tucks the lighter back in her pocket.

"Do you happen to know a Peter Snow?" Louis asks.

Wendy takes a large drag. She looks at the tip of cigarette, then to Louis. "Maybe." She says.

"He was caught poisoning the club culture in Nuremburg, Germany with PMMA five years ago."

"So?"

"So, we have your fingerprints on a door in a drug lab used to create PMMA."

"So?" She takes another long drag from the cigarette.

At this point the cigarette will be gone in no time, Louis thinks. "You learned to make it from your 'daddy' didn't you?"

Wendy is silent. She flicks a few ashes into the ashtray. "Don't you have to get me a lawyer or something?"

"You want a lawyer?" Louis asks.

"Yeah, I want a lawyer." Wendy takes another drag.

"Excellent, I think your real father is going to arrange that as soon as I call him."

"Whatever."

"Just finish your cigarette and I'll go call him." Louis smiles.

Wendy puts the cigarette out in the tin. Louis grabs it and then walks out the door.

"Did she fall for it?" Kristine asks.

"Of course she did. She's got a two-pack-a-day habit." Louis holds up the tin. "She puffed her way right through to her signature on the death penalty."

Rochester Herald Staff writer David Huang reports:

June 17th 11:02pm: A statement is pending, but a source in the Rochester police has confirmed the arrest of a suspect in the string of suspicious drug related deaths over the course of the last four days.

Wendy Johnson, 26, was arrested this afternoon at Cloak Insurance Agency. She has been charged with four counts of murder in the first degree and one attempted murder charge. Bond has not been set yet.

Wendy, a Rochester native, was kidnapped as a nine-year-old from Seneca Park seventeen years ago. Her kidnapper has not yet been identified.

Rochester police believe that Wendy conspired with her partner, Amy Lindow, AKA Tina Smith, to extort money from the Johnson's, steal paintings from their daughter, and Wendy's sister, Julie Mahoney and ultimately kill four others to keep their plans secret.

Wendy even posed as a paralegal to gain access to secure government documentation.

More on this story will be available in Tuesday's Rochester Herald.

TUESDAY

CHAPTER 46

Louis checks the time on her watch; it's nearly five am. The long day, really a series of long days has been well worth it. She rolls the window down to let the last of the cool breeze fill the car. She flips through the radio stations until she hits on the classic "Summertime Blues." She knows the song, but doesn't recognize the artist until after the DJ comes on to tell her it's The Who.

She still has the song bubbling through her head when she opens the door to the house. Her tired mind wanders. She pulls out a large glass and pours herself cool tap water.

Once she put all the pieces together in front of Wendy she was able to get the confession she wanted. The toxicology report from the victims matched the drugs found in the run-down house in Marketview Heights. Her prints were found in the cabin in Naples. Her prints were scattered all over the house in Marketview Heights. But most damningly her DNA from her last cigarette will match the DNA from the cigarettes found in the house. Kristine likes to say that in this day and age you can't get a jury to convict without DNA.

Kristine wanted to know, most importantly, what she was doing playing a paralegal. Wendy didn't want to give up the details. After a bit of prodding from her lawyer, and in exchange for taking the death penalty off the table, she explained. A few of the identities Victoria was pursuing had made changes, changes that required more research from the government's computers. When Wendy saw the ad in the paper for the paralegal, she did some studying, assumed the Marcie Hoyle identity and weaseled her way into the job wearing a short skirt. As they were short staffed already, the City of Rochester probably didn't look too deeply into her background. There is, after all, a Marcie Hoyle with a paralegal certificate. Wendy wrote down all of Marcie's references.

While Tina Smith did her part in getting Wendy behind bars, she too will be seeing the inside of another jail cell. It turns out she was trying to extort money from Mr. Johnson for information on his long lost daughter, her lover Wendy.

Louis walks to the kitchen to start making breakfast. Will should be up at any time, and it would be a delightful change of rolls for her to be the chipper one in the morning. She opens the refrigerator to root around for ingredients to make the one fancy breakfast she knows how to make, frittata. The best part of making a frittata is the lack of structure. As long as it has eggs, veggies, some sort of meat, and starch, and a little bit of cheese to hold it together, it's a frittata.

A short while later she has the makings of a nice frittata, and the coffee is brewed. She checks her watch again, nearly seven. It's unusual for Will to sleep in so long, but who knows what he was up to on a busy Sunday.

She walks up the stairs holding his favorite travel mug. Surely he'll be in a huge hurry starting out this late. He likes to run an eight a.m. meeting sharp.

"Good morning sleepy head." She says opening the squeaky bedroom door.

To her shock, he's not in bed. She peeks into the bathroom, but there's no one there either.

"Will?" she calls. Her heart starts to race. Perhaps he left very early this morning? Before she got home.

She looks back in the bedroom. She heads straight for the bed. On her pillow lies a hand scrawled note:

Louis,

Please forgive me. I've decided to take the job in Washington. I know we need to talk more, but you haven't been around to do the talking. I decided to start the job right away. I know we can figure this out. Either we can do long distance for a while, or you can find a job here. There are lots of security positions, really good consultancies. You could make real money.

I really do miss you. I'll call you Wednesday. I hope you catch your killer by then.

I love you,
-Will

CHAPTER 47

"The service was nice." Aunt Sally whispers.

"Hmm?" Kristine asks, staring into space, not even listening for the answer to her own question. Since they got to the house Kristine has been like a zombie sitting on the soft, overstuffed couch.

Aunt Sally raises her voice just above a whisper, "I said, 'The service was nice.'"

Kristine chokes up, "Yes. It was." She looks over to her aunt sitting next to her on the couch. There are tears in Kristine's eyes, but she refuses to let them fall.

Aunt Sally smiles, "Bryan did so very well with that poem. Who was it?"

"Robert Frost."

Her aunt pats her knee, "It was lovely."

Kristine nods her head silently. She stares over at her sister's knitting basket. There are needles left hanging from the middle of a lacy row. Kelly's life was left in the middle of a lacy row. How could she die and leave everything in the middle for Kristine to finish?

"Are you alright, dear?"

Kristine doesn't look up, but continues staring at the pile of knitting.

"Kristine?" Aunt Sally squeezes her knee, "I said, 'Are you alright?'"

Kristine swallows hard. "I'm fine, I just haven't slept much."

"Oh yes, I know. All the plans for a funeral can be overwhelming. When my husband -"

Kristine interrupts her, "Mom did all that."

"Isn't she a dear? Imagine, having to bury your own child. No one should have to do that."

"Right." Kristine sighs, "Aunt Sally, I'm sorry. I'm just so tired."

"I know dear. You need to have a seat. Let me go get you a cup of coffee."

"Thank you."

Kristine can hear her mother's voice from the other room, "That wasn't the poem I wanted him to read, but it was nice…Yes, well she barely got here in time for the funeral." She can't hear the other end of the conversation, "She does fancy herself the top lawyer in Rochester, NY. But that's a bit like saying you're the head cheese-maker in Alaska. I mean really, who cares?" Kristine's heart beats a bit faster. Her face turns red. "If you want to be a real lawyer, you have to be here in law-making central. Everyone knows that."

"Honey, I think you're getting a bit flushed." Aunt Sally puts her hand on Kristine's face. "Yes, you're burning up."

Kristine strains to hear her mother's voice from the other room.

"Kristine?" Aunt Sally asks.

"Well, if you ask me that boy needs to be here, with what family he has left. With the friends he's made. I don't know why Kristine insists on having him up there. If it weren't for her running me over with the car, I wouldn't have to be in this wheelchair. Then I would be taking care of Bryan."

Aunt Sally looks horrified.

Kristine's heart pounds, she can feel her cheeks redden and then her fists ball up tightly. There's a longing, for once, to stand up for herself to her mother. She stands and shouts into the next room, "Mom, how could you bring up an accident that happened almost twenty years ago? When are you ever going to let that go?"

Her mother wheels her way into the room, followed by her Uncle Fred, her Aunt Millie, her mother's next-door neighbor Susan, the woman who used to babysit her in the afternoons before her mother quit her job. Kristine tucks her face into her hands before she sees anyone else.

"I guess I'll let it go when I stop being crippled." Her mother pounds her fist on the arm of the wheel chair.

Kristine rips her hands out from her face, "Fine. I ran you over with the car. You are the one that tried to teach me to drive without being in the car. You want to know why I moved to Rochester? To get away from you! You think I'm just some flunky lawyer up in Rochester? Well, I'm not." Kristine looks around the room at all the faces. "I'm holding on to my cases with both hands, but I just got a major case back on track. Not by showing up and showing off, but damn hard work. I've got stitches in the back of my head to prove it."

"You should lower your tone." Her mother hisses.

"No. I'm not going to. You've been wandering around in your wheelchair all afternoon, telling everyone that Kelly's life was so perfect. Well, look out world, it wasn't perfect. She had problems just like everyone else. She had problems with Ethan. They were going to marriage counseling. That's where they were coming back from when the accident happened."

"You shouldn't be saying these things... *in front of people.*"

"Get used to it, Mom. You're going to start hearing a lot more honest opinions from me. I have to agree with you on one thing though."

"And what would that be?"

"Dad's wife is a perky, co-dependent, bimbo, but at least she isn't an unbearable, backstabbing, miserable sack like you." Kristine hurries out the back door. Before she's had a moment to think she's standing in a copse of trees. Her nylons are quickly turning to shreds by the thicket. She's too stunned to cry, but too ashamed not to be crying.

"Kristine?" A wavering voice calls. "Kristine?"

"Aunt Sally?" She asks hesitantly.

"That was some speech." Aunt Sally beams a radiant smile.

Kristine shakes her head. "I don't know what I was thinking."

Aunt Sally puts a hand on her back. "I hope you were thinking that you should have done that a long time ago."

"No, I wasn't."

"Well, that's certainly what I was thinking."

"I shouldn't have done that."

"Probably not at your sister's funeral. But your 'unbearable, backstabbing, miserable sack' of a mother should be a bit more tactful as well."

"Did I really say all that?"

"I'm certain you did. You need to stand up for yourself more with her. My husband, God bless his soul, could be as miserable as your mother. The Melton gene is quite cantankerous, as you know."

Kristine smiles, "Yes, I know."

"The only thing you can do is fight back. Your mother will back down. She's been walking all over you for so long, but nothing I've been saying all these years has got her to stop. You have to stand up for yourself, just like you did today."

"I guess you're right."

"You know I'm right. You go back up to Rochester. You win that big case, but make sure you take a few more trips down here to see your Aunt Sally, you hear?"

"I hear you."

"Let's get back to the house. You left that coffee getting cold."

Rochester Herald Staff writer David Huang reports:

June 18th 7:22pm: Rochester police executed another search warrant at the residence of Dennis Baxter this morning. Prior to the hearing to determine if there was enough evidence to continue with his trial on charges of murdering his step-daughter, police found a hidden box containing disturbing photographs of his step-daughter and six other minors.

While the evidence was not yet available for the hearing, four women testified at the hearing to Dennis' behavior toward their daughters. One of the women, Iris Young, tipped the police off to the box and where it would likely be found in the house. She said she found the box, with her daughter's picture in it, while Dennis was living in her house. She burned the box, but suspected he would acquire another one.

Mr. Baxter's lawyer vigorously fought to keep the witnesses from testifying, but Judge Goldstein allowed the women to testify.

Mr. Baxter's lawyer was unavailable for comment after the hearing.

FRIDAY

CHAPTER 48

"Wow, your sister's house is nice." Louis looks around the room. "Look at that clock. Does it really work?"

"Yeah, some guy comes twice a year to work on it."

"Wow." Louis says. She hands one of the bags in her arms to Kristine.

"Red wine in the summer?" Kristine asks holding up the Red Knot Shiraz.

"I'm living dangerously. I really felt it went with the Chinese food." Louis says. "I got something for you too, Bryan."

"What is it?" Bryan jumps up to try and see into the brown bag.

Louis pulls out a foil topped wine bottle.

Bryan looks at her, "I can't drink wine, Aunt Louis. I'm only ten."

His severe face makes Louis smile and laugh. "Don't worry, it's only sparkling grape juice."

Bryan looks surprised. "Did you get the sweet and sour chicken?"

"You bet!" Louis says. She looks over to see Kristine open and shut drawers. "What are you looking for, Kristine?"

"A cork screw. Kelly loved wine, I don't know why there aren't a thousand of them."

"No need." Louis pulls the plastic wrapper from the top of the bottle. She puts her thumbs on the top of the cork and wine makes a pop. "That's the nice thing about

310

this wine, no corkscrew needed." She unpacks the rest of the bag onto the table while Kristine pours two glasses of wine. Before long there is a huge feast in front of them.

Kristine reaches for the box of pot stickers. "How's Will?"

Louis sighs, "He's really enjoying his new job. We had a long talk well into the night on Wednesday. Nothing is resolved, but it's good to be talking without Bert interrupting."

"He does have a way of calling at the wrong time. Ugh, and the way he talks. I don't know how you can stand it." Kristine reaches over to steal a morsel of sweet and sour chicken from Bryan with her long chopsticks.

"Hey!" Bryan squeals.

"He only talks like that to you." Louis laughs. "Will's new manager is quite the charmer. Handsome too. We went to dinner with him last night. He spent the whole evening telling me how fantastic Washington D.C. is. I tried to change the subject, but he found at least forty different ways to inject 'the District' back into the conversation. For instance, did you know that for every nineteen residences in 'the District', one is a lawyer?"

"Yes, as a matter of fact, I did know that." Kristine laughs. "Are you considering moving down here?"

Louis shrugs. She finishes the bite she has in her mouth. "I honestly don't know. Will says I could get a job here in a heartbeat. I'm not sure I want to go from chasing down murderers to corporate security."

Kristine takes a sip from the wine. "You'd be surprised how devious and underhanded corporate security can get. Speaking of murderers…"

"Yeah, I talked to Bert this morning."

"And?" Kristine raises her eyebrows.

"It's a three page written confession. Mr. Johnson shipped in a lawyer from Albany, Leo Rapitas. Do you know him?"

"Never heard of him, but I don't go to Albany that often. Pucket has been trying to figure out how Marcie … I mean Wendy, got a job in our office. McCracken told me he's been storming around the office looking for someone to blame for this mistake. He says I should be happy I'm not there. What I want to know is what was Julie was doing in Germany and what was on that painting?"

"Oh, I thought you knew?" Louis smiles. "Julie was onto the painting theft. But when her father started going nuts about maybe having a clue about her sister's disappearance, she got even more suspicious. She hired a private investigator to dig into Tina's background."

"Wait, how come you didn't know about the private investigator?" Kristine takes another sip of wine.

"No one knew. He was out of town that weekend chasing down a cheating husband." She laughs, "A different cheating husband. The private investigator found Tina's real name and that she was in prison on extortion charges. That's where Tina met the woman we know as Victoria and Wendy, by the way. Only the private investigator didn't know what he had found. He was tracing back the women by their assumed names. Wendy was sloppy. She used the same name in Germany."

"I remember you saying something about Germany." Kristine picks up the wine bottle and pours it into Louis' glass. The last of the wine drips into her glass like a leaky faucet.

"Thanks. Well, Wendy must have been just scraping by in Germany, because at some point she sold a painting under that name to a dealer. Her kidnapper painted the painting, and Julie found it through her art connections. It matched, perfectly, with the weird photo aging Mr. Johnson had commissioned. It was the perfect evidence to convince her father that something was up. She called him and said she was going to talk to him on Saturday to bring proof about what happened to Wendy. Of course, she went home first, where Wendy lined every wine glass with PMMA."

"Yeah, I read that women are more likely to use poison than men. But why didn't Charles die too?"

"She laced the PMMA with real ecstasy, that's how she learned to make it in the first place. It's a pretty complicated process. Anyway, Charles is allergic to ecstasy: he vomited it up before the drug had any time to take effect."

Bryan's nose crinkles, "Eww."

Louis says, "Sorry, Bryan."

Kristine shrugs, "I hate to say it, but I think you should look into the private investigator business."

"Really? Chasing down cheating husbands? Doing background checks? I don't know…"

"I'll bet there are a few cases that might surprise you."

"What about you? Are you coming back to Rochester?"

"Bryan and I decided to give it a try for a year. My Aunt Sally said it would be good to keep a distance between mom and me. We're going to sell the house…" Kristine takes a deep breath and looks around the room. "…and put the money toward Bryan's education. Mom insists he needs to go to private school, but with my salary that would be tough to swing. We have interviews next week at two schools."

"You back in Rochester; that will make it a lot harder to move down here." Louis cracks open her fortune cookie:

```
Need some adventure and enjoyment?
Take a vacation.
```

She hands the slip to Kristine, "Even the Chinese food says I need a break."

###

I hope you enjoyed the book. Please take the time to write some feedback:
http://www.facebook.com/CoriLynnArnold

Acknowledgements:

This book would have been impossible without: The Inklings Calgary Crime Writers, my editor Cindy DeJager, my friends Rob Forteath, Shantha Ramachandran, Jeremy Smith and my loving husband Millard, who waded through many of the drafts, helped me reorganize the pieces into something so much better and who knows how to make a dirty martini.

About the Author:

Cori Lynn Arnold has worked as a hotel housekeeper, handy woman, laundry attendant, radio disc jockey, library clerk, historical photographic archivist, mathematics tutor, teaching assistant, art work framer, photo lab junky, portrait and wedding photographer, high school algebra teacher, Internet security researcher, security analyst, computer programmer and ethical hacker. At the time of publication she is driving across country with her husband and son to start a new life in the North East U.S.

Made in the USA
Coppell, TX
20 September 2020

38418650R00175